Praise for Ally James writing as Sydney Landon

From Alaska with Love

Ally James

JOVE
New York

A JOVE BOOK
Published by Berkley
An imprint of Penguin Random House LLC
penguinrandomhouse.com

Copyright © 2020 by Robin Davis
Penguin Random House supports copyright. Copyright fuels creativity, encourages
diverse voices, promotes free speech, and creates a vibrant culture. Thank you for buying
an authorized edition of this book and for complying with copyright laws by not
reproducing, scanning, or distributing any part of it in any form without permission.
You are supporting writers and allowing Penguin Random House to continue to
publish books for every reader.

A JOVE BOOK, BERKLEY, and the BERKLEY & B colophon
are registered trademarks of Penguin Random House LLC.

ISBN: 9781984806956

First Edition: March 2020

Printed in the United States of America
1   3   5   7   9   10   8   6   4   2

Cover photo of dog in a hat by Jaromir Chalabala / Shutterstock
Cover design by Farjana Yasmin
Book design by Gaelyn Galbreath

This is a work of fiction. Names, characters, places, and incidents either are the product
of the author's imagination or are used fictitiously, and any resemblance to actual persons,
living or dead, business establishments, events, or locales is entirely coincidental.

A heartfelt thank-you to all who have served in the Armed Forces and those who continue to serve. Today and every day I am grateful to you for your courage, your dedication, and the sacrifices that you and your loved ones have made to protect our freedom.

Chapter One

Talk about a family reunion from hell, Sara Ryan thought as she smiled politely through yet another introduction. Her aunt Lydia had relentlessly marched her around the room like a drill sergeant for the last hour. Her brother, Chris, had been smart enough to make up an excuse that got him out of coming, but true to form, Sara let her mother guilt her into it. The bathroom door was only inches away, and she was so close to making a break for it, when her aunt's voice rang out loud enough for the people in the next town to hear. "And this is my niece Sara, Joan's daughter. You know, the spinster. She lives with her brother." *Horrified.* That's the only way to put it. Or perhaps "mortified" was a better word. The entire family appeared to be staring at her with equal parts pity and disapproval. While Sara was frantically trying to compose herself, her aunt patted her on the back before adding, "She spends a lot of time with her mom, since, you know, she's never had a boyfriend. I've told her time and again that she needs to get her nose out of those trashy books she's always reading. Men like that don't exist." Sara wanted to object. There had been some boyfriends. It had been a while, but there had definitely been a couple. *Back before the time of electricity and vehicles.* Heck, she'd had sex before. But how exactly could she go about denying something so personal without making herself sound worse? *Could this get any worse?*

She opened her mouth, intent on clarifying some of the misinformation, but her aunt Ivy suddenly appeared at her other side. *Shit, what now?* Her mother's oldest sister had always been the more outspoken of the three of them, which was normally amusing—but Sara was already at her limit and couldn't take much more. Ivy gave her an exaggerated wink, which resembled someone having a seizure, before saying, "I sure love that Christian fella. Now there's someone who seems like he's got it all figured out. Ana is one lucky gal. He's rich, hot, and knows how to take care of his business." All eyes turned to stare across the room when Ivy pointed to her husband, who appeared to be sound asleep sitting up. "Even Fred likes listening to those audio books." *Oh, dear God, she can't possibly be talking about* Fifty Shades of Grey. *Sweet Aunt Ivy? Uncle Fred?* From the snickers around the room, Sara could only deduce that Ivy wasn't the only one who'd been doing a little reading on the wild side. *Or was it doing a little wild reading on the side?* And while the things being whispered among

2

her relatives might result in years of therapy in the future, it had shifted the attention away from her.

"That's disturbing," an amused voice murmured behind her. Sara whirled around to find her cousin Chloe standing there with a grimace on her face. "Sorry about Mom. She means well for the most part." Chloe was the only child of Ivy and Fred, and two years younger than Sara. She was also single, but no one had called attention to that fact. At one time, she had been very close to her cousin, but Chloe traveled often for her job with a local investment company. And Sara rarely had a night away from taking care of Kaylee, her niece. Truthfully, she had always been a little jealous of her attractive cousin. If her Facebook page was any indication, she had a large circle of friends, whom she was always going on amazing trips with. She was successful, drove a new BMW, and lived in a condominium in the ritzy downtown district of Charlotte. In short, she was living the life that Sara had always imagined for herself—yet had given up on somewhere along the way.

Sara smiled, taking a step closer to her cousin. "Are you kidding? She saved my ass. Everyone looked terrified that my 'spinsterhood' might be contagious. I swear I saw Tasha ready to douse herself in hand sanitizer. Who knew that being single was the equivalent of having a raging STD?"

Chloe snorted as they stared across the room at their cousin. "Trust me, nothing else has touched that body lately—if ever. Now, she's a spinster poster girl. Why in the heck was Lydia calling you out? What'd you do, forget to send her a Christmas card? You know how petty these old hens can be. I swear they all get together and compare notes. If you screw up and miss a birthday for one, but not the other, you're in big trouble."

Sara rolled her eyes, "Happened to you too, huh? Swear to God, I've never heard news travel that fast."

Chloe shook her head, "Um no, not in years. I don't bother with it anymore, and it's the best decision I ever made. Sure, there was some bitching for a while, but now they have no expectations where I'm concerned. If I listened to them, I'd be like Tasha. Just talking about life instead of actually living it." *Ouch.* Sara knew that remark hadn't been aimed at her, but it hit home just the same. She felt like a fake who'd managed to snag a seat at the cool kids' table. Any minute now Chloe would tell her to move her ass back to the other side of the room with Tasha. Heck, come to think of it, even she had brought a guy to the last family gathering. *It's official, I'm a spinster. Is there a Facebook group I should join?* Sara's pity party was in full swing when Chloe elbowed her before saying, "Stop obsessing over it. Lydia's full of crap."

For a moment she considered acting dumb, but why bother? Her pride had already taken a hit, and she didn't feel like pretending the comment hadn't hit home. "I can't say she's totally off the mark. I mean, I do live with my brother's family. And I haven't brought a guy around the family in—it's been a while." *More like never.* But really, who wanted to subject an innocent person to this kind of dysfunctional situation unless things were serious?

She'd been afraid of seeing yet more pity, but Chloe simply gave her a blank stare before shrugging. "Even if you were a lazy freeloader who never had a date in her entire life—which you're not—it shouldn't matter to anyone here. What happened to family supporting each other? It's bad enough that the world passes judgment without knowing all the facts, but who appointed our aunts as judge, jury, and executioner? If you're happy, then screw 'em. If you're not, then change."

While she appreciated Chloe coming to her defense, Sara felt as if she was listening to a self-help seminar. *You've got this, girl. Just go do you. Release your inner power and conquer the world. Blah, blah, blah.* People who had it all couldn't fathom why everyone didn't. "You make it sound so simple to alter your life. Last time I checked, there weren't a line of men waiting at my door, to take me away from all this."

Chloe studied her for so long she had to resist the urge to run a hand over her hair to smooth it. "You really have no clue how attractive you are, do you? I mean sure, you dress completely wrong for your body type and coloring, but even with that, you still have that elusive girl-next-door beauty that most women dream about. If you put yourself out there, you wouldn't lack for attention."

So didn't see that coming. Is she bullshitting me? But there appeared to be nothing but sincerity in her eyes, which was almost more unsettling than a lie would have been. Even more bizarre, she sounded almost envious. Sara resisted the urge to argue, not wanting her lack of self-confidence to be even more apparent than it already was.

But she couldn't resist admitting, "I wouldn't know where to start. It's been so long since I've been on a date that the mere thought of it terrifies me."

Chloe nodded, appearing to understand even though Sara hadn't a clue as to how. Surely she never lacked for men in her life . . . did she? "I get it. After Brian and I broke up, it was at least a year before I went out with another guy." She crossed her arms over her chest and looked down at the floor as she murmured, "I was completely blindsided when I found out he was cheating on me. Never saw it coming. I was so depressed that I almost lost my job over the bastard. After I used up all my vacation and sick days, they were running out of patience. If not for a few good friends showering me with some tough love, I'm not sure how bad things would have gotten before I hit rock bottom." She glanced across the room at her mother and cringed. "I wasn't far from having to move back home with the parents."

Sara had never been one to take pleasure in another's misfortune, but she couldn't help being riveted by Chloe's story. *If she can't hold on to a man, what hope do the rest of us mere mortals have?* She touched her cousin's hand as she said, "I'm so sorry. You should have . . ." *Should have what? Would you have taken or returned her call? Not likely.* Even though she didn't give voice to the last part, they both knew exactly what she was thinking. They were at that awkward level—friends who'd drifted apart and yet fell into old habits when they saw each other unexpectedly. "How'd we get to this point?" she blurted.

"Shit happens," Chloe said matter-of-factly. "But let's

not let it continue. You and I are going to dinner next weekend and don't even think of blowing me off. Tell Nicole to get off her ass and watch her own kid for an evening. Heck, if Kaylee went missing, she wouldn't be able to describe her own daughter to the police. You'd have to do it."

Even though Sara secretly agreed with what she'd said, she still halfheartedly attempted to defend her mostly absent sister-in-law. "Well, I am the nanny. Pretty sure child care is considered the main part of my job."

Chloe gave her a skeptical look. "So they pay you enough to be on duty round the clock? She works like an hour a day doing the weather for Channel 7. How taxing can that possibly be? And what about Chris? He's been out of the military for several years now."

"He started his own business with a couple of his Air Force friends. He spends a lot of time building his customer base." *At least that's what he says when I want a day off.* "He does work from home some, but you know how distracting kids can be. Plus—Kaylee gets upset when I'm not there."

"Of course she does, Sara. You're pretty much the only mother she has. And I know you must be equally attached to her. But she'll grow up and make a life of her own. And you'll realize that a big chunk of yours has passed you by."

"Gee, thanks," Sara muttered around the huge lump in her throat. Way to sugarcoat it. *Does anyone have a bridge I call throw myself off of?*

"That was a bit . . . blunt," she said sheepishly. "I'm used to working around a lot of men who don't have a sensitive bone in their bodies. I could have worded that better, sorry."

Sara forced a smile, hearing the note of regret in Chloe's voice. It had been hard to hear, but she did have a point. Kaylee was already growing up so fast, and when she no longer required constant supervision, what then? *Nicole will make me the full-time maid. Wait, I'm not far from that now.* "It's fine. Can't be in this family without growing some thick skin." She didn't think Chloe was buying into her tough girl act for a minute, but thankfully she let it go.

When Aunt Ivy ushered Chloe away to speak with more relatives, Sara took the opportunity to gather her things and leave. Thankfully her mom was fully enjoying the time with her sisters, and didn't seem to mind when she waved good-bye. Still, she didn't allow herself to relax until she reached the safety of her car.

Even though she wanted a moment to process the hellish reunion ordeal, she didn't dare risk being spotted and marched back inside the building. Her aunts would probably brand her with their version of the scarlet letter. In her case, it would be an *S* instead of an *A*. Heck, being an adulterer would likely have elevated her status in their eyes. *Better a ho than a spinster. I need to get laid immediately.* But short of making out with some guy at the family Christmas party or posting X-rated pictures on Facebook, there wasn't actually a way to prove that she had gotten lucky. *So much for that.*

· Normally she didn't give it a thought, but today she wasn't ready to go home. And since Chris had used Kaylee's cold as an excuse to avoid the reunion, then screw it. Let him and Nicole play parents for a while. It was certainly a role they weren't used to. Their contributions to Kaylee's life were pretty much limited to providing the sperm and giving birth. Oh, she knew they loved their daughter, but they were both career obsessed, which left little time for a demanding five-year-old. When they had friends over, they'd parade her in front of them, pat her head, and hand her off to Sara. Which didn't bother her at all; she loved the little girl as if she were her own—only she wasn't. And lately, she'd begun to wonder if being so close to her niece was a good thing. Kaylee seemed to view her life as some sort of reality television show, in which Chris and Nicole were the supporting cast. The ones you shared a few laughs with from time to time, but didn't miss when they weren't around. But was that good for Kaylee? To want to spend more time with her aunt, playing games, doing crafts, baking, going to the park, dancing . . . Surely long term, she'd rather be doing these things with her own mom.

She spotted Dunkin' Donuts ahead and pulled into the parking lot. An iced coffee always made everything better. *It's coffee in a plastic cup, not a magic lamp.* Even the voice in her head seemed to be unusually bitchy today. Sara was debating whether to go through the drive-thru or inside, when the DJ on the local radio station said something that got her attention. *"Send a card to our deployed troops. Receiving mail from home is a huge morale booster to the men and women overseas. Please take a moment today, and visit our website for all the information. It's a small price to pay for all that they do for us.*" Chris had served two tours in the Air Force, so Sara knew well the sacrifices that were made. Sending a card was the very least she could do.

She sat at a corner table with her donut and iced coffee. Pulling her iPad from her purse, she browsed through her Facebook News Feed, but none of it interested her. Then she remembered the commercial she'd heard and quickly brought up the radio station's website. A few more clicks and she had the information she needed. She knew if she didn't do it now, she likely wouldn't. So she quickly gathered her things, and tossed the remainder of her coffee and donut in the trash. There was a Walgreens at the end of the block, so she walked the short distance and found herself in front of the Easter cards. Not knowing anything at all about the soldier who would receive it, she opted for a generic greeting that would be appropriate for anyone. On a whim, she also bought some stationery to include a letter with the card.

That had been the easy part. But back in her car, with pen in hand, she drew a blank. She wanted to make the person who received the card smile. To take them away from whatever they were facing for a few moments. Maybe make them a little less homesick—at least while they were reading her letter. But how? *Well . . . talking about the weather probably isn't going to cut it. Hey, you think you've got it bad, buddy, I'm a spinster who lives with her brother.* Wait—why not vent to a stranger? At least give them a version of the truth. It was pretty much the only unusual thing to happen to her in recent history, and there was an entire piece of paper to fill.

Dear Soldier:

Greetings from North Carolina. I hope this finds you well and having a much better day than I've had. So I made the unfortunate mistake of attending a family reunion earlier. I know, I know. I can only blame it on a severe lapse in judgment. Let me stop there and fill you in on a bit of my backstory so that you can fully appreciate what transpired.

I am a thirty-five-year-old woman, and I work as a nanny for my brother's family. I have a college degree in business administration, and I was employed in that field for several years. Then my niece Kaylee was born. She has asthma and constantly fell sick when she was put into day care. They hired a few different nannies, but due to my sister-in-law's colorful personality, none of them stayed for very long. When Kaylee was two, I agreed to use my vacation time to help them out of a jam. My brother was going out of town on business, and his wife couldn't get time off from work to watch their daughter. Long story short, I ended up leaving my job and watching Kaylee full-time. I wasn't happy where I was working . . . and it was only supposed to be until they found a replacement. That was three years ago. I'm completely in love with my niece and it's never been a hardship to care for her. But—well, let me get back to the events of the day before I go there.

My extended family is very . . . vocal.

All those words worked. She described the embarrassment that had been the family luncheon, intentionally leaving out Chloe's comments. *What body shape do I have and what should I be wearing?* She pondered that while she filled in her ghastly story. Spinster quarantine. This poor soldier reader. Sara knew it was time to lighten things up a little more. She continued with:

Don't worry, we'll have loads of fun playing shuffle board and bingo. If you play your cards right, I'll let you take my scooter for a ride. That sounded rather risqué.

Risqué? Who even used that word anymore . . . She was so out of practice writing letters.

If you're a woman, this must sound even more insane.

Sara stopped writing for a minute and wondered who would be the lucky recipient of her letter. But did it matter? If it brought a moment of cheer . . . She added a few more lines and then thought about how to sign off her note. Sara Ryan? That seemed too boring. Sara the nanny? Oh Lord.

Even worse. She rolled her eyes and cursed the lack of good coffee in her life. Putting pen back to paper, she wrote:

> *Take care and be safe,*
> *Sara the spinster—and future cat lady*

She hesitated for a moment, then on a whim, included her e-mail address. A reply was doubtful after the letter she'd written, but it could happen. She addressed the envelope, then slid the letter inside the card and added a stamp that she found in her wallet. She also used a few Charlie Brown stickers that Kaylee had left in the car. There was a mail drop on her way home, and she hesitated only a moment before dropping it inside. What did it matter? The person who'd receive it didn't know her, nor was she likely ever to hear from them. She was simply attempting to combine a little self-therapy with spreading cheer to a stranger.

Oddly enough, she was in better spirits. She even found herself humming along to the radio as she pulled into the driveway of her brother's home. Her good humor ended abruptly when she crossed the threshold and heard screaming. She hurried in the direction of the noise and found Kaylee on the floor of the living room throwing a tantrum, while Nicole and Chris stared down at her. "I'll let you have anything you want from Walmart if you'll be a good girl," Nicole coxed. To Sara's amazement, Kaylee went quiet. It was as if Nicole had flipped a switch. When her brother high-fived his wife, Sara couldn't resist the urge to roll her eyes. She'd just witnessed exactly why they had no control over their daughter. Kaylee was a very smart little girl, and she knew how to play them. Naturally there are times that many parents resort to a little bribery to get some much-needed peace, but Sara had a feeling this was not the exception but the rule where they were concerned.

When Chris spotted Sara, he released an audible sigh. Nicole turned to see what had gotten his attention, and frowned down at her watch. "Where have you been? Joan said you left the reunion over an hour ago."

Sara felt the usual irritation when dealing with her snooty sister-in-law. Yet was it really Nicole's fault that she allowed herself to be treated like a doormat? "This is my day off, Nicole. And since that doesn't happen often, I had things to do."

"Sarie!" Kaylee called out as she raced across the room and hurled herself at Sara's knees. "I missed you lots."

"Hey, munchkin," Sara murmured as she let her hand rest on top of Kaylee's head. "I see you've been a good girl while I was gone," she added wryly.

Kaylee moved back a few inches to look up at her. "Mommy got mad 'cause I was playing in her girlie stuff." She did a perfect rendition of Nicole's scowl before adding, "Kaylee Marie, that cost over two hundred dollars. You're grounded 'til you're thirty." *And there you have it, ladies and gentlemen. Successful Parenting 101—hand out ridiculous consequences to ensure your child will never take you or your* discipline *seriously.*

As Kaylee awaited her reaction, Sara was torn between laughter and exasperation. This was far from the first time this particular thing had happened. And no matter how many times she pointed out to the other woman that she should keep valuable things from her daughter's reach, she still refused to heed Sara's warnings. It was almost as if she wanted this very thing to occur over and over so she could be the victim. If that was the case, it had backfired on her today with Sara not here to do damage control. Instead of chastising Kaylee, it took everything she had not to applaud her for neatly turning the tables on her mother. Chris appeared embarrassed that she'd witnessed the episode, which was ironic considering she was on the front lines here every day. "Nic, you could put that lotion in the bathroom cabinet. Kaylee doesn't know that it's that expensive—neither did I, for that matter." He said the last part under his breath, but they all heard it.

"Come on, munchkin, help me put my stuff away," Sara said as she attempted to lead her niece from the room. Not only did she not want to hear her brother and his wife arguing, she didn't want Kaylee to either.

But the little girl seemed determined to dally. "You don't got anything, Sarie," she said as she looked up at Sara in confusion. "What do you need help for?" Sometimes it was a real pain how literal everything was for kids. Another adult would have likely taken the hint, but not a five-year-old.

"Er—I meant, let's go start dinner. I bet you're hungry." When Kaylee opened her mouth, Sara decided to forgo waiting for her reply, knowing they'd still be standing there in an hour. So she bent down to pick her niece up instead.

"You gotta know when to fold 'em, kid," she whispered as she whisked her from the room and down the hallway toward their wing of the house. Luckily, Chris and Nicole's room was upstairs, and Sara's and Kaylee's were downstairs. Without that modicum of privacy, there was no way she could have stayed for so long.

"I missed you," Kaylee said once again, and Sara hugged her before sitting her down.

"Me too, kiddo. I should have taken you with me today." *Maybe I could have passed her off as my kid. Proof I've had sex.*

Kaylee climbed up on Sara's bed and lay back on a pillow as if she'd been thoroughly exhausted by the day. Sara kicked off her shoes and settled in next to her. "Can we go to Walmart and get my toy?"

"What toy?" Sara asked absently, before remembering Nicole's bribery. "Sweetie, you know that you don't deserve a reward, don't you? Remember how I explained that you're to listen to and respect adults?" *Even your mother.* She kept that part to herself and continued on, "Throwing a tantrum to force your mom to buy you something isn't right."

Kaylee was silent for a few moments as if mulling over her words. "But saying mean stuff about your kid isn't good either, is it, Sarie? She said she wished her daughter was a proper young lady. And how Melody was so lucky."

Kaylee recalled her mother's words in a detached voice, but Sara could sense the underlying hurt beneath her almost robotic tone. Melody was a news anchor at the television station where Nicole worked, and also one of her closest friends. Her daughter, Maisie, was only a year older than Kaylee, but they were complete opposites in most every way. As far as she could tell, Maisie was a miniature clone of her well-dressed mother. She'd be surprised if the child even owned any toys. At six, she was so poised, she even made Sara feel self-conscious. Rolling up onto her side, Sara laid a hand on Kaylee's stomach. "Well . . . I bet I know something you can do that Maisie can't." The little girl's eyebrows rose in interest, making her look so darned adorable that Sara wanted to pull her into a big hug, but she managed to resist—for now. "Can you imagine Maisie making dinner? Especially something as messy as spaghetti?"

Kaylee jumped right in, matching Sara's theatrical voice as she said, "Oh no, what if she got the red sauce on her dress? That would be the worst thing ever."

"The absolute horror of it," Sara shuddered as she clapped her hands against her face. Then in her best Southern belle voice she added, "Oh my goodness, this is dreadful. How can I possibly go on my playdate with Mercedes and Lexus? We were going to play the piano and pet Lexus's hairless cat. Now it's all ruined! Simply ruined. My life is over!"

Kaylee giggled, although she probably didn't understand half of it. Which was apparent a moment later when she asked, "They got cats with no hairs? What do you rub, then?"

Sara couldn't help it; she snuggled the little girl close and inhaled the sweet scent she'd come to know so well. There was nothing wrong with how she spent her time. She might not have a boyfriend, or her own home, or even her

17

own child. But this precious little girl deserved love, and Sara knew that her life wasn't a sad existence. For now. *How could I even imagine my life without seeing her every day?* She attempted to quiet the thoughts that swirled in her head and just enjoy the moment with her niece.

She thought back to Chloe's words and wondered if she had been truthful. *"You really have no clue how attractive you are, do you? If you put yourself out there, you wouldn't lack for attention."* Was that all it took to find a man? But then, out of nowhere, came the one thing she couldn't seem to block now, no matter how hard she tried. At some point, Nicole and Chris wouldn't need her anymore. Kaylee wouldn't need her anymore. *Damn you, Aunt Lydia.*

Chapter Two

🐾 🐾

Major Gabriel Randall looked up when an envelope landed on his desk unexpectedly. He was more tired than he thought if he'd missed his friend and colleague's appearance. That was the kind of fatigue that could get you killed in Iraq. People back home might believe that the enemy had been eliminated, but the soldiers here on the front lines knew differently. For every bad guy taken out, there were three more just waiting to take their place. And it was damned difficult to fight someone who had little regard for human lives, including their own.

Gabe had been in the Army for sixteen years, and was in the middle of his seventh deployment overseas—which was more than a lot of soldiers he knew. But since he was single, with no kids, he usually volunteered when someone with his qualifications was needed. He was part of a combat brigade in the Airborne Division, and had spent a large part of his career as a paratrooper. His present role when he was stationed in the States was training new recruits and providing general counsel and assistance to the commander of the unit. His job in Iraq was working with his counterparts on how to best utilize the Airborne units there as well as being a liaison to other bases in the area for training and logistical purposes.

Being deployed was no vacation, but some locations were certainly better than others. Iraq was pretty barebones, and the living conditions were very basic. He had a room to himself, though, and they hadn't yet hit the extreme summer heat, which was impossible to adjust to.

Gabe had always tried to lead by example, so when the food sucked, the Wi-Fi was out, the neighbors were tossing grenades over the fence, and he was close to heat stroke, he still attempted to present a calm exterior. *If I lose my shit, everyone around me does as well.* Even with the embedded reporters and firsthand accounts of soldiers, most would still never grasp what the reality of deployment was really like. The military could post all the cheerful pictures on social media that they wanted, and yes, there were days that were better than others. But it was still fucking hard. The young soldiers, save for a few, had a tough time adjusting. Right down to taking a shit, there was nothing simple about being here.

Even though he didn't have a wife and kids missing him back in Alaska, there were still days he was so homesick he could hardly stand it. Little things like getting into a car and driving to the store were probably what he missed the most. *Freedom isn't free.* That saying was one you learned damned quickly when you stepped onto foreign soil in a hostile country. Sure, there were those who welcomed them, but you can't afford to discount the ones who didn't. He'd never been a man who particularly liked the politics of it all. Whether he agreed with a decision or not, at the end of the day, he had a mission to complete. And he had soldiers that he'd do anything to ensure returned to the people they left behind.

"Oh, come on, bro, I saved you the best one. Aren't you gonna open it? Mine was from a fifth-grade class in Kansas. I'm going to have a flag sent to them before I leave."

Gabe picked up the white envelope from his desk and turned it over in his hands. It had obviously been forwarded from another source, since it was simply addressed to *Dear Soldier.* Maybe it was his imagination, but the writing looked neat and feminine. He'd never admit it, but he kind of liked the Charlie Brown stickers on it. He glanced up at his buddy Jason, aka Captain Jason Keller, and shrugged. "You should give this to one of the younger guys who don't have anyone at home." There were a lot of support groups back in the States that sent food and toiletries on a regular basis. But something as seemingly antiquated as snail mail was a big deal here. Having a handwritten message was worth more than most people could possibly guess. And he tried to make sure all of his soldiers were covered in that area.

"Got more than they can open in a week," Jason assured him. "You know the mail has been backed up for a while, so there was a shitload that came in today." Jason pointed to the one Gabe still held in his hand, "Take one for yourself just this once. It's probably from a school like mine. I'll have another flag flown for you to send out to them."

"Yeah, sure." Gabe nodded, knowing it was pointless to argue. He put the envelope down and pushed back from his desk. "Time to feed the troops." Every so often, the senior commissioned and noncommissioned officers served lunch to the troops. It was a way to interact in a more relaxed manner, as well as show appreciation for their hard work. Should they run low on food, he'd eat one of the stale candy bars he kept in his desk for the days he was too busy to go to the chow hall.

The troops were in good spirits as they enjoyed not only a good meal but some much-needed time off. Gabe had been through enough deployments to detect the underlying current of melancholy that hung over the noisy room, but most appeared to be pushing it aside as they joked around with their fellow soldiers.

By the time everyone was served and he'd made the minimum amount of small talk, he was ready to unwind before he caught a few hours' sleep. But the assholes who decided to shoot grenades over the fence had other ideas. Gabe had long ago become desensitized to the sounds of explosions. And most would never be more than an annoyance, but it still required investigation and, at times, retaliation. Thus, another day had passed before he noticed the unopened envelope pushed to the side of his desk. Again, he almost ignored it, but he needed a break. *Something that lets me pretend I'm anywhere but here, if even for a moment. Let's see what you've got, kid.*

And that's what he expected when he opened the card and unfolded the paper tucked inside. To see a child's handwriting. Possibly a picture drawn at the bottom. Instead, he found himself reading a letter that had him not only smiling but laughing by the end. Considering he hadn't done it often lately, it sounded rusty even to his own ears.

Dear Soldier:

Greetings from North Carolina. I hope this finds you well and having a much better day than I've had. So I made the unfortunate mistake of attending a family reunion earlier. I know, I know. I can only blame it on a severe lapse in judgment. Let me stop there and fill you in on a bit of my backstory so that you can fully appreciate what transpired.

I am a thirty-five-year-old woman, and I work as a nanny for my brother's family. I have a college degree in business administration, and I was employed in that field for several years. Then my niece Kaylee was born. She has asthma and constantly fell sick when she was put into day care. They hired a few different nannies, but due to my sister-in-law's colorful personality, none of them stayed for very long. When Kaylee was two, I agreed to use my vacation time to help them out of a jam. My brother was going out of town on business, and his wife couldn't get time off from work to watch their daughter. Long story short, I ended up leaving my job and watching Kaylee full-time. I wasn't happy where I was working . . . and it was only supposed to be until they found a replacement. That was three years ago. I'm completely in love with my niece and it's never been a hardship to care for her. But—well, let me get back to the events of the day before I go there.

My extended family is very . . . vocal. I'm putting that kindly for your benefit. Don't want you to think I'm the type of person who is mean to old people and animals. Anyway, one of my aunts totally blindsided me in front of the entire family unit by announcing that I'm a spinster who lives with my brother. And that I've never had a boyfriend. Which, by the way, isn't true. I had a very active social life before I became a nanny, and I still meet up with friends often.

Since when is being a good person a crime? I thought my relatives were going to give my brother a medal of honor for supporting his deadbeat sister. Then place me in quarantine before some poor innocent person caught my spinsterhood disease. Either that, or ship me off to a retirement home to live out the rest of my golden years. Obviously, I missed the memo that says you're put out to pasture when you reach your mid-thirties. If you, my new friend, are around my age, I'll see if I can get a discounted rate at the local old folks' home. Oh wait—you didn't know you were over-the-hill either? Well, thank goodness, I'm glad it's not just me. Don't worry, we'll have loads of fun playing shuffle board and bingo. If you play your cards right, I'll let you take my scooter for a ride. That sounded rather risqué. Don't get excited, I was speaking of my future motorized chair—bedazzled, of course. According to my family, I've never given a single ride of the other variety, so get that notion right out of your head. If you're a woman, this must sound even more insane.

I should probably end this now. It's already gone off the rails and crashed into a brick wall. You're quite possibly scanning for a return address to forward to the authorities. I promise, I'm harmless. A bit of a disaster when it comes to words, but that's it. Oh, before I forget, I have a very serious question for you. Which character from the movie Top Gun *would you be? Goose or Maverick? If you've never watched the movie before, then do so immediately and get back to me. Cue the music from* Jeopardy. *I'll be waiting.*

Take care and be safe,
Sara the spinster—and future cat lady

He read the letter twice more before reluctantly laying it down. By sharing her own amusing tale of woe, the stranger, a woman named Sara, had made him feel lighter somehow. The stress of the last twenty-four hours had been subdued as he found an escape outlet in her words. And for that, he was more grateful than she'd ever know. He owed her at the very least the courtesy of a reply. Yet as his fingers hovered over the keyboard, he could come up with nothing that even compared to her humor. The few lines he typed sounded stilted and formal. Had it really been so long since he'd put himself out there to someone not affiliated with the military? Well, he couldn't discount his parents and sister, but that was different. He and his dad said a few words, but after that, he mostly listened while his mom and sister talked, and they seemed fine with that. In fact, it was hard to get a word in most of the time. But for some strange reason, he wanted this Sara to like his e-mail. For it to make her smile in the way her letter had him. *But how?* He could tell her he Googled tips on how to write a great letter to a woman. And he actually considered doing just that, then thumped the desk in disgust. *Unless pity is what you're going for, buddy, you should go back to the drawing board.* He was still sitting in the same position ten minutes later when Jason stuck his head in the doorway. "Hey, we gotta go, man. Got that promotion ceremony in a few." Gabe nodded as he began gathering his things. Then before he could talk himself out of it, he sent a brief response to Sara. He had too much on his plate to be stressed out over something so trivial. He doubted he'd ever hear from her again anyway, so why expend energy worrying about it?

Sara:

Thank you for the card and letter you sent. I enjoyed them both. I am thirty-seven, which my mother points out often, so I can relate to your situation. Skip the cat, though, and get a dog. I have one that I miss.

Regards, Major Gabriel Randall, US Army, Iraq

PS . . . I'll take Maverick since Goose meets an unfortunate ending.

Gabe winced as he read over the short response. He'd written warmer and more engaging e-mails to his boss than he had the woman he wanted to impress. Being career military had taught him to get his point across using his words sparingly. He'd long ago lost all social graces, it seemed. Not that he had many to begin with. He was a man who believed in getting to the point. There was no sugar coating, nor chitchat. It was all about the fastest way to accomplish the objective. In business, time was money. But in war, time could be your worst enemy. You work long hours not only because there's always something that needs to be done but also because you need to dull the ache of being away from everyone you know. There was no looking forward to the weekend. Saturday and Sunday were no different than the five days before them. You get up and go to work, then come back to a tiny room where you stare at the walls or watch Netflix. Then you attempt to sleep in an uncomfortable bed. When you're as tall as he was, your feet were usually dangling off the twin-size mattress.

He knew firsthand that the first month of being deployed in a combat zone, you woke with your heart racing as the sounds of fighter jets landing and taking off shook the thin walls around you. And, of course, the announcements when there were bombings near or inside the base. The latter can be terrifying for the newbies, but even they become accustomed to all of that after a while. *Life in the suck zone.*

Speaking of time, Gabe glanced down at his watch, then cursed under his breath. Unless he was dealing with an emergency, he was never late for anything. Yet his musings had done just that, to the tune of two minutes. He jumped to his feet and hurried out of the office. *This is all on you, mystery lady.* It was painfully obvious that he was more Major Randall than Gabriel Randall, which made sense given how many tours he'd done. That also made him good at his job, so that wasn't a total negative. *But what would the woman who wrote the letter think?* It shouldn't matter, and Gabriel knew that. The brief moment of receiving something unrelated to war, unrelated to risk, unrelated to woe, was just that. A brief distraction, something he'd probably not receive again given his succinct reply. Duty called. Back to real life.

Sara was lying in bed flipping channels. She'd already tried reading, but nothing seemed to keep her attention. Normally she was thrilled when Kaylee went to bed early without a struggle, but without the distraction of her niece, she found the evening to be endless. At one point she'd drifted off to sleep herself, which had been a big mistake. Because now she was wide awake, with no end in sight.

She'd just settled on a rerun of *Sex in the City* when the
e-mail alert on her iPad sounded. She absently picked it up
from the nightstand and scanned the preview. *Wait, what?*
The e-mail subject read: "Thanks for your card." It had
been almost a month since she'd mailed the card to the radio station. She'd hoped for a reply, but hadn't really expected one. *It's probably spam, don't get excited.* The
sender's address was Gabriel.T.Randall.mil@mail.com.
*Looks official enough. Why in the heck am I still sitting
here guessing?* Sara hesitated another moment, then took a
deep breath. She had no idea why she was so nervous. *This
is nuts. Open the damned e-mail already.*

She straightened her shoulders and braced herself before
clicking the button. Her pulse leapt as she read the message:

Sara:

*Thank you for the card and letter you sent. I enjoyed them
both. I am thirty-seven, which my mother points out often,
so I can relate to your situation. Skip the cat, though, and
get a dog. I have one that I miss.*

Regards, Major Gabriel Randall, US Army, Iraq

*PS . . . I'll take Maverick since Goose meets an unfortunate
ending.*

Okay, admittedly it was rather brief. And her spam mail
from her Internet provider was way more animated, but

still. Her letter had reached a deployed soldier. Once again, her fingers were hovering as she debated a reply. He hadn't asked her any questions, nor made any type of overture toward continuing their communication. He hadn't exactly said he was single either. Although she thought he alluded to the fact when he mentioned his mother giving him a hard time about his age. So what if she'd written him a book and he'd responded with a paragraph? He probably figured she talked enough for both of them. *Screw it, what have I got to lose?* She might never hear from Gabriel again, but this qualified as the most exciting thing to happen to her in ages. *And this year's spinster award goes to . . .*

Sara pushed that depressing thought aside. She'd dwelled on her aunt's words more than enough since the reunion from hell last month. Gabriel was no doubt breathlessly anticipating her reply. She didn't want to keep him waiting. *Dare to dream, sister, dare to dream.*

Dear Gabriel:

It's great to hear from you! It sounds like we have a lot in common with the whole age thing. Although I'm not sure men are considered spinsters. Assuming you're single, of course. I think you'd just be called a bachelor. That hardly seems fair, does it? My nickname brings to mind the little old lady in the deck of Old Maid cards. While yours makes me think of that reality television show where the men get to pick from women who look like supermodels. You lucky thing. Plus, the whole uniform thing clearly gives you the

*advantage. From my experience, it seems to make even
unattractive men appear sexy. Camouflage is a real miracle worker. Kinda like a Wonderbra. Not that I'm saying you
need it. (The uniform, not the bra.) I'm sure you're handsome. Heck, everyone has something that works for them,
right? At least one feature that others notice. Not sure
what mine is. I can touch my nose with the tip of my
tongue. Wait, I don't think that counts.*

What is your dog's name?

Be safe,

Sara

Sara read it over twice more, thinking it sounded even
more insane than the first note. Yet he'd responded to it,
hadn't he? If he'd done it out of pity, then shouldn't she stay
with what worked? She hit the Send button, then picked up
her cell phone to call Chloe. Surprisingly enough, they'd
stayed in touch after the reunion. Not only had they gone out
to dinner once, but she'd also met her for lunch a few times.
Of course, Kaylee had been along as well, but Chloe didn't
seem to mind. They'd even gotten into the habit of calling
and texting each other most days. It was the closest thing to
a friend that she'd had in years. But ever the pessimist, she
wondered how long it would be before her cousin got involved with some guy and disappeared. That had happened
to all of her friends from high school and college. They got
married, had families, and were just sort of gone. It wasn't

that they were inconsiderate people, it was simply that their lives went in different directions and they ended up spending time with people they had more common ground with. At one time she'd spent time with Shannon, a woman who lived right across the street. But between Sara having such an unpredictable schedule and Shannon having her second child, their friendship had turned into more of a friendly wave when they saw each other in passing. They had gotten a quick cup of coffee together a few months back, but those occasions were few and far between now. There were a couple of other single women who lived nearby, but they appeared to have their own network of friends and showed no interest in branching out. Unfortunately, it made it all too easy to end up a virtual recluse, with her main source of company and entertainment coming from a five-year-old. *Don't forget dear old Mom.*

When Sara's father had died unexpectedly of a heart attack a few months after Kaylee was born, she saw first-hand what a bad thing it could be for one partner to coddle the other. Her father had controlled everything. Her mother had never paid a bill before, nor did she have a clue as to how much money they had in the bank. By being the man of the house in all aspects, he'd essentially ensured that his wife wouldn't be able to stand on her own feet should something happen to him. Sara knew he hadn't done it maliciously. He doted on his wife and wanted to take care of her. He didn't want her to be upset over anything. Even though the doctor said that his heart attack was caused by blockages in several major arteries, she knew that the stress he had to be under at times couldn't have been good for his health.

So now, Sara had taken over the finances for her mother. And Chris handled any type of repairs. For a while she attempted to get her mother involved each month when she went over the household account, but she'd wring her hands and make a million excuses why she couldn't. Eventually it seemed easier and faster to do it herself. *Hello pot, meet kettle.* Their father had probably come to the same conclusion years ago, so how could she hold it against him? And if Sara was bad, Chris was worse. He treated their mother like fine china. And in his defense, their mother seemed to be a master at working them to her advantage. She had the "poor me" act down to a science. Plus, if she met any resistance, she could, and would, produce tears in five seconds flat. It was actually kind of impressive. Poor Kaylee didn't stand a chance. Not only was her mother emotionally manipulative, but her grandmother was too. It's totally genetics. *At least Kaylee has me.*

Basically, what it all boiled down to was that Sara had two kids to take care of. And Kaylee was the only one who wanted to learn new things. Their mother was firmly committed to being coddled, and didn't seem to care who it inconvenienced. Sara loved her mother, but a part of her had also started resenting the fact that she seemed to want and expect her daughter to put aside any thoughts of having a life of her own. Before their father died, her mother had urged Sara to get out more. To meet someone and settle down. But that encouragement had packed up and skipped town. And in its place were guilt-laced words, such as "I don't know what I'd do if you left me too, Sara." Or the ever-popular "I'm so lucky you decided not to get married." When exactly was that choice made? *Congratulations, Sara, you've won a lifetime supply of mommy-sitting. Step right up and claim your prize.*

"Hellooo, I know you're there, I can hear you breathing." Sara nearly jumped off the bed as her cousin's raised voice came through the line. She'd been so busy brooding over her mother that she hadn't been aware of pressing the speed dial for Chloe.

"Er—sorry about that." She laughed as she reclined against the headboard. "I was a little distracted and missed you answering."

"That was about five minutes ago," Chloe said wryly. "I just put the call on speaker while I dried my hair." *Oh crap, had it really been that long?*

If anyone would understand the deal with her mother, it was Chloe, but Sara didn't feel like rehashing another exciting episode of "Why my world sucks ass" right now. She'd save that for a rare evening out and a fishbowl margarita. *Better make that several if you're going to get through it without sobbing uncontrollably.* "I got a response," she said excitedly. "Can you believe it? I was floored. I really had no expectations to begin with, and what few there were had pretty much dwindled away by now."

"Sara, that's wonderful," Chloe exclaimed before asking, "Exactly what are we talking about? Wait—is this about the letter to the manager of the Walmart down the street from you? I hope you scored a gift card. That was a nasty cut you got off that dilapidated shopping cart. That's a law-suit waiting to happen. Good for you."

For a moment she drew a complete blank. *Walmart? What th*— "Oh no, it's not that," she replied, remembering her rant about being stabbed by a rogue cart. "Remember the Easter card I sent to the radio station? The ones they were forwarding to deployed soldiers?"

"Er—vaguely," she replied. Sara could almost hear the wheels turning in Chloe's head as she racked her brain. It was tempting to let her go awhile longer, but she was too excited to share the news. So she repeated the details once again, then added, "Anyway, tonight I got an e-mail from Major Gabriel Randall."

Chloe whistled under her breath, "That name reminds me of either a naughty pastor or a virginal nerd. Well, actu-ally he could be both things. What'd he say? Did he send a picture? Wait, did you send one?" She was firing off ques-tions so fast that Sara was beginning to wish she'd texted her instead of calling.

"No, he didn't send a picture, and neither did I. This was to support the troops, not try to pick them up." Chloe asked her to read the e-mail, which took only seconds.

"I've been more stimulated by bad Mexican food. Talk about lack of personality. Did he at least toss an emoticon or two in there? Something—like anything—to show he's not an android."

Sara laughed, having had similar thoughts. "Maybe it's

a military thing. Wouldn't it have been more surprising if he used some kind of Snoop Dogg lingo?"

"I guess you've got a point. Although it would have been funny as hell. Have you responded? I assume you're going to . . . but you should wait a few days. Don't want to seem too available, you know? Act like you're a social dynamo. It took a while, but you finally managed to get back to him. Also, keep it as brief as he did. You know how impatient men can be? Leave him wanting more, not nodding off while reading your mini-series."

Sara inwardly winced. "Chloe, this isn't a dating app. I'm simply writing to one of our soldiers who is off fighting to ensure our freedom. Our interaction isn't about finding a man . . . and I doubt he'd be thinking anything like that about me either. It's just a program to look after our soldiers." She felt a little uneasy at Chloe's assumption. She'd never been the type to give so that she could get something in return. And she certainly hadn't sent the card hoping for a date.

"You're so right. Sorry, Sara. Did you write back already?" she asked with less enthusiasm.

Sara chuckled. "I did. It was short, though. He didn't say much, so I didn't have a lot to go on." And that was an understatement. Still, Sara knew what the contact was about. Support for the men and women serving our country.

"What did you write?" She was tempted to lie, but in the end, she read the e-mail exactly as it was written, fully expecting another lecture. But surprisingly, Chloe giggled. Not just a polite chuckle either, but a full-fledged roar of laughter. "You sound like a basket of crazy," she gasped out. "That was freaking great, I love it." Talk about a back-handed compliment. *Is she screwing with me?*

"Um, really? You actually approve? I thought it was a bit . . . eccentric. He's probably picturing me as one of those chicks that wears pajamas with flip-flops out in public."

"Who gives a crap? After that, even I want to hear more from you. The world is full of way too much polite chatter. People waste hours with pleasantries without ever giving you a real glimpse into who they are. You may have sounded bat-shit nuts, but you were funny. And a sense of humor is rare and underrated. I'll tell you something else: I've known you our whole lives, and just that little bit makes me see you in a different light, Sara. Your personality literally leaps out. You sparkle."

"Sparkle, hey? Did I mention in my first letter that I wrote about bedazzled wheelchairs?"

"No. You totally left that bit out." She laughed. "See what I mean? This is great, Sara. You never know, this could become a little fledgling romance, although if you look at my track record with men, I obviously need advice more than you do." The last was said in a joking manner, but Sara could hear the sad undertones in her cousin's voice. She wasn't even close to getting over the jerk who had broken her heart. But Sara also knew that Chloe shared in bits and pieces, most of them unexpected. If Sara tried to pry, she'd shut down fairly quickly.

"I thought Gabriel made my night, but you may have topped him," Sara said sincerely. "Thank you for what you said, that means a lot to me. I'm not normally one to joke around so easily with a stranger, but there's something about the anonymity of e-mail that feels freeing. We've never met in person, nor will we ever. So I can be whomever I want, you know?" *Sara the spinster has left the building, folks. At least where Gabriel is concerned.* "Oh crap, I've gotta go. Kaylee is calling." Sara sighed, already on her feet and crossing the room. Regardless of what she was doing, she could always hear the little girl. *Just like a mother should.*

"Well, far be it from Nicole to actually get off her butt and check on her daughter. Gotta have her rest so she can deliver that one hour of work tomorrow." Even though she didn't respond to the insult, Sara couldn't help agreeing. She was in no way paid enough to essentially be Kaylee's primary caregiver. Luckily, she did it out of love and not for the money.

Sara said a quick good night and laid her phone on Kaylee's nightstand as she lowered herself to the bed next to her. Oddly enough, as she rubbed her niece's back and whispered soothing words to lull her back to sleep, she thought of Gabriel. She'd looked up Iraq and knew there was a seven-hour time difference. Was he having breakfast now? Was he one of those wretched morning people who woke up cheerful? As she continued to ponder the mystery that was Gabriel Randall, she wondered if he had any idea how much one brief e-mail from him meant to a stranger in North Carolina. A woman who was lonelier than she'd ever admit—even to herself.

Chapter Three

🐾 🐾

This is damned ridiculous. You're a seasoned soldier. You've been shot at, dodged bombs, and shaken hands with four sitting presidents. You bow to no one, remember? Even as he ran through the reasons why he shouldn't be excited as he stared at his in-box, it didn't change the fact that he was. The notification had come through on his phone as he was finishing breakfast in the chow hall. The last cup of coffee he chugged was now burning like acid in his stomach. He'd rather take a bullet than have any of his troops ever find out about this. The fact that she'd even written back was nothing short of a miracle. *Pity e-mail?* Remembering the letter he'd sent her, he feared it might be a brush-off. *Dear Soldier: E-mail me when you remove the stick from your ass. Kind regards, Bored in North Carolina.* She'd word it a little better, but he was half expecting that when he finally opened her e-mail.

Dear Gabriel:

It's great to hear from you! It sounds like we have a lot in common with the whole age thing. Although I'm not sure men are considered spinsters. Assuming you're single, of course. I think you'd just be called a bachelor. That hardly seems fair, does it? My nickname brings to mind the little old lady in the deck of Old Maid cards. While yours makes me think of that reality television show where the men get to pick from women who look like supermodels. You lucky thing. Plus, the whole uniform thing clearly gives you the advantage. From my experience, it seems to make even unattractive men appear sexy. Camouflage is a real miracle worker. Kinda like a Wonderbra. Not that I'm saying you need it. (The uniform, not the bra.) I'm sure you're handsome. Heck, everyone has something that works for them, right? At least one feature that others notice. Not sure what mine is. I can touch my nose with the tip of my tongue. Wait, I don't think that counts.

What is your dog's name?

Be safe,

Sara

Gabe felt a smile once again tugging at the corners of his mouth. She was so adorable. He'd read her first letter so many times he knew it by heart now. Sara was quirky, and that appealed to him. It was only a letter, and he had no idea if she'd write more, but it gave Gabriel something he'd gone without for years: someone other than his family checking in on him. While he wasn't lovesick by any stretch of the imagination, he felt he understood the goofy expressions some of his soldiers wore when they heard from their significant other. It wasn't that there hadn't been women in his life. He'd been lucky enough to meet some amazing ones. But somehow, he was always uninvolved when he deployed. There was no one pining away for him at home. Well, other than his dog, Trouble. And his affection could be bought by food and petting. Come to think of it, he was typical of a lot of males in that regard.

Gabe figured it was better not to subject someone to his long absences. It didn't seem fair to ask them to wait for him. And if there's one thing he'd witnessed over and over again, it was the strain that military life could put on a relationship. So many of the couples he knew with one person enlisted ended up either divorced or living separate lives. That's not to say he wouldn't be willing to try a committed relationship if the right person came along— but thus far, that hadn't happened. He'd loved before, but he'd never been in love. Not the kind he dreamed of years ago, before he turned into the cynic he was now. Although if he was honest with himself, he knew he wasn't a cynic at his core. He'd just never made *finding* love a priority, and at this point in his career, it still wasn't in the cards.

It wasn't as if he believed that Sara, this mythical creature who was interested in corresponding with him, had just happened upon his life to be his forever love. That would be foolish thinking, and if there was one thing Gabriel was not, it was foolish. Nor illogical. Contact with Sara would be brief and entertaining. He doubted her intention of writing had been anything other than an obligatory greeting to the overseas soldier she had been assigned. *Should I nip this in the bud now? Although what's the harm in writing back and forth for a bit?* He could delete her e-mail and let it go. But—he just couldn't do it.

Military mail was a pain in the ass at times. What if he changed his mind and it was not in the recycle bin? That thought alone made him feel a little queasy. So maybe he wouldn't get rid of her e-mail yet. No harm in letting it sit there. The trick was not replying. Gabe grabbed a nearby folder with some information for the morning meeting and hurried from his office. He would stay busy until the urge had passed.

Two hours later, Gabe felt like a junky deprived of his fix. His knees were bouncing up and down, and he was chewing gum as if his life depended on it. *It was mean not to send a quick message. A gentleman doesn't ignore a lady.* He knew that last one was a reach, but still, he'd take any justification at this point. It was almost alarming how much he craved hearing from this Sara again. And he knew for that to happen, he had to do his part. Before he could wage another inner battle, he opened her e-mail and hit the Reply button.

Sara:

*Yes, I am single and my dog's name is Trouble. After being
surrounded by our uniforms for many years, I don't think I
share your views on them suiting everyone equally well. I
would agree that touching your nose with your tongue isn't
necessarily a feature. And I've never given any thought as
to what mine would be.*

Thanks,

Gabe

Gabe shook his head in defeat. He hadn't thought it could
get much worse than his first written disaster, but this one was
a strong contender. *Why can't I just talk to her like a friend?*
If he was this uptight with all women, that might explain why
they weren't exactly beating his door down. Again, he wondered why it suddenly mattered so much to him. As intrigued
as he was with his new pen pal, a part of him resented her as
well. He had more than enough shit to keep him awake at
night. Now, thanks to her, he was actually giving thought to
being liked? When had he ever given a damn about anyone's
approval? He'd moved up in the ranks of the military through
hard work, dedication, and precision, not kissing ass. Same
thing applied to other areas of his life. He was there if needed
and stayed out of things that weren't any of his concern.
*You're the social butterfly of Anchorage, Alaska. Winning
them over everywhere you go with that personality.*

Before he wasted more of his day on self-analysis, Gabe hit the Send button and logged off his computer. He'd never been happier to know he was needed at the airfield. At least that would keep his mind off *her* for a while. *Get out of my head, lady,* he inwardly groused as he crossed the runway. As if afraid he'd jinxed himself, his next thought was, *Please write back.*

Sara smiled as Kaylee walked toward the car. One of the teachers opened her door and waited for the little girl to settle inside before closing it behind her. When she'd started the half-day kindergarten a few months earlier, it had really made Sara think about her own future. In her mind, Kaylee would always be the baby she'd fallen in love with at first sight. Oh, she knew there was no fear of losing her job for years to come, but by then her chances to have a family of her own might have diminished. *Well, you don't exactly have any baby daddy prospects lining up to take you off the market.* That might be true, but as Chloe had mentioned more than once, Sara wasn't likely to meet someone sitting at home every night.

What about Gabe? She'd *met* Gabe, and was enjoying chatting back and forth with him. Even if his messages weren't particularly long. Surely that counted as *meeting* someone, and who knew . . . maybe she'd gain her confidence back and be able to find someone closer to home.

They'd been running late that morning, so Sara had rushed Kaylee out of the house to get to school. Then she'd spent the last few hours grocery shopping and running errands for Nicole. Returning the other woman's clothes wasn't her job, but her sister-in-law didn't seem to get that.

Now that she finally had a moment to breathe, she couldn't help the rush of anticipation at the thought of her new online friend. She hadn't checked her e-mail, but considering how pained he sounded in his previous one, she was doubtful he'd jumped right in and answered quickly. As Kaylee chattered on and on about her preschool crush, Jimmy, Sara found herself counting the minutes until they were home, which was a first for her. Normally she attempted to prolong their time out, knowing it would make the afternoon shorter and also help Kaylee burn off some excess energy. "Sarie, can we go to McDonald's?"

Oh crap. Wait, that's perfect. "Absolutely, sweetheart," Sara said brightly as she took the next exit. Even though Nicole rarely ever cooked, she frowned on her daughter eating fast food. Something Sara usually agreed with. But once in a while, Kaylee deserved a treat. And with the afternoon seeming to loom before her, she felt like today was a perfect day for a splurge.

Like most people, she got bored sometimes by the routine of her days, but Kaylee was very good at keeping her entertained. Lately, though, she longed for . . . more. She could blame the whole attack of discontent on her aunt Lydia. Having your life scrutinized in front of a roomful of people not only was embarrassing, but kind of brought some hard truths home. The mirror you could no longer avoid. And even though she was thrilled to have met Gabe, it also made her yearn for someone special in her life. There was a restlessness within her that hadn't been there before.

Strangely enough, the McDonald's atmosphere was fairly low key when they arrived. Within a few moments, Sara had their tray, and Kaylee was impatiently holding open the door to the play area. Usually the excited squeals of the kids would have her cringing, but she was so distracted she barely noticed. Kaylee looked longingly at the slide and back at her as they took a seat at a corner table. "Sorry, sweetheart, you know the rule. You need to eat at least half your food before you play." She couldn't help laughing as the little girl took a big bite of her burger from one hand while holding an apple slice in the other. It appeared she was gearing up to race through her meal. "Please slow down. You don't want to choke."

"Okay, Sarie," Kaylee mumbled around the apple slice, which was now in her mouth. The pained look on her face clearly said that Sara was trying her patience, but she didn't complain. Even at five, she was smart enough to know that it would just delay the fun. She knew that all parents felt as if their kid was the best at everything, and Sara was no exception. Kaylee was absolutely precious. A combination of smart, stubborn, sweet, and so damned funny. *Don't forget you're not her mother.* Nicole and Chris were the ones who would be front and center at every major moment in this child's life, as they should be. *And you'll be standing to the side next to your mother.*

When Kaylee finished her food, Sara had her phone out

before the girl had taken two steps from the table. "Have fun, sweetie, and remember your manners," she called out absently as she impatiently logged into her e-mail. And there it was . . . another reply from Gabe. She clutched her iPhone as if it would take flight if she didn't hold it tightly. Yet she did nothing more. After all of her eagerness, she sat staring at the screen. *Why am I so nervous? This is nuts. I don't even know him. How come this is so important to me?* But she couldn't deny it did feel important to her. Meeting him had given her an excitement she hadn't felt in so long. And she was afraid each time that either she'd never hear from him again or he'd simply brush her off. *His brief responses aren't exactly begging you to continue contacting him.*

Before she found an excuse to delay any longer, she quickly opened the e-mail and smiled at the short paragraph. He certainly wasn't one to waste words.

Sara,

Yes, I am single and my dog's name is Trouble. After being surrounded by our uniforms for many years, I don't think I share your views on them suiting everyone equally well. I would agree that touching your nose with your tongue isn't necessarily a feature. And I've never given any thought as to what mine would be.

Thanks,

Gabe

She did a quick check and saw he'd sent it only a few hours after hers. *That had to mean something, right? Maybe he enjoys talking to me as much as I enjoy his letters.* Chloe would be horrified, but she hit the Reply button instead of waiting until later.

Gabe:

Why did you name your dog Trouble? There must be a story there. Don't leave me hanging here. As for the uniforms, you're a guy so I think I can safely assume that although you might be more of an expert on females, I am clearly in a better position to judge the males. OK, OK, I realize the fact that I haven't had a date since electricity was invented might call my credentials into question, but I still believe I'm a more thorough judge than you are. Now you're over there thinking I sound like the world's biggest pervert, aren't you? Spinster Sara spends her days cruising military bases, and her nights scouring the Internet for a little camo eye-candy. That's my kink, Randall. Run, soldier, run! Since I have no clue as to what you look like, I can't pick a favorite feature for you, but if we're going by talent, like my tongue to the nose, yours would clearly be your chattiness.

Back to you,

Sara

She couldn't help laughing at what she'd written. "That's my kink"? There was no way she could send that. He really would think she was a nut. Her finger was hovering over the Cancel button when Kaylee barreled into the table. Sara's drink went crashing to the floor, and tea seemed to cover everything around her. "I'm sorry, Sarie," Kaylee cried out as she looked down at the carnage she'd accidentally caused.

"It's fine, sweetie," Sara assured her. "Could you grab some extra napkins while I pick everything up?" Sara turned to lay her cell phone on the table and she noticed the screen. *Message Sent.* "Oh crap," she whispered. Somehow in the commotion she'd hit the button. The downside of using a phone for correspondence was that the small screen size left little space between selections. She'd done it a few times before, but it had never been a big deal. Usually she ended up sending a half-finished e-mail and had to explain it. But how could she tell Gabe, "Sorry, that whole pervert part was a joke. You weren't supposed to see it."

Sara felt something tugging on her shirt, and she glanced over to see Kaylee staring up at her. "I'll clean it up, Sarie, don't cry." She realized she was still standing where the little girl had left her, probably looking as upset as she felt. But the sinking feeling in her gut had nothing to do with their sticky surroundings. She already worried each time that she'd never hear from Gabe again, but this time she was almost certain of it. *Unless he wants your 900 number.*

"Aunt Sara's tummy isn't feeling too well, honey," she

murmured as she patted Kaylee's back gently. "How about using your strong muscles to help me and we'll be done in no time." And she was right—that particular mess was taken care of and forgotten moments later. Unfortunately, the one she'd made with her wayward finger would probably haunt her for far longer. *Scouring the Internet for a little camo eye-candy? What the hell, Sara?*

Chapter Four

It was after nine in the evening, but Gabe was in no hurry to go back to his room. Why bother? His office was far less claustrophobic, and the Wi-Fi was definitely better. Some nights he'd stay there and watch a movie or television show until after the crowds using the dorm showers had diminished. Right now, they'd be herded in the tight space like cattle, and that was just a little too much closeness with his troops. He tried to ignore the small tingle he felt as he propped his feet on his desk and casually opened his e-mail folder. He'd intentionally avoided checking it for the last few hours, trying to pretend he wasn't as anxious as a teenage boy with his first crush. *It's deployment boredom—everyone has it.* Even as he made excuses, he couldn't mistake the jump of his pulse as he saw her name in his unread messages. He pondered waiting a while longer to open it, but that was carrying it a bit too far. After all, if a tree falls in a forest and no one sees it, did it happen? *Really, man?* Even his subconscious was shaking its head at that rationale. A few keyboard taps later and he was anxiously scanning her letter.

"Ookkkaayy," he muttered to himself. Her choice of words got more interesting every time. He had to admit, his eyes had locked on "kink" right away. He knew she was joking around. Although there were some big military bases in North Carolina, he couldn't see her trying to pick up men outside Fort Bragg. She didn't seem the type. What she was to him was a breath of fresh air. She was hilarious, quirky, and damned entertaining. He liked that she didn't appear to filter her replies to him. *Hell, for all I know, this is the heavily edited version.* He laughed aloud at that thought. Come to think of it, he smiled or laughed every single time he heard from her. *Bet she can't say the same about your zero personality responses. She's definitely getting the short end of the stick.* He was beyond curious about her. Now, more than ever, he'd love to know what she looked like. Not to judge her appearance, but simply to put a face with the words and sense of humor that he enjoyed so much. He could send her a picture of himself and possibly prompt her into sending him one in return, but that seemed kind of like a pickup attempt. *Dear Sara: I like piña coladas and getting caught in the rain, how about you?* She'd probably enjoy that line. Although corny, it was less robotic than his usual prose. He flexed his fingers, ready to send back another masterpiece. Or in his case a disaster-piece. He knew he'd come across as cooler if he waited until the morning before responding, but that would delay getting another e-mail from her. And dammit, he couldn't bring himself to go to bed without making certain that was a possibility. *Pathetic, Gabe, really sad.*

Sara:

I found my dog at a rest area.

That's what you're leading with, Randall? She mentions kink and camo eye-candy, and you lead with how you met Trouble. He was certain Sara wanted to know about how this dog decided Gabe would be his owner and he hadn't really had a say in it. Still, she'd asked, so he answered. As he wrote, he pondered when the last time was that he simply *chatted* with someone. A drink at a bar stateside really didn't count, did it? Once Gabe had tapped out his six or so lines, and a few eye rolls thrown in for good measure, he hit Send and got off-line.

Shit. He'd tried to seem more human this time, but he wasn't sure how successful he'd been. With his family, he could just ask questions about relatives, but with a stranger, it was much harder. There was no common ground to discuss or shared acquaintances. She was a civilian, so that automatically excluded her from a big chunk of his usual conversations. Plus, there wasn't much he could elaborate on concerning his current mission. Most of it was classified, which could be a hard point to get across at times.

No need to sit around obsessing over his lack of writing skills. His message might not be great, but it was definitely an improvement—or at least he hoped so. *Couldn't get much worse, buddy.*

Sara awoke when something kicked her in the side. "Ouch, what th—?" A moment later she had her answer as she reached out to flip on the bedside lamp and turned to see Kaylee sleeping sideways next to her. "Kaylee Marie," she grumbled as she moved the little girl's feet away from her. She was surprised she hadn't noticed her before now. *Probably because you stayed up late checking your e-mail constantly.* "It was only a few times," Sara said under her breath. Then felt insane for arguing with herself. It wasn't as if her inner Sara didn't know the score, so lying was kind of useless. A loud snore filled the room, and she smiled. Hard to believe such a tiny thing could make so much noise.

There was over an hour before they had to be up, so she debated going back to sleep. *Or you could surf the Internet. Just to kill some time.* More denial, but habits were hard to break. Unable to resist the urge, she grabbed her iPad off the nightstand and saw the mail notification on the lock screen. "It's probably not even from him," she whispered, and got a snort from Kaylee in response. "Hey, don't give me that attitude, kid; one day this'll be you. All tied into knots waiting to hear from some boy." Another snort sounded, almost as if she were following along with the conversation perfectly. With damp palms and the now familiar hum of anticipation, Sara clicked a few times and there was Gabe's name, right under a spam message saying she'd won ten million dollars. "And my horoscope said nothing about good fortune." She deleted it, and moved on to the one she really wanted.

Sara:

I found my dog at a rest area. I left my information on the billboard there, but no one ever contacted me. He ran up to my truck that day and promptly pissed on one of my tires. I told him he was going to be nothing but Trouble, and it stuck. Your kink cannot be staking out military bases, otherwise you'd have been disillusioned about the so-called miracle of camouflage long ago. And I've never run from anything in my life, although I should have a few times. I'm not a man who does idle chat well, sorry.

Gabe

Sara grinned, feeling kind of melty inside at his story of how he'd found his dog. Even though his e-mail was brief once again, she still thought it showed more of his personality. *Why does he never ask me questions?* The hardest part of communicating with a stranger was keeping the conversation ball in the air. And Gabe didn't make that easy. She hated to rattle on about herself or silly stuff all the time, but he didn't leave her much choice. If he'd ask about her, it would give her an idea of what he might be curious about and she could expound on it. Otherwise, she'd blurt out whatever came to mind and that could be dangerous. *He must like it. He's still responding.* She hoped the radio station had received a lot of letters, so that other deployed military personnel had someone to talk to as well.

Chloe had said to be herself. If her gorgeous cousin thought she was engaging, then maybe Gabe felt the same way. *Be fun, Sara. He doesn't have to know whether that part of you exists beyond the computer.* This time, she didn't even try to talk herself into postponing her reply. It would only lengthen her wait in return. So she settled back against her headboard and began typing.

Gabe:

I loved the story of Trouble, it made me smile. Bet you've had to answer the question of his name more than once. You found me out, I have never been on a covert op at a military base. But I've checked out my fair share at the neighborhood Walmart. You can rest easy, though, I've never tailed any of them home, so you're safe—for now. Believe it or not, I'm usually a person of few words. Some would say I'm an introvert, except with my niece. She simply won't allow anything other than full participation when I'm playing Barbie or Minions with her. If you're impressed by my witty conversation, you'd be spellbound by my voice-over talent. I do a different variation for every stuffed animal the kid has. We get some funny looks out in public when I'm channeling Daddy Pig from Peppa Pig.

What are you doing right now? I'm still in bed. My niece woke me up with a foot to the head. It was a rude awakening, to say the least, but it allowed me to read and respond to your message, so it might be considered a good thing, right? After all, I know you eagerly await my replies as much as I do yours. That last part isn't a joke in case you're wondering. I really do look forward to hearing from you each time.

Have a great day, Gabe :)

Sara

After she sent the message, she debated getting up and doing something productive, but she'd likely wake Kaylee up in the process and it didn't seem worth it. So she snuggled back down into the soft cocoon of her covers and used the remaining time to daydream about a man in Iraq who was occupying more and more of her thoughts. And she wondered—or rather hoped—whether it might be possible that he was experiencing the same thing.

Chapter Five

🐾 🐾

Gabe was yawning when he jumped the short distance from the Blackhawk helicopter to the ground. He'd spent most of the day at another base meeting with some bigwigs who'd flown in for a brief morale visit. Normally his lieutenant colonel would be along as well, but he'd flown back to the States a few days ago for a couple of weeks. The whole dog and pony show was something he'd never enjoyed. He preferred leaving that to others, but as with most any job, there were politics involved to some degree. And even if nothing ever came of it, he felt strongly that everyone in Washington needed to see the conditions that the troops were forced to deal with at some dangerous locations. No better place for that than Iraq. He'd barely been able to keep a straight face when they took a few bites of the tasteless food. He wondered how they'd feel after eating basically the same menu every week for months. Most deployed soldiers shed any extra pounds pretty damn fast. He was almost certain they weren't interested in sleeping on a narrow cot in a tent with a dozen other soldiers while hoping the shit air-conditioning kept the temperature inside bearable. Then there were the ever-popular trailers that were made into bathrooms. You quickly lost whatever modesty you might have after a few weeks of doing your business in such close quarters.

He knew it could be a slow process to make improvements to bases in a foreign country. There was likely more red tape involved than even he knew. And the most urgent needs had to be addressed first. But he never passed up an opportunity to point out how even small things, like decent Wi-Fi and hot water, were big morale boosters to the soldiers who spent so much time away from home.

After his demanding day, he wanted nothing more than a shower and bed. He didn't give a shit if the chlorine was so strong in the water it stung his eyes—as long as it was hot tonight, he'd be happy. Lukewarm water was usually about as much as they could hope for, but you learned to deal with it. Plus, with summer temperatures reaching well over 100 degrees, it didn't matter much half the year.

As tired and grimy as he was, though, he found himself walking to his office instead of to the dorms. He didn't bother to tell himself it was for business. No, it was her—Sara. He could attempt to check his e-mail from his room, but the Wi-Fi there was shit and he was too tired to retrace his steps if it didn't connect tonight. He stopped to briefly exchange a few words with the evening shift before finally closing the door behind him. He dropped heavily into his ever-squeaking desk chair and signed onto his computer. *Please be there.* Rationally he knew that eventually he wouldn't have a reply waiting. She had a life outside of being his pen pal. But he'd become addicted to the respite her cheerful words gave him.

Gabe released the breath he hadn't been aware he was holding when he saw her latest message. He was happier than anyone with a pound of sand in their shoes should be, but if nothing else, life here taught you to embrace the little things that came your way. And she brought those moments to him every time he heard from her. He found himself smiling at her words. When he reached the last paragraph, he read through it twice.

What are you doing right now? I'm still in bed. My niece woke me up with a foot to the head. It was a rude awakening, to say the least, but it allowed me to read and respond to your message, so it might be considered a good thing, right? After all, I know you eagerly await my replies as much as I do yours. That last part isn't a joke in case you're wondering. I really do look forward to hearing from you each time.

Have a great day, Gabe :)

Sara

From Alaska with Love

He winced in sympathy over her being awoken with a foot to her head. But what really stood out was her admission of looking forward to hearing from him. Was she simply being nice? He should probably consider it a generic pleasantry, but he didn't really think that was the case here. She genuinely appeared to enjoy their correspondence as much as he did. Which, in turn, made him feel kind of special. *She's probably saying the same thing to ten other soldiers.* He froze as that unwelcome thought flittered through his head. He didn't even know this woman. They could pass on the street and he'd be none the wiser. He was being ridiculous. He should hope that she was bringing the same kind of magic to others as well. Did his fellow soldiers deserve it less than him? *Asshole award, right here.* And with that, he dropped back into his chair and hit the Reply button.

Sara:

Nothing wrong with being an introvert. You already know by now that I don't use ten words when two will do. I could blame it on the military, but it's just me. Everyone has their part to play in the game of life. If we were all the same, where would that leave us? I like the image you present of doing the voices with your niece. And every kid is probably embarrassed by adults at some point. It's those times they'll remember when they're older, and not the serious stuff.

Right now, I'm in my office. I'm dirty and tired from traveling today. Looking forward to bed and a few hours of sleep to recharge. I like your e-mails too.

Talk soon,

Gabe

As he read over his response once before sending it, Gabe gave himself a mental pat on the back. *I'm definitely getting the hang of this.* Not that it was great by any stretch of the imagination, but it wasn't the worst he'd sent either. He'd even written two paragraphs. He'd have to check back to be certain, but he thought that was a first.

Just then a knock on his door jarred him back to the present. One look at Jason's stark expression told Gabe two things: Something was very wrong, and there would be no sleep for him that night.

Sara was sitting at her mother's kitchen table sipping a much-needed cup of coffee as she went through the bank statement for last month. She'd been up since before 4 a.m. thanks to her mother accidentally setting off her burglar alarm and calling in a panic. With Chris out of town, it left her to make the early morning drive across town to deal with something her mom could have easily handled. Naturally, Nicole hadn't been thrilled to discover she would have to take over getting her daughter up and to school, but after Sara had sweetly given her the choice of coming here or staying in bed another few hours, she'd opted for Kaylee detail. *Poor thing, I hope she can do the weather on eight hours' sleep.* She laughed softly, thinking Chloe would have appreciated her sarcasm.

As Sara wrote out the few checks needed for the monthly bills, she once again vowed to have a talk with her mother. Most of the bills were on autopay, so there was very little to deal with. Plus, she needed to understand her finances. It shouldn't be necessary for her to call her son or daughter every time she wanted to make a purchase. Sara had tried to explain how much more privacy she would have if she simply handled this on her own. She was an adult, and it was her money. She didn't need permission to use it. Yet every time Sara had broached the subject, she was met with a dozen excuses as to why she couldn't do it. Maybe she should discuss it with Chris first. If they presented a unified front, it might be easier. Plus, it was past time he stopped treating their mother like a child. Sara would never get anywhere without his support. *Why couldn't he see that this would benefit him too?*

She loved her brother, but he tended to bury his head in the sand to avoid confrontation of any type with the women in his family. He let Nicole have her way, even though she knew at times he didn't agree with her decisions. And he did the same with their mother. It was easier to him than risking tears or anger. Sara was the only one he didn't seem to mind pissing off. *That's because you always let it go, and he knows it.* As she was processing that unpleasant thought, her mother wandered into the kitchen dressed neatly in blue jeans and a sweater. She knew from the bank statements that she had an appointment with her hair stylist every six weeks like clockwork. Which was obviously money well spent because her short bob was neat and sassy, and Sara couldn't detect a hint of gray among the dark strands. Even though she was proud to have such an attractive mother, it made her pat her own sloppy ponytail self-consciously. She'd also thrown on a pair of yoga pants and an oversized shirt when she'd been abruptly woken earlier, a fact that her mother's sharp glance didn't miss. You'd think a woman who needed help as much as her mother did would be a little less critical of the daughter supplying it.

She leaned in to drop a kiss on the top of Sara's head before saying, "I'm exhausted. The darned alarm going off in the middle of the night took years off my life. Have you any idea how startling it is to be jarred from a sound sleep by something such as that?"

Gee, I have no clue, Sara thought wryly, not bothering to point out that she'd done the same thing to her. "Maybe you can catch a nap later," she added dryly. That certainly wouldn't be happening for her, as she'd be leaving straight from there to pick up Kaylee.

Her mother looked pointedly at her clothing again. "Were you going to the gym this morning, dear? You know there are much more . . . figure-flattering choices out there. Those types of knits don't look good on anyone, unless you're a tiny thing like Nicole." *Wow, an insult* and *a comparison to Nicole. She* is *cranky today.* Even though her mother wasn't what you'd call close to her daughter-in-law, they had a sort of mutual admiration thing going on. They were both very appearance conscious and worried far too much about what others thought of them. *Don't forget self-centered.*

As irritating as it could be at times, she also felt sorry for her mother. She knew that she focused on silly stuff because she was lonely. The adjustment to her new life had been hard for her. Their father had lavished compliments on her, and she still dressed as if the man who'd been dead for five years now would walk through the door any moment. Every time Sara came close to losing her patience, she tried to put herself in her mother's place. What must it be like to unexpectedly lose the man you'd been in love with most of your adult life? How do you go from that to living alone? To feeling as if you're special to no one? Sure, there were children and a grandchild, but that wasn't the same. Then it hit her with the force of a lightning bolt. *Chris gets it and I don't.* While she felt compassion for her mother, maybe she couldn't understand the full spectrum of her grief because she'd never been married or really even been in love. Sure, five years seemed like a long time, but to her mother, twenty-five probably wouldn't be enough to get over the loss of her soul mate. Yes, she needed some independence, but with the epiphany she'd had today, Sara decided to let it go—all of it. Instead, she opted for the complete opposite response. "You look nice today, Mom. But then again, you always do," she said sincerely.

Her mother froze, with her coffee cup halfway to her

mouth, as if stunned by her remark. *Have I really been so insensitive? It's not her fault I gave up on my dreams; the buck stops with me.* "I—thank you, Sara, that's very sweet." She looked down at the table for a long moment. When she glanced up again, her eyes were suspiciously moist. *Crap, why hadn't I kept my big mouth shut?* "Can you mail those on your way out?" she asked, pointing toward the nearby envelopes. "I'm meeting my friends for lunch soon, and you know how I feel about being rushed. It ruins my day." She looked at her watch and clicked her tongue. "Speaking of, shouldn't you be on your way to get Kaylee? What if you get held up in traffic? I don't want my granddaughter standing in front of the school waiting after the others have gone. That reflects poorly on the entire family, don't you think?" *Had I imagined those tears? Surely I must have, because emotional mom, if she was ever there, has changed places with disapproving mom.* In a strange, and yes, dysfunctional way, she knew how to deal with that version of her mother better since it was the one she got most often.

"Sure, Mom, I'll take care of it," she said as she began gathering her things. She'd been keeping up with the time and knew she would easily get there ten minutes early, as she always did. Kaylee had never been picked up late, no matter how many times Sara had been forced to juggle things that Nicole or Chris threw her way at the last moment. They seemed to have total faith in her ability to multitask, even if her mother didn't. *Either that, or they just don't concern themselves with anything other than their needs.* That last catty thought was unfair and she instantly felt petty. A fact that she blamed on too little sleep and an overabundance of coffee. It was normal to have some less than flattering opinions of your employer, at least she hoped it was. Unfortunately in her case, they were also family, which could get complicated in the best of circumstances. And really, it was completely her fault that they tended to take advantage of her. She'd as good as condoned it by never complaining. It wasn't likely they'd gotten the memo that she was suddenly unhappy with a big chunk of her life. *Be the change you want to see.* That might not be the exact wording, but she'd read something along those lines before. She talked for another moment, then gave her mother a hug. By the time she'd said good-bye, the other woman was actually rolling her eyes and making no pretense of hiding her exasperation at Sara's lack of urgency. *Just once it would be nice to be recognized for the good job I do with Kaylee instead of being second-guessed constantly.* And therein lay the problem. *No one recognizes my needs. No one cares about* my *needs.*

Sara wanted to check her e-mail before she left the driveway, but she figured her mother would come outside to see what the holdup was. So she waited until she got to the school. Luckily, she had fifteen minutes to spare, so she quickly scanned her new mail and felt that usual leap of excitement at seeing his name there. *Gabe Randall, is it possible I've gotten addicted to you?* A quick glance showed this message to be longer than his usual ones, which thrilled her even more.

Sara:

Nothing wrong with being an introvert. You already know by now that I don't use ten words when two will do. I could blame it on the military, but it's just me. Everyone has their part to play in the game of life. If we were all the same, where would that leave us? I like the image you present of doing the voices with your niece. And every kid is probably embarrassed by adults at some point. It's those times they'll remember when they're older, and not the serious stuff.

Right now, I'm in my office. I'm dirty and tired from traveling today. Looking forward to bed and a few hours of sleep to recharge. I like your e-mails too.

Talk soon,

Gabe

Giddy. She was ridiculously breathy, giddy from his letter. When she'd written that she looked forward to hearing from him, she hadn't believed he'd return the sentiment, yet he had. And he even included a closing this time. *Talk soon.* In the pen pal world, that was as good as a promise to write again. Of course, this made her even more curious about him. And it seemed that when she opened up, he did as well, albeit on a smaller scale—but still, the proof was there before her. She wanted nothing more than to reply immediately, but Kaylee was getting in the car now, and she wouldn't have a chance until they got home. Sara loved this time with Kaylee, so no *new* friendship with a soldier would interfere with that.

It was difficult, but she put Gabe firmly on the back burner while she talked with her niece about her day. Hearing her animated conversation never failed to make her smile. She loved her so much. "And Billy told Abby she got cooties, and made her cry. So I stepped on his foot, but he didn't cry. That's why I'm not on green today, Sarie. When you step on someone's toes, even if they're mean, you're going straight to yellow."

She couldn't help it—the matter-of-fact explanation of her drop in the behavioral chart had Sara laughing out loud. She hadn't been able to imagine such a system would work at keeping rambunctious kindergartners in line, but Kaylee was almost obsessed with staying on the good color. That was why she didn't feel the need to scold her for the slip today. It was rare that she received anything other than praise from her teacher, and she was proud of the little girl for defending her friend. "I can see how that would happen." She nodded. "But I'm sure you'll be back on track tomorrow. Hey, look, kiddo," she said, drawing her attention to where snowflakes were hitting the windshield. "We need to stop at the store and stock up. It might be a few days before we're out again. I'm sure your mom will be working longer hours handling the weather updates as well." It was rare that they had snow in the spring, but it had been a weird winter. The unusually cold temperatures, along with record rainfall, had combined for more of the white stuff than they'd had in years. She was so ready for summer.

"It's very important work." Kaylee did an almost perfect impersonation of Nicole. She wasn't making fun of her, though. She was simply repeating what she'd been told. Watching her mother on the news every day was something she rarely missed. Sara wondered at times if Nicole wasn't more like a beautiful stranger the little girl looked up to. *The supporting cast.* She pushed that troubling thought aside as they reached the grocery store and parked. It was frantic, as it usually was when bad weather was expected, but they managed to get all they needed. A short time later, when everything was put away, Sara gave in to Kaylee's pleas to go outside for a few minutes. And even though there was only a dusting of snow on the ground, they still had a blast playing in it. She took a few pictures and sent them to both Chris and Nicole, as she tried to do daily. *They're missing this beautiful girl's childhood. Moments they'll never get back.* She took one last one of her and Kaylee holding rabbit ears over each other's head. That one was just for her. She had hundreds of them, and each one told a different story.

A couple of hours had passed by the time Kaylee was coloring and Sara had some time to herself to write back to Gabe. She used to enjoy playing Candy Crush or surfing the Internet as a way to relax, but now either responding or reading back over their old messages was her favorite pastime. She hated how long it had taken her to reply this time. She could have sent a rushed note, but he deserved to have her full attention. She wondered what sorts of things he'd want to know from home. *Where does he live when state-*

side, anyway? He'd probably like hearing about their snow-ball fight, and really, what else could she tell him about her day? *Helped my beautiful and incapable-of-independence mother with her finances . . .* So snowball fight it was.

She had no idea where the idea of sending him a couple of pictures had come from. As she stared down at the one of her and Kaylee that she planned to attach, she wondered if it was a good idea. Her face was flushed and her hair was standing up in a couple of places. She looked exactly like someone who'd recently rolled in the snow. Surely she had more flattering ones she could send. She was still staring at the images in indecision when Kaylee startled her by saying, "We look pretty, Sarie." Her innocent approval was enough for Sara. If Gabe didn't agree, then too bad. He was her pen pal, not her future husband. Her appearance shouldn't matter.

Her bravado ended the moment she hit the Send button. *Crap, what have I done?* She wanted nothing more than to get the e-mail back, yet that wasn't possible. There was nothing she could do now but wait for his response. *Time for a distraction.* "Kaylee, how about we make homemade pizzas for dinner tonight?" She smiled as her suggestion was met with a roar of approval. *Don't leave me hanging, Gabe.*

Chapter Six

🐾 🐾

Gabe lay on his back in his small bed and stared up at his phone screen yet again. He'd lost count of how many times he'd looked at the picture Sara had sent him earlier. He'd barely been able to control his excitement while he'd scrolled down until the two images popped up. The first had been shallow outlines in the snow, clearly the angels she'd mentioned. But the second one . . . wow. He didn't think he was capable of that heart-melting feeling he'd read about. But when he saw the beautiful, smiling woman with one arm around a beaming child's shoulders as they both made rabbit ears atop the other's head, his insides had turned to mush. Her cheeks were pink and her eyes fairly glowed from within with vitality and mischief. She had long, dark hair that was hanging to one side from a ponytail, and her figure looked lush and curvy in the formfitting clothing she was wearing. To put it crudely, she was every wet dream he'd ever had. And she had no idea how much he needed the smile she'd given him. Unfortunately, he couldn't tell her for probably another twelve hours.

Jason had delivered the news earlier that they'd lost a soldier to friendly fire. Of all the casualties in this endless war, those were the losses that he had the hardest time accepting, senseless and avoidable accidents that cost the life of another. Worlds were forever changed and there wasn't a damned thing he or anyone could do to make it better.

When something like this happened, the base went on a communication blackout until the situation had been handled and proper notifications had been made. Usually that was around twenty-four hours. He shouldn't have even gotten Sara's e-mail until much later, but he had temporary leeway to send a couple of official messages before he was once again off-line. He couldn't have guessed how much that correspondence would help him deal with this latest tragedy.

Even without Wi-Fi, there was work he could do, but he'd temporarily lost his ability to give a shit about it. There was also the fact that he hadn't slept in going on two days now. The biggest workaholic had to hit the wall at some point, and he was pretty much there. As spent as he was, he couldn't make himself put his phone away. He'd long since memorized every single feature he could see in her picture. He was a logical man, not given to flights of fancy. Yet he was captivated by her and he had been even before he knew what she looked like. *You've been in the desert too long.* An argument could certainly be made for that, yet he was practically an old pro at this life by now. He'd spent almost seven of the last sixteen years overseas. And that didn't count the other TDYs, or temporary duties he'd been assigned to in various locations. He tended to travel a lot and had long since learned how to pack light and live out of a suitcase. Like everyone, he had bouts of restlessness. Most of those were upon returning and adjusting to life stateside again. Being away from all the luxuries many citizens took for granted sucked, but there was a simplicity here. Each day was basically the same, and your focus was entirely on the mission. Naturally you worried about things at home, but the fact that you couldn't do shit about it relieved a little of that stress. In a sense, going back was like leaving nine months of solitary confinement and suddenly being dumped out into a bright, sunny day. Although it was a beautiful thing, it was also blinding and disorienting until you adjusted. Everyone around you understood all the societal rules and nuances, some of which you simply forgot. In a word, you often felt lost.

He'd thought the younger guys struggled with that the most. The seasoned soldiers such as himself tended to joke it off as no big deal. Yet his rapid attachment to Sara made him question whether this lifestyle was beginning to wear on him. The biggest thing he should know to avoid was a woman with such close ties to her family. There was no good way to ask someone like that to move around as often as he did. And that wasn't the worst of it. Having a woman in his life meant not only that she would be uprooted from her loved ones but that she'd eventually be left alone in a place she wasn't familiar with while he deployed to somewhere like Iraq for another nine-to-twelve-month tour. With the number of wars the United States engaged in now, there was no end in sight to the amount of times an active service member would be sent overseas. *Who would sign up for that?*

Gabe could write a book about why it was a bad idea for him to become infatuated with a woman at this stage in his career, yet that ship seemed to have already sailed. It shouldn't have come as a total surprise to him. He'd been unusually restless the last few years. Really since he'd relocated to Alaska. Even living close to the big city of Anchorage didn't distract from the unspoiled beauty of the state he'd grown to love. He was still years away from retiring, and chances were high that he'd end up moving several more times before his career ended, but unless something changed, he wanted Alaska to be where he started his civilian life when his military one was over. He hadn't been exactly enthusiastic when he got his orders for Alaska. Would have been nice to end up somewhere with less snow. But for the most part, you went where Uncle Sam needed you, which was how he'd ended up in Anchorage. He could freely admit now that he'd been wrong. He loved the unspoiled beauty. The way the few hours of sunshine a day during the winter glistened off the snow-heavy tree branches. The white mountain peaks that looked like something out of a magazine. The crisp clean air that made you want to pause simply to inhale it. The vibrant colors of the Northern Lights that shimmered and swirled against the backdrop of Anchorage's skies in the winter months. And the people—which was an unusual thing for him to list as a plus. Normally he tended to keep to himself. He was polite, but distant. Why bother forming attachments when it was a temporary layover for him? Yet he had done just that. Anchorage might be a large city, but he'd never felt anonymous there. Neighbors watched out for each other, and the servers in the local restaurants remembered how you liked your coffee. He knew he wouldn't be there more than another year or so, but he was putting down roots for the first time. In Alaska, he'd finally found a home.

The one good thing about deploying so often was that he'd managed to put away a tidy nest egg for the future. Right now, he was renting a cabin away from the hustle and bustle of Anchorage, but if he moved there permanently, he'd be looking to build exactly what he wanted. He'd never given much thought to sharing that vision with someone else, but in such a short amount of time, she'd made him consider an alternate ending to the solitary one he'd imagined. It wasn't that he was dead set on being a lifelong bachelor; he just hadn't seen the need to ponder an alternative lifestyle—until now. He was very much a "cross that bridge when you come to it" kind of man. Dealing in the here and now, or situational control, as the Army referred to it. *I sound like a brochure for the freaking military.*

A loud yawn escaped him as his eyes began to blur. Ready or not, his body was shutting down for a while. The last thing on his mind as he drifted off into an exhausted slumber was the beautiful woman from the picture. Only in his dreams, she was laughing by his side instead of with the little girl.

"Why in God's earth did I send him my picture? Temporary insanity, that's all I can come up with. We had a good thing going, but now it's just the sounds of silence. I scared him away," Sara muttered before taking a sip from her glass of wine. When Chloe had called and invited herself over, Sara had been more than happy to welcome her. With Nicole sleeping at the station and Chris still out of town, she was desperate for a distraction. Normally she would have taken Kaylee somewhere, but the icy roads made traveling too risky. Chloe's neighbor had offered to drop her off on his way to work, and obviously she was bored enough to take him up on it. So now they sat cross-legged on the floor in front of the fireplace in lounge pants and T-shirts, having their version of an adult pajama party. When Kaylee had gone to bed, Chloe had brought out the bottle of wine she'd brought along with her.

"Let me see it," Chloe mumbled around a chip she'd just pushed into her mouth. When Sara didn't respond, Chloe made a grabbing motion with her hand. "If you want my honest opinion, then show me the damn thing."

Reluctantly, she scrolled through her camera roll until she located the image she'd sent Gabe. She studied it for a moment before handing it to her cousin. Granted, it was no glamour shot, but she didn't think it was *that* bad. If Gabe was so picky and critical of a woman's appearance, then screw him. The last thing she needed in her life was someone else making her feel bad about herself. *I've got a family to do that, Randall.*

"Are you kidding me?" Chloe asked, sounding baffled. *Well, damn, even she thinks it sucks. Why didn't I ask her opinion before I sent it?* "Sara, this is an amazing photo. Probably the best one of you I've ever seen. You should use it as your profile picture on Facebook." *Wait—was that sarcasm?* But even as that thought occurred to her she discounted it, because there was nothing but sincerity in Chloe's tone. "I have no clue why you haven't heard back from him, but I can promise you that there is nothing at all wrong with that picture. Remember when I read the e-mail you sent to him and I said it sparkled?" Sara nodded slowly, feeling herself beginning to relax. "Well, this image was made to go with that letter. It picks up on everything that I pointed out to you and more. This says without words that you're vibrant, funny, loving, *and* a flipping knockout."

Sara could feel the heat rushing into her face at Chloe's comments. *She almost seems to envy . . . me. That can't be possible. She has it all.* "Please—look at that piece of hair sticking up on the side of my head. And I'm so pale, I nearly blend in with the snow." Sara cringed in embarrassment.

Instead of laughing along with her, Chloe shook her head. "Why do you always do that? Whenever someone pays you a compliment, you immediately draw their attention to what you consider a negative. And it's not just with me either. I've heard you do the same thing at family gatherings." Chloe held up her hand, as if knowing what she was going to say. "I'm not talking about the reunion. I think Aunt Lydia took center stage with the spinster thing. Even you couldn't top her there." She leaned over and placed a hand on Sara's arm, giving it a gentle squeeze. "Seriously, though, I'm not saying it to be mean. Quite the opposite. We all have built-in protection mechanisms, and that's yours. Insulting yourself before anyone else can do it. But here's the thing—the majority of people were never going to hurt you in the first place. And the ones who would are assholes and their opinion doesn't matter."

Although she was embarrassed to have her cousin pick up on something she'd done for so long that it was almost second nature to her, she couldn't deny that it was an ugly habit. She did it partly because having attention focused on herself made her uncomfortable, but she had to face that fact that her low self-esteem played a role as well. *Never let them see you sweat.* Or, in her case, never let them hurt you when you can do it yourself. Sara ran a hand through her hair self-consciously. "You're absolutely right. I once worked with a lady who did the same thing. Funny thing is, I'd never noticed any of the things she brought to my attention. But after that, I couldn't stop seeing them."

"Yep, precisely." Chloe nodded. "She retrained your brain. It's why you never tell a guy what size you wear. Because chances are they think you're way smaller until you toss out something that contains the word 'large.' After that, when they look at your ass, yeah . . . big."

Sara giggled; she couldn't help it. And it seemed to be

contagious because, seconds later, Chloe joined in, and soon they were leaning against each other laughing hysterically. In the midst of it all, she couldn't help thinking how much she'd missed having a close friend. Someone to share moments like these with. Not only had she given up dating, but she'd pushed aside most of her relationships. She'd read once that it was often those who thought so little of themselves that willingly marooned themselves on their own island of self-loathing. *Was that me? To not know that my cousin thinks highly of me and thinks I'm pretty?* Sara almost felt ashamed that she'd sunk so low that she not only expected criticism but possibly condoned it by not answering back. *Built-in protection mechanisms. Mine were walls.* Was Chloe right? *This says without words that you're vibrant, funny, loving, and a flipping knockout.* Was that how other people—those not in the asshole territory—saw her?

When she thought hard about it, she couldn't even remember when this behavior started, but clearly it wasn't the way to continue living life. *Vibrant. Funny. Loving.*

Unfortunately, while she'd remained in limbo, the world had continued on without her; she hadn't joined in as part of it. *That has to change.* Both Gabe and Chloe had shown her what she was missing. Having a boyfriend, someone she connected with like Gabe, would be great . . . but what she wanted most of all was simply a life of her own. And only she could make that happen.

Chapter Seven

🐾 🐾

Gabe couldn't believe how anxious and excited he was to be back online again. *I need the escape from reality badly.* The communications block had been lifted an hour earlier, but he'd been forced to sit through a meeting before he could make it to the privacy of his office. It had been almost two full days since he'd written to Sara, and he hated that she had no clue why he had stopped writing to her. Yet another hardship on those back at home. Technology was wonderful, and did an amazing job at lessening the hardship of deployments, but things still happened that were beyond their control. Even though they'd still worry, family members who'd been through this with soldiers before understood it. But Sara likely had no clue. *Should I have warned her ahead of time?* That was the problem with connections like this—you didn't really know what protocol to follow. If he were dating or married, then of course he'd have covered the part about not panicking if he abruptly disappeared. Naturally, a significant other would still be concerned, but at least they knew the possibility of downtime existed. Sara had popped into his life so suddenly, he hadn't had a chance to think of anything other than how much he enjoyed talking to her.

He knew he could easily sit there another hour and obsess, but he had an e-mail to send. So he pulled up her last message and hit the Reply button.

Sara:

I'm sorry I've been off-grid for a few days. We had an incident, and when that happens, comms are taken down for a while. It's standard protocol and unfortunately it happens far too often. I wish I could have gotten word to you, but what little outgoing mail we're allowed to send during that time is monitored.

Thank you for the pictures. You couldn't have sent them at a better time, as they gave me something else to focus on other than what's been going on here. I've pretty much seen it all, but . . . I guess the day I become immune to the loss of human life is the day I need to resign my command. And I think you're right about the only true path to peace. I love my country and I'm proud to do my part, but I think these wars will be fought long after I'm gone. Soldiers have to find a way to accept that the sacrifices that we and our loved ones make are part of a big, long-range goal.

Instant gratification doesn't exist here. There are many types of victories, and one of the most important is keeping your sanity while being away from everything you've ever known for months at a stretch. You've made a difference for me. I loved the pictures. Your beautiful smile, your joy, it held me together.

Gabe

He knew his letter was too serious and bordering on gloomy, but he'd just started writing, with nothing other than an apology in mind. He'd ended up pouring out a piece of his soul, something he'd never done like this with anyone. Even though her messages were usually funny and upbeat, he remembered the one about her aunt calling her a spinster. No matter how much she joked about it, he sensed the underlying hurt. Granted it was a much different scenario, but it had shown him immediately that she had a compassionate heart. A big part of talking to someone in this way was being able to read between the lines. And with her, he felt a type of kinship. He could be wrong, it had certainly happened with other things, but somehow he didn't think so. She was special. *Please don't let me be wrong about her.*

Gabe pressed the Send button and felt as if a weight had been lifted from his shoulders. Not being able to contact her had bothered him more than he could have imagined. And now he had her reply to look forward to. He picked up his phone and glanced around his empty office sheepishly before looking at his home screen. The picture she'd sent him was now his background image. Just seeing her face somehow made his day better. He knew it was crazy, and he'd never admit it to anyone else, but he was in serious danger of falling for a woman he'd likely never meet.

Sara was usually a bit sad to drop Kaylee off at school. She missed the little girl while she was gone, even though she attended for only a few hours. The house always seemed entirely too quiet without her constant chatter. Plus, today was one of those rare times when Nicole was picking her daughter up, so she wouldn't see her until late that afternoon. But after being snowed in with a bored and restless five-year-old, Sara was more than happy to give her niece a hug and say good-bye. Unfortunately, Kaylee didn't feel the same way. "I wanna stay with you, Sarie." She scrunched her face up into an adorable frown before adding, "Billy gets on my nerves really bad. And now I gotta put up with perfect Maisie. Those big bows in her hair are ugly. She doesn't even have a bike, only a doll with a face that breaks if you drop it. Who wants something like that?"

Ah, now I see. Sara understood she wasn't the only one in the car who struggled with self-esteem. She mentally cursed Nicole for not seeing that by praising her friend's daughter so much, she was filling her own with insecurity. If Kaylee were more confident in her relationship with her mother, it might not be an issue. Regardless of her feelings toward her sister-in-law, she didn't think the other woman

did it maliciously. She probably believed Kaylee would see
Maisie as a role model. Unfortunately, it was having the
opposite effect. Kaylee resented and felt inferior to the little
girl. Sara had broached the subject with Nicole before but
had gotten nowhere. Nicole didn't like her input on parenting philosophies. She'd point out that since Sara herself
wasn't a mother, she didn't understand how things should
be. She'd wanted to tell her that she spent more time with
Kaylee than Nicole did, but it was one of many times she'd
bitten her tongue for the sake of family peace. But none of
that mattered now. She had to remain positive; otherwise, it
would influence Kaylee's mood further, and she didn't want
that. So she pulled her car out of the line and over to the
side before putting it into Park. Then she turned and put a
hand over her niece's. "Sweetie, listen to me," she said gently and waited until Kaylee was looking up at her. "You've
barely seen your mom in days because of the snow. She's
taking off this afternoon just for you. She's missed you so
much. You're going to have such an amazing time." When
Kaylee appeared skeptical, Sara reached up and tapped her
forehead lightly. "You better keep notes for me up there. I
want to hear all about it tonight."

"It'll be all 'bout Maisie," Kaylee said with an eyeroll
that had Sara grinning despite herself. "She'll have one of
those big bows in her hair again. They're always pink too,
Sarie. Does she not have any other colors?"

Don't laugh, don't laugh. Keep it together. Sara bit her
tongue so hard she was surprised it was still attached. The
kid was so darned cute, it was nearly impossible to remain

composed. Then she did something that she knew every parenting book preached against, but dammit, she wanted Kaylee to have fun with Nicole and not dread it so much that she missed out on what could be some much-needed mother-daughter bonding. She lowered her voice conspiratorially and motioned Kaylee closer. "Can you keep a secret?" Kaylee's eyes widened as she nodded enthusiastically. "Your mom says all that nice stuff about Maisie because she feels sorry for her." She pointed to Kaylee's blue jeans, with the colorful butterfly and rainbow patches. "See how adorable and different you're dressed? That makes you very unique. Do you know what that word means?"

Kaylee sat there for a moment appearing deep in thought. Finally, she said, "It's a good thing, right? That's why you're smiling, Sarie."

Nodding, Sara said, "It's a great thing. You're different in the absolute best way." She pointed to where Kaylee's heart was located before adding, "You glow on the inside and outside. You're like a shooting star crossed with the brightest sun. You're so very special, and your mom just wants other kids to feel as awesome as you make her feel."

"Really?" Kaylee whispered.

"Absolutely, sweetheart," Sara said confidently. "Now remember, this is just between us. We don't want your mom to stop doing her good deeds, do we?"

"Oh no, Sarie, we don't. Maisie needs lots of those too. She might wear some yellow one day if Mommy keeps trying."

"Wow, I bet you're right." Sara grinned. "Now let's get

you in school so you won't be late. And before you know it,
your mom will be here to pick you up, okay?"

She couldn't believe the difference that one little bending
of the truth had made in Kaylee's attitude. She was practically bouncing on the seat in excitement. She didn't consider
it a lie because she knew Nicole thought her daughter was
special. She just didn't know how to communicate that in a
way that Kaylee understood, at least not yet.

Sara eased the car back into the drop-off line and said
good-bye to Kaylee before pulling back out into the street
and heading to the mall. Since she had a rare day off, she
planned to do some long overdue shopping and of course
return some items for Nicole. She parked on the end next to
Starbucks and ordered a white chocolate mocha latte and a
blueberry scone. She found a quiet table near the back and
settled down to enjoy her breakfast. When she pulled her
phone out of her purse and saw the e-mail alert, her heart
skipped a beat. *Don't get excited. It's not him. You probably won't hear from him again. It's over.* She kept repeating
some version of that to herself, but her fingers trembled as
she clicked to check her mail folder and saw his name. *Oh
my God.* She leaned over as if to block the rest of the world
out as she began reading his message.

Sara felt the tear slide down her cheek before she even
thought to stop it. Gabe had said so much in his letter, but it
was what he hadn't fully put into words that moved her. The
grief and fatigue that he was feeling hung so heavily through-
out his message. She wanted nothing more than to go to this
man—this stranger that she barely knew—and put her arms

around him. Tell him everything would be all right, even though she had no clue if it would be. Sometimes you just needed to hear the words, kind of like with Kaylee earlier. Even the strongest people require comfort, since it's human nature to seek it from another when the world appears bleak.

Almost without thought, she hit the Reply button and typed out:

I'm here for you, Gabe. I wanted you to know that before I took the time to write more.

Sara

She was so lost in her thoughts that when a chair scraped loudly across the floor, she jumped in shock, having completely lost track of where she was. Luckily, no one seemed to pay her any attention. She took a sip of her coffee and was setting it back down when her e-mail alert flashed. She clicked on it and was surprised to see another message from Gabe. Although for the most part they e-mailed each other fairly quickly, she'd never received a response instantly before. Somehow it made it feel like a more personal exchange. As if he were close by and not thousands of miles away.

Thanks Sara, that means a lot to me. What are you doing?

Her hands trembled in excitement. They were having an actual conversation. Somehow, she hadn't expected that. *Slow down. He's likely not sitting there breathlessly await-*

ing your reply . . . like you are his. Oh, come on, he might be . . . I'm officially losing it, I'm arguing with myself now.

I'm at Starbucks having some coffee. Plan to brave the mall after the caffeine kicks in. How about you?

And even as she tried to remain calm, she still found herself staring at her phone after hitting the Send button. Her patience was rewarded when another e-mail came in.

I'm at the coffee shop too. Trust me, it's nothing fancy, but over here, it's about as close to luxury as you can get. Hey, do you have any instant messaging programs? It would be easier to talk that way. I use WhatsApp with my family. Or if you use an iPhone, we could try the iMessage app. I get it if you're not comfortable doing that. No pressure at all, Sara.

This was as close to a date as she'd come in years. Heck, she probably couldn't have been much more excited had he proposed marriage. She didn't have the app that he'd mentioned, but she'd been an Apple girl for years, so she was very familiar with the messaging program.

I'd love to do that. I do have an iPhone and the e-mail address I've being using is also my iMessage one, so use that. This is exciting!

She might have gone slightly overboard with that last sentence, but she wanted him to know that she had no reservations over talking to him in that way. Although it may have bordered more on desperate than anything else, but she wasn't going to worry about it now. Just then her message indicator flashed, and she quickly opened it to see his name there.

GABE: Sara?

SARA: Yep, it's me. Hey!

GABE: Thanks for doing this. I realize we're strangers and you can't be too careful these days, but since we've already been e-mailing . . .

SARA: I'm glad you suggested it. Are you already off work?

GABE: I'm never really off duty in the conventional sense here. I try to meet with the soldiers in a less formal environment when I can. So, I'll buy them a cup of coffee and then talk about any issues they might be having. They're more likely to open up away from the office.

SARA: Ah, that's a good idea. I'm sorry about what happened there. I assume someone was either injured or killed?

GABE: Don't take this the wrong way, but I'm not at liberty to discuss it. I know people talk and word gets out, but I try to adhere to the rules. If you'd like to read about it, I imagine it'll hit the news in the next day or so.

SARA: I get it. I should have guessed that. No offense taken, Gabe. Are you doing all right? You sounded kind of down in your e-mail earlier. I was worried about you.

GABE: No need to be concerned. Things like that never get easier, but you compartmentalize as best you can and focus on the job. Deployments are mentally and physically taxing, so you have to learn to shut out the stuff that'll make it worse.

SARA: How long do you plan to stay in the Army? Do you have a number of years in mind or maybe a career goal?

GABE: I'm not exactly sure. I'll be eligible for full retirement benefits when I hit the twenty-year mark. So that will definitely be happening. I wouldn't mind making Lt. Colonel or even Colonel. But that's not an absolute must. How about you? What will you do when your niece is older? Do you plan to stay on with them or maybe return to your previous profession?

SARA: That's a good question. One I don't have an answer to yet. I can say that I've been giving it a lot of thought lately and I know that I want to make some changes in the near future. I love Kaylee dearly, but she's already in kindergarten.

GABE: I'm guessing what sounds simple will be anything but. You've been with her for a long time. It will be rather traumatic for both of you to be separated, won't it?

SARA: You have no idea. I can't imagine loving my own child any more than I do her. I've been right there to see her grow from a toddler to an amazingly funny, sweet, and loving little girl. Frankly, it will be pure hell not to be with her every day. But . . . she also needs to form a closer bond with her parents and that won't happen while I'm there fulfilling that role.

GABE: Ah, gotcha. They're content to sit back and let you handle all of her care? Do you do anything else for them or is your job strictly looking after your niece?

SARA: Lol, oh, I am the nanny, maid, personal assistant, and any other title you can think of at one time or another. But that's a whole different story.

GABE: I hear that. Guess that's the risk of working for family. What do you do when you're not working? You get time off, right?

SARA: Oh sure. I hang out with friends. Take some weekend trips and stuff like that.

GABE: Hey, Sara, sorry to be so abrupt, but I've gotta run. I have a meeting at the other end of the base in ten minutes. I'll hit you up later. Have a great day.

SARA: You too, Gabe. Bye.

She was absurdly giddy at their real-time chat and sad to see it end. She found him so easy to talk to. Of course, the fact that they weren't face-to-face took the awkwardness away, but still, there hadn't been any long pauses on either end. The only time she'd even hesitated had been over the flat-out lie she'd told about her social life. It sounded so damned pathetic to admit that she didn't have one at all outside of spending time with her cousin. *I sit at home every night. My best friend is a five-year-old.* It made her wish she hadn't told him about the whole spinster episode. Because now she felt as if she had to avoid being seen in that light by Gabe. Which sucked, because she didn't like the dishonesty. But she also didn't want him to see her as some pathetic homebody who had absolutely no life. How could a man as accomplished and obviously driven as he was respect her lack of ambition? *Since when is it a bad thing not to be a bed-hopping party girl?* But wasn't there a fine line between too much socializing and not enough? He almost certainly had a lot of friends considering how many people likely worked at his base back home. *Probably no shortage of women around either.* She still had no clue what he looked like, but she hadn't been kidding about the wonder-camouflage. Women were drawn to men in uniform, be it policemen, firemen, or soldiers. *Geez, am I actually jealous? I've never even met this man in person. I have no right to feel possessive about someone I don't know.*

Glancing at her watch, she was surprised to see that she'd been in Starbucks for well over an hour. She got to her feet and tossed her empty cup away before making her way out into the mall. As she was walking toward the first store, she couldn't help thinking that everything seemed brighter this morning. Gabe had changed her life for the better in such a short amount of time. There was a spring to her step that hadn't been there for years, and a happiness in her heart that had her smiling at everyone she passed. She knew she needed to keep things in perspective. Her connection with him was fragile and almost certainly temporary. The more attached to him she became, the harder it would be to lose him. Just thinking of it was tough enough. How would she deal with the reality when it happened? Because eventually it would. If nothing else, his deployment would end and he'd return to his real life. How long would he need a pen pal then? From what he said, there was next to nothing to do in the way of socializing where he was stationed now. So he was, in a sense, her captive audience. She was a distraction, and it was possible he was as intrigued by talking to a stranger as she was. But what about when the new glow wore off? *Congratulations, you're hereby promoted from spinster to Debbie Downer.*

Screw it. For once she was going to go with the flow and see where it took her. It was too late to be cautious. Besides, being that way her whole life had gotten her exactly nowhere. She might end up getting hurt, but wasn't that a part of living? Chloe had been hurt by her cheating ex, but she didn't give up on life. Gabe had struggled through countless deaths and near-death experiences, she was sure, but he still wanted to serve more time in the Army. Both Chloe and Gabe seemed to believe in Sara, but ultimately it had to be belief in herself that made her want to change. So would she grab these moments of happiness and hope they were part of a road map that led her to the next chapter? Everyone had to start somewhere, and at thirty-five, she had a lot of catching up to do. If nothing else, she figured it was likely to be a hell of a ride.

Look out, world, it was Sara Ryan's turn to shine.

Chapter Eight

He'd officially lost his mind—and if he wasn't careful, his heart—to a woman he knew only online. When he described his new pen pal to Jason, he'd been regaled with tales of some television show called *Catfish*. He refused to look the damn thing up on YouTube, as Jason had laughingly urged him to do (after suggesting to him that Sara could actually be a Sam). When he'd shown him her picture, he shrugged and suggested she got it off the Internet. He'd been offended on her behalf. *Why must everyone make good things into something ugly?* It wasn't the other man's fault, though. It was Gabe's for telling him in the first place. And no matter how much he wanted to discount everything he'd said, he hated the tiny niggle of doubt that was planted where there had been none.

They'd been talking multiple times per day for several

weeks now, and it had become such a big part of his daily life that he couldn't imagine not telling her good morning or asking about her day. And more than anything, he loved waking up to find a text on his phone waiting for him. It felt so good to have someone thinking of him. Whether she realized it or not, she was making a huge difference for him here. Hell, he'd even been asked a few times recently why he was smiling. One of his soldiers told him he hadn't been aware he actually had teeth.

He wasn't really concerned that much about appearances, but he damned sure wanted to verify that she was indeed a woman. *You're such a paranoid asshole.* He hated himself for it, but thanks to Jason, he couldn't quite get past the notion that he could be made a fool of fairly easily. So with that thought in mind and because he genuinely wanted to hear her voice, he had decided to suggest they FaceTime. They could stick to audio, or if she was okay with it, they could use video as well. Naturally he hoped she'd go for the second option just to put the whole thing to rest, but he could understand if she wasn't ready for that step yet. He was a little nervous about it himself. A quick glance at his watch told him that Kaylee should be at school by now, so he typed a quick message to her.

GABE: Good morning, Sara. Hope your day is going well. Hey, wanted to see if you were interested in trying FaceTime. Thought it would be kind of cool to hear each other. We can do the phone call only—or video if you're OK with it. Completely up to you, no pressure.

After he hit Send, he sat on pins and needles waiting for

her response. When he saw the little bubbles indicating she was typing, he held his breath. *How in the hell is it that I can remain totally calm while fighting a war, yet turn into a basket case over asking a woman to chat?* To hell with the guys finding out, he was embarrassed enough at himself without anyone else making fun of him.

SARA: Wow, I'd love that. Give me five minutes, though. I literally rolled out of bed and took my niece to school. I'm not sure I even took the time to brush my hair. Someone kept me up late last night . . .

You'd think he'd won the lottery, as excited as he was at her agreement. *Wait, she hadn't indicated which one she wanted to do.*

GABE: I'm sure you look beautiful, regardless. Just let me know when you're ready. No rush. I know I sprung this on you suddenly. Oh, are we doing a phone call or video? Need to know before I make the connection.

SARA: I'm at home alone, so it doesn't matter to me. Do you have privacy to video chat? If so, I'd love to see you.

Was it too late to back out? Gabe wondered uneasily. It had been his idea, but now he was on the verge of panicking. He never really gave his appearance any thought. He knew he was in good shape, thanks to years of running and strength training. Being physically fit made deployments easier to handle. And even though his bedroom was far from a revolving door, he'd never found it difficult to find a woman when he longed for female companionship. The opposite had been mostly the case. Yet he couldn't help being uneasy. He'd come to look forward to talking to Sara every day. What if FaceTiming changed everything? Rationally he knew that he'd adjust and life would go on, but he didn't want that. Before he could obsess any longer, she was back.

SARA: OK, ready when you are, Gabe.

He blocked out everything and focused on the task at hand. He always worked better that way. Overthinking wasn't wise in his line of work. It would drive you crazy. All too soon, his iPad was waiting for her to answer. And then there she was. Like a punch to the gut, he knew he'd have been better off had she been a dude. Because the woman smiling shyly while waving a hand was more dangerous to him than anything he'd ever faced. This time his heart was on the line, and he feared that the beauty before him might be the one thing against which he had no defense.

Am I drooling? Dear God he's so freaking hot. Sara was very much afraid she looked and sounded like an idiot. But since the moment Gabe had asked her to FaceTime, she'd been more rattled than she could ever recall being. And seeing the handsome man on her iPad screen did nothing at all to help her relax. Maybe she was biased, but he reminded her of a mix between Taylor Kinney and Bradley Cooper. His hair was much shorter, but those eyes. Something about them was so unusual, and his tanned face seemed to make them almost glow. *Down, girl. Oh shit, what did he say?* From his expectant look, it was obvious he was waiting for a reply. "Er . . . could you repeat that? I think our connection lapsed for a second." She mentally patted herself on the back for that brilliant excuse. He might think she was an airhead, but at least she hadn't been forced to admit she was ogling him. "I said that you look just like your picture. I asked if I am what you were imagining. Well, if you've given it any thought." *Was he blushing? Surely not. Must be the lighting.*

"Of course I've wondered. But you're way better than I envisioned." *Yikes, that didn't come out right.* "Not that I thought you'd be ugly or anything," she added quickly, "but you're really handsome." *Understatement of the year, baby.*

"Oh," he murmured, looking down for a moment. He ran a hand over his cheek before saying, "Thanks. I—I'm glad you think so." Then he grinned, and Sara had to fight the urge to fan herself. *Holy hotness, Batman.* "Although it could be the miracle of the camo, as you called it. Maybe I should have worn my civilian clothing so you could make an accurate assessment. I'd hate for you not to recognize me out of uniform."

"Trust me, there's no way you'd be unattractive, regardless of how you were dressed," she said honestly. *He is blushing. I can't believe I said all that.*

"What are your plans today?" he asked, as if wanting to shift the focus from himself. Somehow that made him more endearing to her. He clearly wasn't a man who wanted or needed his ego stroked. She thought she detected a hint of relief in his expression at her approval of his looks, but he'd been ready to move on after that. It was just another area in which they were alike.

She checked the time on her iPad. "I need to leave to

pick up Kaylee soon. Then it's the usual girl thing for us. I'm not certain about this evening. I never know what Nicole has in store for me."

"Don't you usually meet up with friends a few times a week?" he asked.

"Oh—yeah, but I haven't spoken to anyone yet, so I'm not sure when that'll be. Everyone stays so busy." She hadn't wanted Gabe to see her as someone without a life. A simple girl with no aspirations who spent all her time with her niece or running errands. Was it time to tell Gabe the truth? Was this a test conversation to see if there was anything there between them? At least she did have Chloe now, so her social life wasn't a total fabrication. But still . . . truth or *fabrication . . . aka lie*.

"Please go out and have a decent meal for me." He shuddered. "I'm so tired of the food here that I have to force myself to eat enough to survive on."

"That bad, huh?" she asked sympathetically. "Wait, can I send you a package? Maybe some of your favorite things that you can't get there?"

He appeared shocked for a moment, and she wondered if she'd overstepped the bounds of their relationship. Then he grinned and she nearly swooned. "Normally I'd decline, but I'd sell my soul for a bag of Doritos and a pack of Oreos."

She couldn't help laughing at his hopeful expression. In a way, it was as if she was meeting him for the first time. His e-mails were so reserved, and even though he was more relaxed via texts, she could still sense that he was on guard. But FaceTiming seemed to really bring his personality out.

Maybe it was because she could see the different expressions flit across his handsome face. "Consider it done, Major. If you'll send me your address, I'll get a box in the mail to you this week."

"I'll text it to you when we hang up. If you're sure you don't mind, Sara, I'd really appreciate it. We have some different groups that donate stuff fairly regularly—but I try to leave that for my soldiers. Something as small as a pack of cookies can be a big morale booster, and they all deserve it. Hey—it's ten thirty your time, do you need to get going?"

Sara jumped, having completely lost track of everything but him. "Crap. Yeah, I'm sorry but I gotta run. Thanks for letting me know. I'd zoned out."

"You're welcome." He smiled. "I have some things to take care of as well. But—I really enjoyed this. Maybe we can do it again soon."

"I'd love that." Sara nodded enthusiastically. She stood up and began gathering her things before realizing that she was giving Gabe a close-up view of the lower half of her body. *Yikes.* Another moment and she'd probably have had her backside plastered against her screen. "Oops, sorry. I have to go," she added regretfully.

"Not a problem." He chuckled. "I'll text you later. Have a good afternoon, Sara." He waved once, then ended the connection.

I miss him already. She could no longer deny that the quiet, confident man serving overseas had made a major dent on her heart.

Chapter Nine

👣 👣

Gabe stared in wonder at the big box sitting atop his desk when he returned from dinner. He recognized the flat-rate decals from the postal service, but he'd never received one with stickers and drawings on the outside of it. And after a day in 100-plus temperatures, where tempers were short and tensions were high, it was about the most welcome sight he could imagine.

He approached it cautiously and stared down at the return address label. *It was from her—his Sara.* The possessiveness of his train of thought should have had him freaking out, but he didn't feel any panic. Rationally, he was aware that the woman in North Carolina whom he'd never met in person didn't belong to him, but he gave himself a pass since you tended to live in your own type of world while you were deployed. *Damn, I sound like one of the newbies here. Lovesick and irrational.* Again, he let it go. Everyone was allowed to lose their shit at least once, weren't they?

He felt a grin pulling at his lips as he stared at the package she'd sent him. He almost hated to open it since the cardboard was like artwork. He suspected that the drawings were done by her niece. Either that or Sara was strictly at the stick figure talent level, just as he was. There was what appeared to be a dog, a cat, a house, a butterfly, and the sun. There were also some Charlie Brown stickers similar to the ones she'd used on her Easter card envelope.

Grabbing a pair of box cutters, he carefully sliced through the tape, and the edges seemed to burst apart. When an individual package of Oreos popped out, he had to exert considerable control to keep from ripping it apart like a wild dog. As he sorted through all the items she'd included, he was beyond touched at how much thought and effort she'd put into the package. Not only had she bought what he'd mentioned, but she'd also added about a dozen other types of things as well. Many were in zippered baggies, he suspected to save space by removing them from bigger containers. How on earth Sara had guessed that socks were something he desperately wanted was beyond him. *She listens. She listens to more than my words.* There were bases with large stores, but the one here was pretty limited and didn't carry a lot. There was also a small bag of toiletries and miscellaneous items such as eye drops, allergy cream, hand lotion, and Chapstick. He'd mentioned how tasteless the food was, so she'd included a couple of containers of various spices as well as hot sauce. Then an assortment of protein bars, trail mix, and even Rice Krispies Treats. He wasn't in the market for a wife, but if she were here right now, he'd be damned tempted to drop to one knee and pop the question. This was quite possibly the nicest thing anyone had ever done for him. And her thoughtfulness and generosity were yet more reasons why he was so captivated by her.

Since their first FaceTime chat several weeks back, it had become almost a daily routine for them. Due to the time difference, sometimes it was brief, but even five minutes made his day. Their conversations flowed so easily. He found himself opening up as he never had with another person. Naturally, he knew a big part of it was the ability to relax, thanks to the distance between them. There was no awkward first date in a restaurant sitting inches apart. Or wondering if he should go in for the goodnight kiss or wait. Everything like that was taken out of the equation. And with it, he was able to simply enjoy the witty, beautiful woman with the sparkling green eyes, sexy Southern accent, and infectious laugh.

His troops had long since grown bored with teasing him about his improved mood, although they did jokingly send their thanks to Sara for making him less of an asshole. He'd have been offended if it weren't basically true. He was a better person with her in the picture. Thinking of her had him picking up his phone to send her a text:

GABE: Hey, guess what I got? He took a quick picture of the package and attached it.

SARA: Yay! It finally got there. Do you like all the things I included? Since you wouldn't give me any ideas other than Doritos and Oreos, I had to guess.

GABE: You did an amazing job. I didn't want you to feel obligated to buy a ton of stuff. I'd have been happy with anything from you. But this . . . seriously, you made my day. Thank you so much.

SARA: My pleasure. You probably figured out that Kaylee helped me. She insisted on handling the decorating.

GABE: Sure, blame it on the kid. It's OK that you can't draw a straight line, sweetheart. I still like you.

SARA: Lol! That's good, because I have absolutely no talent in that area. But . . . it wasn't me. I did get a few weird looks at the post office, though. Probably because the dog on the back looks like it has a penis hanging out. I'm pretty sure that was meant to be a long, floppy ear instead . . .

Gabe flipped the box around searching for the drawing in question. Then he saw it and started laughing. It did indeed resemble a dick, remarkably so. He wondered how he'd missed it the first time.

GABE: Ha-ha, I found it! That kid is something else. She's got a bright future ahead doing nudes if she decides to pursue an art degree.

He was awaiting her response when his door opened. He glanced up to see Jason standing there, frowning. It felt like déjà vu, and he had a sinking feeling there had been another accident.

GABE: Gotta run. Back when I can.

It was abrupt and he knew she'd be concerned, but it couldn't be helped. As much as he loved talking to her, he was a soldier first, and could immediately switch into his role of major, which was an absolute necessity in moments like these. He knew she understood, but it reminded him once again why he'd never wanted to have someone at home who would worry about him, and vice versa. There was no pulling back now, though. Right or wrong, he was falling for her. He had no clue how what was happening between them would translate in the real world when he left Iraq, but he was more certain each day that he wanted to find out. As he was walking beside Jason to the front gate checkpoint, it hit him: *I called her "sweetheart."* And that was the last thought that crossed his mind before all hell broke loose.

She'd been mildly apprehensive when Gabe ended their conversation earlier that morning without their usual drawn-out good-bye. But she knew that there were a lot of demands on his time on base. She figured he'd likely been interrupted by someone and hadn't had the privacy to say more. That had been eight hours ago. She was careful not to be one of those people who texted constantly. He always contacted her when his schedule allowed, and other than saying good morning and good night, she generally waited for him. But she'd texted him three hours ago when she hadn't heard anything. And once more a few hours later. And none of those messages were marked as read yet. Which was really worrisome. Because even when he couldn't stop to respond right that moment, he usually read her texts fairly quickly. He'd explained that very thing to her a while back.

Nicole had been out on a girls' night, so it had been just Sara, Chris, and Kaylee for dinner. She'd been so distracted, Chris had asked her if she was alright. He'd had to repeat the question a few times before he nudged her arm with his hand. She'd assured him she was simply tired, but he didn't seem convinced. She knew her family had noticed the changes in her the last few months since she'd met Gabe. Considering how invisible they made her feel at times, it was rather surprising how quickly they picked up on her newfound happiness. Her mother had inquired if she'd met a man. Not wanting to lie, she'd laughed it off. *You've fallen for him without the courtship.*

Even her self-absorbed sister-in-law questioned whether she'd changed her makeup or done something different with her hair. When Sara said no, Nicole had shrugged, as if the conversation hadn't been worthy of any further consideration. Yes, indeed, she might as well be carrying around a sign that said she had a secret crush. She wondered if Gabe had picked up on her growing feelings. She wasn't brave enough to put them into words or ask him if maybe he was experiencing the same thing. But she didn't try to hide the fact that he was very important to her. He might not realize it, but he treated her in a similar manner. Everyone in his office seemed to know of her. He'd often comment on mentioning something she'd said to people there. It was as if they were an official item. They'd grown so close that she was almost surprised each time she pondered the fact that they'd never been together in person. He had made mention a few times recently, though, of taking that step when his deployment ended. He'd even jokingly invited her to Alaska to visit him. She felt that he'd been intentionally testing her reaction to see if she was agreeable to it.

She was pulled from her thoughts by a soft snore coming from Kaylee's small body. She'd been sitting beside her after reading her a story. Normally it would have taken much longer to lull her into sleep, but apparently Sara's preoccupation had taken care of it. Poor kid, she knew she had been a bit distracted lately, but luckily the different time zones meant that her schedule with Kaylee wasn't really affected by her time with Gabe. She walked to her room and shut the door behind her before grabbing her iPad and sitting on the bed. She quickly typed in the name of Gabe's base in Iraq, as she did on a regular basis, and scanned Google for any recent news. And there it was, in bold headlines from an hour earlier. SUICIDE BOMBER KILLS THREE. DOZENS INJURED. Sara felt a wave of dizziness assail her. *He's fine. Just busy dealing with the chaos.* Yet even as she tried to convince herself, the reality of how easily she could lose him hit her with an intensity that took her breath away. How could she allow herself to love a man whose job put him in harm's way on a daily basis? She had to wonder if she was strong enough to even attempt it. If she was already having these kinds of doubts, what did that say about their future, if it should come to that? Didn't a man that brave deserve a woman strong enough to stand by his side? The voice in her head said that if she had to ask, then she wasn't really the one for him . . . nor would she ever be.

Chapter Ten

🐾 🐾

One again he'd disappeared on her, and all he could think of was letting her know he was okay. It had been a couple of days since he'd been abruptly pulled away. And even if the comms hadn't been taken off-line, he doubted he'd have had a second to contact her. It had been absolute insanity since a suicide bomber had managed to get through the front gate and take three soldiers out with him, and injure another fifteen. Only three casualties were from American troops, but the whole incident was entirely unacceptable. The base had been crawling with bigwigs from the United States and their coalition partners. He'd been in meeting after meeting, as every single move from the days before had been questioned and new safeguards put into place. It felt like too little, too late, but that was the nature of the beast. For every hole they plugged, the enemy came up with another dozen to get around them.

It was morning for him, so it was nighttime in the States. There was a good chance he'd miss her altogether, but at least she'd have a message waiting when she woke up.

GABE: Hey, Sara. I just read your texts. You're right, sweetheart, we were off-line again here. I'm sorry it has taken so long to get back to you. Are you awake?

He sat there staring at the screen of his phone, hoping to see the indication that she'd read the message, but so far there was nothing. *Come on, be there, please.* He was considering sending another, hoping she might have her alert on and the sound would wake her. Normally he tried to keep from disturbing her this late, but damn, he'd missed her so much.

SARA: Gabe! I've been worried about you. I saw an article in the paper earlier about what happened over there. Are you all right?

GABE: Oh, sweetheart, I'm fine. I wish I could have gotten word to you. I hated to think of you being upset. I know we discussed the fact that things like this happen, but I realize that's of little comfort when you have no way to confirm that I'm uninjured.

SARA: I did know that, but I got a little nervous when I read that story.

GABE: I'm sure I would have felt the same way in your position.

SARA: I'm relieved to talk to you. And don't be concerned about me when and if this type of thing happens. I'll be fine. I know you need to keep your focus on what's happening around you.

GABE: Thanks, sweetheart. I . . . missed you. More than you know.

SARA: Aw, same here. You're such a part of my world now that things weren't the same without you.

GABE: You realize that by the time I head home, we won't be able to tie our shoes without talking to each other about it first, right?

SARA: Lol, you've got a point there. We may need an intervention.

GABE: Or a plane ticket.

He couldn't help noticing the prolonged pause after his last comment. Damn, he wanted to see her, to hug her. Of course, he couldn't deny the physical attraction, but that was secondary at this point. He'd never rush her into that until he was sure she was ready. Naturally he understood that a woman couldn't be too careful, and he was more than willing to put whatever safety measures in place that would help her feel more secure. *I can't believe I'm the one pushing for a face-to-face. I don't do complicated, and there's no way this would be easy.* Just the distance between their homes would make a relationship extremely difficult.

SARA: I really want that. I can't imagine you being back in the States and us not meeting.

GABE: Then we'll make it happen. Hey, sweetheart, I've gotta run. I have a briefing in 10. And you need your sleep. We can FaceTime tomorrow when we both have some privacy. Sleep well, beautiful.

SARA: Thanks. Be safe. Good night.

Gabe quickly gathered together what he needed for his daily meeting and hurried out of his office. He'd always been the person who was early to everything. But since meeting Sara, he wasn't late, but he damn sure was no longer the first to arrive. *It's called having a life outside the military.* But with the good, there was also the bad. And today that came in the form of guilt. He felt like shit for the worry he'd obviously caused her the last few days. It was exactly the reason he was still single. Worse than that, though, was the warm feeling it had given him to know she cared enough to be apprehensive. *I'm such an ass.* She'd also been agreeable to meeting in person when he returned stateside. He'd let that ride for a while. He was grounded enough in reality to understand that their connection was fragile and could be derailed far too easily. He certainly wasn't going to make travel arrangements this early in the game. That was too much pressure on both of them. But he was more excited than he'd have thought at the possibility of taking what was happening between them to the next level if all continued to go well.

"The smiling thing is getting downright creepy," Jason said as he took a seat next to Gabe.

"Don't be jealous, honey, you're still my favorite," Gabe murmured under his breath, causing the other man to laugh.

Jason batted his eyes in a pathetic feminine imitation. "I've moved on. Donaldson makes me feel pretty."

Sergeant Matt Donaldson shrugged his shoulders, going along with the banter. "What can I say, I know how to make 'em happy, Major."

"That's not what I heard," Warrant Officer Chris Camron tossed out from across the table. "Otherwise you wouldn't have received a care package containing nothing but packing peanuts."

"She forgot to put the other stuff inside," Matt argued. "It was an oversight, that's all."

"Yeah, right, and that didn't occur to her *until* you received the box weeks later? Shouldn't she have noticed some stuff sitting around?" Chris asked skeptically.

Jason shook his head before pointing to Matt and saying, "Dude, I hope she's hot, because she's obviously not the sharpest crayon in the pack."

As the banter continued for a few more moments, Gabe couldn't help thinking how irritating he used to find this type of thing. He'd wanted everyone to blow off steam on their own time and not when he was ready to get down to business. Although he still had those moments occasionally, he found that now he was better able to connect with his soldiers on a personal level because he was less rigid. That didn't mean that he'd allow anyone to slack off, but he would joke around at times and also share a meal with them instead of eating something at his desk while he worked. Regardless of whether he ever met Sara in person or not, he'd always be grateful for the ways in which her kindness had improved the morale of the soldiers under his command. Then he took a moment to marvel at her words. She wasn't even his girlfriend, yet she blew him away with her comprehension of his reality. *Don't be concerned about me when and if this type of thing happens. I'll be fine. I know you need to keep your focus on what's happening around you.* Like the men and women who surrounded him daily, Sara Ryan had his back. And God, that felt incredible.

Chapter Eleven

🐾 🐾

Sara sat across the table from Chloe at her favorite Mexican restaurant. Nicole and Chris were going to a barbecue at Chris's friend's house, and since it was a family thing, they were taking Kaylee with them. They'd also invited Sara, but she declined, choosing to have dinner with Chloe instead. She figured that if she went with her brother and his wife, she'd end up babysitting all the little ones while the adults enjoyed some kid-free time. It had certainly happened before. The look on Nicole's face had been priceless. The horror. She could almost hear her sister-in-law's internal monologue: *Sara's not coming? This is meant to be my night off and she can't give us that time?* So not sorry. But tonight, she was in a mini-panic and needed advice.

"Wow, I can't believe how quickly the time has gone by. You and Gabe have been talking for months now."

"I know," she marveled. "I sent him that card in April and he e-mailed me a few weeks after that. It's been almost seven months." *And they've been the best of my life. He makes me so happy.*

Chloe grimaced. "That beats my record. Maybe I need a pen pal too. So you're beginning to freak out about it, aren't you? Is he putting pressure on you now to meet him?"

Sara shook her head. "No, of course not. We've both made references to doing stuff together in the future, but that's it."

Appearing perplexed, Chloe asked, "But didn't you say that you two were closer than ever?"

Propping her face in her hands, Sara nodded. "Yeah, we are. I know it's weird, but he's like my boyfriend. Actually, he's the best one I've ever had. I know, I know, that's sad considering we haven't so much as held hands. But he's so attentive, thoughtful, and he even worries about me. I'm not used to that. The last time I had the flu, all my family could harp on was how it would affect them. Yet when I had a cold last month, he reminded me to take my medicine and asked how I was feeling every single time we talked. He even urged me to see a doctor—heck, he even threatened to make the appointment for me if I wasn't better in a few days."

"He sounds too good to be true," Chloe said lightly, but she heard the note of uncertainty in her voice.

"Don't you think I've told myself the same thing a million times? I keep waiting for my rose-colored glasses to fog up, but that hasn't happened. Don't get me wrong, he's human and has days that he's a little moody. But I'd be worried if he didn't. He'll even warn me when he's had a rough one and is not feeling that social. He doesn't try to make me believe that he's perfect, but he also never takes it out on me."

"Well, there's no sense in sitting around waiting for him to bring it up. Why don't you come out and ask him to visit you? This isn't the dark ages where the little woman waits on the man to handle everything." She pointed to where Sara's phone was sitting on the table. "Go ahead and text him now while I'm here for moral support. You need to know where you stand anyway. I don't want to sound negative, but I find it a little concerning that he hasn't already tried to make plans. I question whether he might already have someone at home waiting for him."

"That's not it at all," Sara said firmly.

Chloe gave her a look full of sympathy. "Sweetie, you may be too close to the situation to be objective. To a lot of people, this whole situation would sound a tad suspicious. I mean, I could be wrong and he might be one of those people who does everything at the last minute." Then she lowered her voice and murmured, "Or there may be a Mrs. Gabe."

"You're wrong," Sara argued, wishing Chloe wasn't so forthright. *Or you could have kept your big mouth shut.*

Despite her denials, Chloe was like a dog with a bone. She simply would not let go of her suspicion about Gabe. Which made Sara feel like crap, since she could quite easily put the whole thing to rest. But in order to prove his innocence, she'd have to admit her guilt, which she hadn't counted on. Yet even though her cousin wasn't likely to ever meet Gabe, Sara still didn't want her to have a bad opinion of him. She tried once more to change the subject to no avail. Finally, after Chloe mentioned Gabe possibly lying not only about his marital status but about his location as well, she found herself blurting out in exasperation, "For God's sake, he thinks I'm coming to Alaska at the end of the month. Chloe, he bought me a plane ticket weeks ago."

Chloe was temporarily at a loss for words. *That certainly shut her up.* "But why did you say you hadn't made plans if you have?"

Sara stared at her cousin, surprised by what she considered a dumb question. "You, of all people, have to understand I can't go. Kaylee started first grade a few months ago and she's having a tough time adjusting. Plus, Mom is just beginning to get around better after spraining her ankle."

Chloe settled back on her seat before crossing her arms over her chest. "Correct me if I'm wrong, but don't you have a brother *and* a sister-in-law? Not to mention the fact that your mother could easily take care of herself. You're a member of the family, Sara, not their servant."

"You just don't understand," she said defensively. "You're an only child and both of your parents are still alive. You're free to do whatever you want to, but not all of us are that lucky."

"What a cop-out." Chloe laughed. "You've done nothing but talk about this amazing man that fate practically tossed at your feet. Yet now that he's not going to be thousands of miles away in another freaking country, you're terrified. I thought you cared about him. But it sounds as if you've just been playing games."

Sara felt the blood drain out of her face as each of Chloe's accusations hit her like arrows to the heart. "I—no, that's not it. I do like him—more than that, in fact. I'm absolutely crazy for him. But I didn't want to lose him—so I said I'd go visit him when he got home. It . . . seemed so far away then. I thought there was a good chance we either wouldn't still be talking, or I'd be able to find a way to put it off for a while—until later. But—"

"Later is now," Chloe finished for her. Her cousin ran a hand through her hair, releasing a long sigh. "Sara, what are you going to do? It's not the money so much as the expectations you've given this man. He's sure enough of his feelings to not only invite you to visit but to pay for it as well. I don't know exactly what your conversations consist of, but I don't think they're just a lot of dirty talk. Although I hope you've tossed some of that in," she joked before looking serious once more. "I know you call each other endearments, you've admitted that. Not many men would do that unless they were invested in more ways than a simple flirtation."

"I think we passed that a while back," Sara whispered as she stared down at her drink. "I'm scared, Chloe, because it all seems to be happening so fast now. My family doesn't even know he exists. I mean, they are aware that I talk to someone a lot, but considering I haven't been on a date, they're not overly curious about him. Can you imagine what their reactions would be if I suddenly announced

I was going to Alaska to see a soldier that I've never met before?"

"You're a grown woman, Sara, you don't need their permission," Chloe pointed out. "I agree that you should have leveled with them a while ago. Then after the shock wore off, you could have all made arrangements for everything to be covered while you were gone. Instead, you have, what, two weeks before you're due to leave?"

"Pretty much," she mumbled. "And he's so calm about the whole thing. As if it's never entered his mind that I might not come."

"Sara," Chloe said firmly, then waited until she made eye contact. "You either have to tell him or your family. This is only going to get worse if you wait. If you care about him and want to keep him in your life, then level with him."

"But I'll lose him." Sara uttered the words that terrified her the most.

"Maybe." Chloe nodded once, not bothering to sugarcoat it. "But it's your only hope. With every day that passes, you're digging a bigger hole. Put on your big-girl panties and do some damage control before it's too late."

Chapter Twelve

A crowded airport had never felt so good, Gabe thought as he looked around Charlotte Douglas International. He'd been flying for the better part of two days now. Actually, three if you considered all the time changes. This last leg had taken him from New York to his destination in North Carolina. Despite all the risks he'd taken in the line of duty, the one he was embarking on now somehow struck him as the biggest. *I shouldn't have listened to Jason.* Yet the other man had made sense. How could he expect a woman he'd never met to travel to Alaska to visit him? The scenario was probably described in every article out there as what *not* to do. When he'd mentioned their plans to his friend, he immediately pointed out how risky that must sound to Sara's family and friends. Then he asked if he'd be comfortable with his own daughter taking a trip to meet a stranger if he had kids. *Hell no,* had been his immediate response. So he managed to alter his plans to part ways with his group in New York. Jason would be on hand to ensure that everything went smoothly on the last legs of their flight. Normally he'd be expected to be on hand for the whole welcome home celebration, but his boss had been willing to accommodate his request.

With Sara's trip to Alaska fast approaching, this was really the only way he could come to her first. He even managed to book a seat home on her flight, so they'd be traveling together. He debated letting her know he was coming, but he knew how nervous she'd get. She still insisted on having a few minutes' notice before they Face-Timed so she could "look presentable." She joked about scaring him away with her messy hair and lack of makeup. But to him, she didn't need any of that. She had a natural beauty that the cosmetic companies made a fortune trying to sell women. He told her that very thing, but she'd brushed his compliment aside, saying something about looking as pale as Casper the Friendly Ghost. She wasn't comfortable with praise; he'd noticed that pretty early on. He thought it pleased her, but more often than not, she made a joke at her own expense. It was a strangely endearing show of insecurity. Most of the women he'd been out with were the opposite. Confidence could be attractive, but when it bordered on conceit . . . not so much. She might insist on brushing her hair and touching up her makeup, but he was really glad she didn't show up for their video dates wearing a damned prom dress. When the weather was cooler, she usually had on either jeans or gym clothes, and if it was warmer, it was the sundresses. Those were his personal favorite because they showcased her feminine curves.

Gabe stopped by the restroom before slowly making his way to the baggage claim. He'd learned years ago not to be in a rush to collect his luggage. It was better to arrive later and miss everyone tackling each other over a generic black suitcase. He'd shipped most of his things from Iraq to his neighbor's house. It was much easier traveling with just a carry-on. Although in this instance, that hadn't worked out, since the overhead compartments had been full. It was a pain in the ass, but he hadn't argued. He was too distracted by the woman he'd soon be surprising in person. Luckily, he had her address, since he'd insisted on buying her plane ticket. She'd argued and said she would pay him back, but he wouldn't take her money. After all, she was flying over three thousand miles to visit.

He'd have to go to the base for some post-deployment protocol, but he'd have several weeks before he returned to his regular schedule. He often wondered if that was necessarily a good thing. The military felt like it was the least they could do after separating you from your loved ones for long months. Yet reintegration was always a challenge, and from personal experience, he found it went better the sooner he got back on his normal routine. Otherwise, he had too much time to dwell on everything he'd experienced while he was gone. He could see a few weeks to take care of all the shit that had piled up while you were away. But post-deployment leaves could easily run for a month.

Most of the soldiers he knew were going stir-crazy before it was over.

Gabe easily snagged his green duffle bag and looked around until he spotted the sign for the car rentals. He'd reserved one with a GPS, since he wasn't about to attempt to find his way around without one. He figured he'd pick up his car then go see her. He'd slept a good portion of the trip, so he wasn't too tired. Plus, he couldn't imagine being this close to Sara and waiting another day to see her. He only hoped that showing up unannounced wouldn't scare the hell out of her. In his mind, after her initial shock wore off, she'd be thrilled by the visit. *Every stalker probably thinks the same thing.*

He would have never guessed in a million years that he'd begin his deployment single and end it damn near head over heels for a woman he'd never laid eyes on in person. He couldn't wait to hold her in his arms. To smell her skin and hear her laughter. Even though they video chatted often, it still wasn't the same as being in the same room together. Several months back, she started mailing him a card every week. And in one of those, she sprayed her perfume. He must have sniffed that damned thing a dozen times a day. It seemed to fit her so well. It was light and sweet, with a hint of something sexy. In a word, intoxicating. Like a sap, he'd kept every letter she'd ever sent. He'd read through them all again during his flight. Now they were safely put away in a large manila envelope.

Sara had turned what were usually endlessly long months into some of the best moments he'd ever experienced. He was almost sad when his time was over because he'd gotten so used to their routine. But he was also excited about starting what he hoped was a new chapter with her. It wouldn't be easy, he knew that. They were strangers that knew each other better than a lot of married couples. Since there hadn't been the complication of sex thrown into the mix, they'd actually communicated with words instead of jumping into bed, then finding out how the other liked their coffee. Hell, he didn't think he'd ever been this well acquainted with anyone he'd dated in the past. Might explain why he was still single. For a man as level-headed and cautious as he'd always been, this was a huge leap of faith. She might not know it, but the fact that he was here spoke volumes about his feelings for her.

He opened the door to his midsized SUV and tossed his bag into the passenger seat. In less than an hour he'd be with her. He only hoped it was the dawn of a new beginning and not his first true heartbreak. He'd never been so nervous over meeting a woman before.

Sara was tired and irritated. It had been one of those weeks. Kaylee had been unusually uncooperative, and her mother, who was staying with them until her broken furnace was repaired, hadn't been much better. Which unfortunately coincided with the start of Nicole and Chris's vacation. They were leaving for Mexico with some friends tomorrow afternoon, but until then, they were all home and annoying the hell out of her. She'd been beyond grateful when Nicole had announced she was going shopping. Her sister-in-law had probably planned to enjoy a few hours of alone time, but her mother had jumped at the chance to go to the mall. She hadn't missed the beseeching look Nicole had thrown Chris, and even though he acted dumb, she was sure he'd picked up on the hidden plea to accompany them. It had gotten even more amusing when their mother attempted to talk Kaylee into going as well. Sara was certain Nicole couldn't imagine a worse hell than shopping with her mother-in-law and five-year-old daughter. But Kaylee had taken a page from her father's book and said no.

When the door shut behind the two of them, Chris released a loud sigh. "I'll pay for that later, but it's worth it for some peace. I swear, Nicole and Mom are driving me crazy. They're worse than a bunch of kids hyped up on sugar."

Kaylee walked over and wrapped her arms around Sara's leg and made a sound similar to her father's. It seemed they were all relieved to have some quiet time. "I've got nothing." Sara shrugged. "I'd love to say I'm enjoying all this togetherness, but—not so much. Is it just me, or is Mom extra annoying today? I literally cannot get away from her. I resorted to staying in the bathroom because she was trying to organize Kaylee's toys by size, color, *and* condition. This was after she arranged the contents of the kitchen cabinets. I don't know about you, but I'll certainly sleep better tonight with everything in alphabetical order."

"She's trying her best to get into my office and 'improve my flow.' Not sure what that would entail, and I don't intend to find out." Chris shuddered. "For someone who has been limping around for weeks, she's certainly spry. She didn't even think twice about the shopping trip."

They were still standing in the foyer joking around when the doorbell chimed. All three of them jumped guiltily. "It's not them. They would have used their key," Sara whispered.

Chris stepped forward, looking through the peephole. "It's some guy. First time I can recall being happy to see a salesman."

"Buy whatever he's hocking," Sara smirked as she turned to walk away.

"Um—hello. I'm here to see Sara. Is she available?" Sara froze in place. *That voice. No . . . it couldn't be. He's on his way home.*

Chris was looking over his shoulder, obviously puzzled by the stranger asking for her. She shook her head, trying to communicate her panic to him without putting it into words. *It's not him. There is no way . . .* "Could I get your name?" Chris asked, clearly having no clue as to what to do. Men didn't show up at their door out of the blue asking for her.

Kaylee had gone oddly silent, as if sensing her distress. "Sure, should have led with that. I'm Gabe Randall. Sara isn't exactly expecting me. I hoped to surprise her." *Can't breathe, can't breathe.* She was very much afraid she was going to pass out. *He's here—Gabe. My Gabe. Why? How? Oh my God.* "You must be Sara's brother. I've heard a lot about you. I thought it might put your mind at ease if you all met me before the trip."

Even though Gabe couldn't see her, Chris was openly

staring at her now. She had no idea what he'd picked up on there, but what he did next was clearly meant to protect her. "No, I'm her husband. Exactly how do you know my wife?"

"Chris," she whispered in horror, shaking her head frantically. "No, dear God, don't tell him that." Sara moved out of the shadows and shoved past her brother until she was face-to-face with the man who had been the center of her world for the past seven months. For a moment, she could only stare. He was even handsomer in person. Tall, dark, and fit, with eyes that were even more piercing in person. Only instead of the affection she'd gotten used to seeing in them, they were now filled with confusion, anger, and, worst of all, hurt. *So much hurt. Oh God. Why is Chris doing this? I can't believe he's here.* "Gabe." She choked out his name as she extended a hand toward him.

Yet he simply stood there, with his arms crossed over his chest. "Are you here to talk to my mommy?" Kaylee asked as she moved to Sara's side. *Kaylee, not you too.* Sara closed her eyes briefly, knowing the little girl assumed Gabe was someone for Nicole. It wasn't unusual for clerks from the station to stop by to drop off and pick up mail for Nicole. But her question sounded even more damning in light of Chris's absurd claim. And Gabe's now ashen face told her that he thought the worst. This entire fiasco was fast spinning out of control. Considering the damage that her family had already inflicted, she couldn't risk trying to reason with him in front of them. So she put a hand on his shoulder and nudged him back a few inches so she could step outside and shut the door behind her.

She stood for a moment, drinking in every feature. Yet his expression told her that she was not welcome there. "Gabe. My brother is joking. How long are you here—"

"No, I'm thinking the joke is on me, Sara. You lied to me about everything. You're not the spinster nanny, you're the mother. How did you manage to pull it off? We talked so much. Does your husband travel or something?" Before she could reply, he held up his hand. "You know what? It doesn't matter. Hell, I wouldn't know if you were telling the truth anyway." The pain in his voice ripped her heart out when he said, "I trusted you, Sara. I fucking let you in and you lied to me. Is this how you get your kicks? Seems like *that* is your kink." *No. No, this is not happening. How can he not believe me?*

"I'm not married, Gabe!" she yelled out, desperate to salvage the mess she'd made. "I swear to you, Chris is my brother. He said that because he could see that I was panicking and he was trying to protect me. If he'd known who you were—"

"I felt it was the right thing to do to come to you, Sara. And I'm glad I did. I'll make sure I get a refund on the ticket to Alaska." She opened her mouth, then closed it again. What could she say? She'd been too much of a coward to tell everyone about the man she had met online. And maybe a part of her hadn't believed it would ever happen that they would one day meet in person. This was a disaster. How could this have happened? *Lower than dirt. I'm the worst excuse for a person ever. He's even more amazing than I realized, and I've hurt him.*

I hate myself.

She had no idea what she should do next, but she found herself blurting out an explanation. "I was afraid to let myself get excited. I was already so attached to you that I didn't think I could handle it if you changed your mind after your deployment. So I tried not to think about it. To get my hopes up . . ."

He ran an unsteady hand over his face in a gesture that was so familiar to her that it made her heart ache. She knew him so well—yet not at all. *How did things get to this point?* "I swear, I don't know what to believe. In hindsight, showing up unannounced wasn't such a good idea, that's for sure."

"Why did you?" she asked him softly, barely able to resist the urge to touch him. The only thing that stopped her was the certainty that he didn't want her to get any closer. *Why would he?*

His expression was blank as he stared back at her, but the pained expression was still there in his eyes and she had to fight to keep from glancing away. "I knew you'd get all nervous and I didn't want that. Shit, you get flustered if you don't have time to prepare to FaceTime. I changed my flights. Thought it would be a nice surprise after the initial shock. But now "

"You did all this for me?" she asked. *Please don't walk away, Gabe. Please listen.*

"Great plan, huh?" he said sarcastically. "Remind me to stick to the script in the future. Oh wait, you're not likely to be around for that, are you? Maybe I can have it put on a T-shirt or something more reliable."

"I'm so sorry." She gulped as the tears threatened to flow. The fact that she'd held them back this long was nothing short of a miracle. "I never wanted to hurt you, Gabe. These months with you have been . . . the best of my life. You don't know how much I looked forward to each day because of you. I—I've never felt this way about anyone before. And I was afraid . . . it was too good to be true."

"Sara—dammit, don't you think I've felt the same?" he snapped, before inhaling roughly when a tear rolled down her cheek, followed by another. "Don't . . . please. Regardless of how angry I feel, I can't stand to see you cry."

"I'm sorry." She hiccuped, but couldn't stop the outburst of emotion now that it had started.

"Jesus." He sighed. She felt hands on first her shoulders, then her back, before she was pulled into a warm embrace. The scent, there it was. His cologne. He'd sent her a letter from Iraq and had added it, just as she'd put her perfume on some for him. "I need to leave. I'm tired and frankly a little overwhelmed. Returning to the States is challenging enough without playing the starring role in a sideshow."

"It's not like that. Please believe me. Where are you going to go?" she asked, suddenly terrified that she'd never see him again. *He probably doesn't believe a word you've said. Why would he?*

He put his hands in his pockets as he rocked back on his heels. He did look exhausted and completely distant—so different from how she was used to seeing him during their hours on FaceTime together. "I booked a hotel room. I'm going to go check in and crash for a while."

"And after that?" she asked quietly. *Run like hell.*

He shrugged his broad shoulders before saying, "What does it matter to you? How long were you planning to stay in the fantasy world we created? You know what? Don't answer that." He turned away, and Sara was sure he was going to go. But then he turned back, and even though there was still so much hostility in his expression, he managed to say more softly, "Why'd you agree to come to Alaska? You went so far as to let me buy you a plane ticket. This isn't about the money, so don't offer to pay me back." *How does he do that? Read my mind so easily.* "Why didn't you come up with an excuse? Buy yourself more time? Especially if, as you've stated, you thought I'd lose interest in you when I got home."

"Because I wanted to meet you. Gabe, I wasn't lying when I said these have been the best months ever for me."

His lips curled into the smirk she'd always thought was so flipping cute. But today, it made her more uncomfortable. She'd never been at odds with him before. He always treated her so gently. She had no doubt he knew how to get his point across to his soldiers with the minimum amount of words. But that wasn't her Gabe—until now. *All my fault, I did this. He doesn't see me in the same light anymore.* Opening his arms, he said, "Well, here I am, Sara, in the flesh. All you have to do is reach out and take a chance. I've literally laid myself at your door."

She felt trapped in a prison of her own making. She wanted to run off into the sunset with him, yet she had obligations here. *I should have told my family about him. Why didn't I?* "Gabe . . . I can't just walk out on my life," she said imploringly. "My brother and his wife are going on vacation tomorrow. And my mother is staying here until her heating system is repaired. She won't watch Kaylee for more than a few hours, so there's no way she'd do it for an extended period. If you'll give me a little more time, I can—"

"Stop, Sara, enough with the excuses. You have a flight booked in a week. If you want to give whatever this is between us a chance, then you'll be on it. I was planning to go with you, but now I'll see if I can change my ticket and go back sooner."

"Wh—what if I can't get everything together that quickly?" she asked, knowing he was still angry, but never expecting what he said next.

He glanced down the street, as if gathering his thoughts. "Whatever we've been doing ends here. I did my part. I committed to the next step by coming to you. We won't continue our virtual relationship after this. I'll cut off communication with you and move on. I cannot and will not put my world on hold to be your e-boyfriend. I'm not a teenager, Sara, I'm thirty-seven years old. Even though I was wary, I bought into the fact that people meet in unusual ways every day and it works out. I took a chance on you once—but that's as far as I'll go."

"Gabe," she whispered as the tears started once again.

Only this time he made no move to comfort her. Instead he turned on his heel and was a few feet away when he stopped and faced her one last time. "Your pictures and FaceTime didn't do you justice. You're beautiful, Sara."

Then he added the phrase she'd used in one of the first e-mails she'd sent to him: "Ball's in your court." And with that he was gone—and it felt like he took with him a large chunk of her heart. And the other part? It was shattered. Torn. *The man I'm certain I'd begun to love is walking away, and I can blame no one other than myself.*

Chapter Thirteen

🐾 🐾

Somehow, she made it back inside the house, although she couldn't remember moving. Chris was sitting on the bottom of the stairs when she opened the door, but Kaylee was nowhere in sight. "What in the hell was that all about?" he asked in bewilderment. *Oh, you're confused? Join the club.*

She debated continuing on past him, but she had nothing left. Plus, even though she and her brother had never been what you'd call confidants, she needed to talk to someone about the absolute train wreck she'd just caused. He slid over a few inches and motioned for her to sit next to him. If she looked anywhere near as bad as she felt, he probably thought she'd collapse at any moment. "His name is Gabe Randall, and we met about seven months ago," she said quietly. *It's over. No more messages, no nothing. Over, Over, Over.*

It was obvious by the note of confusion in his voice that he was even more lost now. "Okay . . . if you *met*, then why did he seem like a stranger to you? And you damn sure weren't rolling out the welcome wagon for him. That's why I said you were my wife. Hell, I thought maybe some weirdo had followed you home from the grocery store or something. Although I couldn't figure out how he knew the things he did."

She pinched the bridge of her nose, trying to collect herself so she could tell him what was going on. She needed to get it out before Nicole and her mother got back. She couldn't face them joining in this mess. "It's a long story, but one of the radio stations that I listen to was collecting cards back in April to send to deployed soldiers. I filled one out and mailed it to them, and it ended up in Gabe's hands. He e-mailed to thank me and we formed a friendship . . . that turned into more." *Understatement of the century.*

At the mention of soldiers, she had Chris's complete attention. Even though he was no longer in the service, he still considered it a second home and the troops his family. "He's active duty? Which branch?"

"Yes, he's a major in the Army. He just finished his seventh deployment overseas."

"I see. That's impressive," he said sincerely. "How long has he been in?"

"For sixteen years. He's stationed in Anchorage, Alaska. He bought me a plane ticket to go visit him."

"I thought you'd seemed . . . different lately, but I couldn't quite put my finger on it." *And you didn't care enough to bother figuring it out.* But then she felt bad for her bitchy reaction. He was trying now, wasn't he? "What I can't understand is why you wouldn't have come to me. I might not have been Army, but I have contacts who would check him out for you. I hate to say this, but there are a lot of guys who use their uniform to impress women. For all you know, he might be married with a half-dozen kids running around. You've led a pretty sheltered life, Sara. You don't know what it's like out there. It would be so damned easy for someone to take advantage of you. I mean, you even gave him your address. Not only did you put yourself at risk, but my family as well."

She looked up at him, not bothering to hide the hurt she felt. "Oh, excuse me, I thought I was your family as well." He felt bad; it was clear on his face. She also knew she was being overly sensitive because of Gabe. If she could pick a fight with her brother, then she wouldn't be so focused on what she'd lost. *You mean threw away. You had a choice—you made it. Spinster.*

"God, I suck at this." He laughed before bumping his shoulder against hers. "I never seem to say the right thing to you. So I just didn't bother to try after a while. I know I've been a shit brother, considering how much you've given up for us—for Kaylee. I should have said it way before now, but I hope you realize that I appreciate you and all you've done for us. I haven't a clue what we would have done if you hadn't agreed to help us. Nicole and I—we need to do better. I always wanted to have a relationship with my kids the way we had with Dad. You know—be a friend and a parent. You and Kaylee are like that, but I don't know how to be."

Even though this was not at all the time she would have picked to have a heart-to-heart talk with her brother, it did provide a temporary diversion. "I've loved being with Kaylee," she said honestly. "You have an amazing daughter. And I might not know much about kids, but the main way that bonds are formed is by being there. Spending time with them. Listening to their hopes and fears. Because even at that young age, they have plenty of them to discuss. You have to become a main character and not part of the supporting cast."

"Okay, that makes sense," he mused. "I'm going to talk to Nicole while we're gone, and we're going to make some changes when we get back. We both lead busy lives, but that's no excuse. You shouldn't have to shoulder all the responsibility for raising *our* child. That must have put so much pressure on you. Obviously, you needed an escape; otherwise, this wouldn't have happened today. We'll give you more time off so you can have a social life with people you actually know. I'm sure Chloe could introduce you to some of her friends."

As he continued outlining his plan to get her some socialization, she could only sit there and listen to him incredulously. *He's trying to fix me, as if I'm broken.* Then what was really going on hit her. *He's scared.* This thing with Gabe today had shaken not only her but him as well. But for two very different reasons. She was devastated over hurting the man she cared so much for. She also couldn't imagine not talking to him every day. He'd become such a big part of her world. But Chris . . . he was clearly panicked at the thought of her leaving them behind and starting a life of her own. Not only was his daughter spoiled by her constant presence, but so was he. Her exit would cause a major upheaval for them. They were so used to Sara handling Kaylee's care and whatever things they couldn't get to. There were essentially three people in their marriage, instead of two. She was the one who took care of all the details they didn't want to deal with. There was no way that he'd have ever approved of Gabe, regardless of how much the other man impressed him. Because he could only see the potential disruption he could cause. "I think I'm going to go lie down for a while," she said when he'd finally paused. "I've got a bit of a headache."

"Well, of course you do," he said as he leaned over to kiss the top of her head. *Wow, affection too? He's really freaked.* "Don't worry about any of this. If that guy bothers you anymore, let me know and I'll take care of it. You did the right thing—sending him on his way. Even if he has been truthful with you about everything—which I seriously doubt—your life is here. Responsibilities that neither of us can walk away from. Outside of your job, we have a mother that depends on both of us. Everyone has dreams, but they have to be balanced with reality. I can see how you would have been easily led astray by some pretty words—and whatever other nonsense he filled your head with. I'm just glad I was here when this happened. No telling how difficult he might have been if he hadn't known I was right inside, watching."

Talk about a glass of ice water over the head. His motivational talk bordered on insulting. She knew his heart was in the right place, but again he made her sound more like a wayward employee than his sister. *Is that all I am to him?* Sara got to her feet, having hit her limit for the moment. She desperately needed a quiet space to process the last hour—and to cry. She had no idea what she even said to Chris before she walked off. She covered the last few feet to her room in a dead run. She closed the door and locked it before leaning her back against the hard surface and sliding down until she was sitting on the floor with her arms wrapped around her knees. Then the dam burst and all her anguish came pouring out. She couldn't remember crying like this since she'd lost her father five years earlier. All she could see was Gabe's stricken expression as he stared at her. She'd hurt him—badly. She wanted nothing more than to make it up to him. *But how?* He said the ball was in her court now, but she'd also picked up on his unspoken threat. It wasn't an open-ended offer. He wouldn't wait for her, and there were no guarantees that he'd forgive her either way. She had one shot, and the window was already closing on it. Unless . . . she could reason with him. Make him understand that she needed just a little longer. She jumped to her feet, intent on getting her iPad to e-mail him. But even as she tried to reassure herself that it could be that easy, she knew in her heart that it wouldn't. His statement had implied she had a chance, but she was very much afraid that it had been over between them before the words had left his mouth.

How could I have been so damned gullible? Gabe had counseled his soldiers countless times on not taking anything at face value, especially relationships. *Always trust your gut. If it seems too good to be true, it likely is.* He'd said some version of that at least once a month. Yet he'd jumped headfirst down the same rabbit hole he'd advised against and had been blissfully happy doing it. Until today, when he'd been made an utter fool of. He had a hard time even thinking about the scene at Sara's door without being equal parts furious and embarrassed. He might have been wary a few times along the way, but it had never seriously given him pause. She'd been so amazing it dazzled him. And not in the sexual kind of connection that a lot of his soldiers had fallen victim to. Although she was a beautiful woman and he was very attracted to her, it had been more than that between them. Her outgoing personality, along with her sweetness, had lured him in. Had she just been some hot bimbo, he would have given her the brush-off quickly. *Was it all an illusion? What she wanted him to see?*

Instead of checking into the hotel, Gabe drove straight to the airport. He was lucky enough to get a seat on a flight that left in two hours. He'd even been upgraded to first class, thanks to his military status. So he turned his car back in and had a beer at the sports bar. By the time the plane was boarding, his limbs felt heavy with fatigue. He stored his bag in the overhead bin and settled in next to a middle-aged businessman who seemed no more interested in small talk than he was.

This wasn't the way it was supposed to go. He'd warned Sara that he would cut all contact with her, and he meant to stick to that. But damn, it was hard. He felt as if he'd left a part of himself behind. She'd slowly become the center of his world over the last seven months. His confidant. *His release.* How did he go back to a life without that—without her? He was certain she'd be more than happy to pick up where they left off and continue their e-relationship, but that wasn't enough for him. He'd been counting the days for the last month until he could be with her in person—and until today, he assumed that they both had. He couldn't fathom settling into limbo, where there was nothing beyond FaceTime, texts, and phone calls. Those were amazing tools when you were deployed and forced to be apart from the person you loved. But that all ended when you came home.

A part of him wished he hadn't surprised her today. He'd still be in that rosy bubble until she didn't get on the plane. *Maybe she will now that she knows you're serious about her.* That seemed about as likely to him as winning the lottery. His odds of being a millionaire were probably better. As much as it sucked, he needed to accept that the fantasy world they'd been living in was over. He wasn't naive enough to believe it would be easy. For the first time, his heart literally ached. And even after all the humiliation he'd suffered at her hands, a part of him couldn't stand leaving her behind. It felt wrong to him somehow. *I seriously need to grow a pair.*

Yet he did believe her. At first, he'd been ready to convict her without a trial based on the damning evidence. But most of the pieces had fallen into place when they'd been talking outside. And no husband would remain in the house after what had transpired inside. Yeah, he could give her a pass on all that. But what ticked him off was whether or not she was actually going to come see him in Anchorage. He couldn't give a shit about the cost of the ticket. What really got him was how far she'd let it go without hitting the brakes. If she'd expressed concern and wanted to wait until after he was home to make plans, he'd have understood. But she hadn't. Instead, she pretended to be just as excited as he was about their upcoming meeting. Knowing all the while that she had no intention of following through with it. Quite simply, she made him feel like a fool, and that was a first for him. It made him question his judgment. Was his head really so easily turned by a pretty face? He hadn't believed he was such an easy target.

Gabe also had to wonder at what point she'd have made her excuses if he hadn't shown up at her house. Would she have left him standing at the airport in Alaska until the crew had exited the aircraft?

The flight attendant was making the final announcements when his phone vibrated. Normally he'd have already put it in airplane mode, but he'd been too distracted to pay much attention to flight preparations. His gut twisted painfully when he saw that it was a text from her. *Shit. Don't read it.* Yet even as he told himself that, he clicked to open it.

SARA: Gabe, I'm so sorry about what happened. I do want to come see you. Very much. If you'll please give me a little more time. Everything I told you about my family arrangement is true, and therefore, they will need to cover everything I do while I'm with you in Anchorage. I hope you can forgive me. I care for you more than you'll ever know. I miss you. Sara

He'd never been more grateful to feel a plane beginning to taxi toward the runway than he was now. He put his phone in the correct mode, which meant he kept his promise not to contact her. He hated how weak he was where she was concerned. He found it almost physically painful to ignore her message. She'd been a priority in his thoughts for so long that it was going to be a very hard habit to break. In Iraq, whenever he had a spare moment to himself, saying hello to her was the first thing he'd done. She'd pretty much assumed the role of his girlfriend—or heck, even his wife. He'd talked to her more than he had his friends or family.

He was at loose ends now, similar to what you'd go through after a breakup. The pain, the confusion, the doubts, the sense of loss. He wasn't sure he even realized what a key part she'd played in his world until today. If this bothered her half as much as it bothered him, then he almost felt sorry for her. After all, he did care for her—a lot. Regardless of how they'd met, he'd felt a connection he'd never known before, and *that* would be hell to walk away from. *Today is bad enough.* They *could* easily be one of those couples you read about that met on the Internet and spent years talking but never took it further, though somehow he doubted that.

Could he keep her in his life as a friend? He could . . . but he didn't see the point. He couldn't be platonic with her. The spark between them was too bright. They might not have crossed over into straight-up sexting, but they weren't innocent pals either. But if this was the end . . . then like any other loss—and he'd had many—he'd mourn and continue on.

He leaned his head back as the plane took off, gripping the hand rests as he always did until they reached cruising altitude. He glanced over at the guy sitting beside him, thinking once again that Sara should be there. He wasn't a man given to romantic daydreams, but he'd imagined them holding hands at takeoff because she'd mentioned she was always nervous then. He'd have attempted to distract her. Probably made some reference to a past joke they'd shared or told her more about his home in Alaska. They'd never been at a loss for words, and even with the adjustment to physical proximity with each other, he didn't see it being awkward, at least not for long. *I may never know now. If she doesn't make any overture to rearrange her family responsibilities, then I'll have to conclude that it was only real to me.* The words of her text kept bouncing around his mind, though, too hard to shut off. Too tempting to dismiss. *I care for you more than you'll ever know. I miss you.* God, he already missed her too.

Damn, he needed to at least believe that it was insecurities that had made her deceive him. He didn't want his sweet, sassy Sara to be anything other than the woman he'd come to know so well. *There's only one way she can prove that to you.* That's what it boiled down to. Otherwise, he'd never truly be rid of that inkling of doubt that she wasn't the person he thought her to be. And it was sheer torment to have the image of the woman he'd developed such deep feelings for ruined. *Distance yourself. Pack it up and shut it down.*

Piece by piece, he pushed her out of his head, sealing that part of his mind off—for now. He knew he wouldn't be able to keep her locked away for long, though. Because he'd never had to compartmentalize someone who was not only in his head but in his heart as well. He had a bad feeling the same rules simply didn't apply, but a guy could hope.

Chapter Fourteen

🐾 🐾

If Chloe made that annoying sound of disbelief one more time, Sara was afraid she'd lose it. She'd called her cousin for an emergency meeting as soon as Nicole and Chris had left the next morning. Her mother had even volunteered to babysit Kaylee that evening so she could meet Chloe for dinner. She'd been too distracted and too grateful to marvel at that unusual offer. It had been twenty-four hours of hell, and she'd about hit her limit. "Could you maybe say something instead of making that hopeless humming noise?"

"I'm trying to process here," she grumbled. "This is seriously a big mess," she added. *Way to state the obvious.*

"I'm aware of that," Sara snapped. "Crap, sorry. My nerves are a little frayed. As if dealing with the whole Gabe thing wasn't bad enough, I also heard my brother and his lovely wife talking about me last night."

"Whoa, what?" Chloe choked out. "You didn't mention that."

Shrugging, Sara said, "It wasn't my priority. It hurt, but not nearly as much as what happened with him."

Chloe gave her an expectant look, then waved a hand in exasperation. "Do you want me to guess?"

They were in a corner booth in their favorite Mexican restaurant, and Sara paused to take a long drink of the jumbo margarita Chloe had ordered for her. "Well, Kaylee had Nicole's makeup case hidden in her room, so I found it and took it upstairs so she wouldn't wake us up looking for it before they left. Their door was cracked and I heard my name, so I stopped—and listened. Chris was telling her about Gabe and what had happened earlier. Which pissed me off, but I wasn't really surprised. I figured he would. You know what she asked him first? If Gabe was ugly. As if she couldn't believe anyone attractive would be interested in me."

"That skinny bitch," Chloe snorted. "She's just jealous and you know it. She can't stand the thought of anyone getting more attention than she does."

Sara smiled, secretly agreeing. Nicole certainly liked the spotlight. She often thought it was one reason she didn't connect well with her own daughter. She saw her as competition for Chris's attention, which was absurd. "Anyway, you know men. Chris just said he hadn't noticed. Then he told her he'd tried to talk some sense into me, but he was still worried I'd take off and he didn't know what they'd do if that happened."

"That should scare the hell out of them," Chloe said as she popped a chip into her mouth.

"Nicole giggled," Sara murmured, unable to hide the hurt that she felt. "Then it turned into hysterical laughter. I should have walked away then, but I was kind of rooted in place. Chris asked her what she found so funny. When she could breathe, she said, 'Losing your sister is the last thing I'd worry about. She isn't going anywhere. She's far too comfortable here, and why wouldn't she be? She's got it made. Kaylee practically takes care of herself now, so what's there to do? Sit around and watch television all day?'"

"I'm so going to kick her bony ass when she gets back," Chloe hissed. "I swear I've never liked that self-absorbed airhead. What did Chris say?"

Sara's finger drew circles in the moisture left behind on the table by her glass as she said, "He pointed out that I do a lot of things for them outside of Kaylee. He also mentioned them doing more with her so that I could have more time off. Nicole said if they did, then my salary should be cut. After all, I don't have any living expenses, so I really shouldn't even be drawing a paycheck." *Knowing that your sister-in-law thinks even more lowly of you than you thought possible is extremely painful. Yet they're happy for me to raise their daughter.*

When Sara looked up, Chloe's eyes were so wide, they were almost crossing, and her fingers were attacking a napkin so intently that the poor thing was in shreds in seconds. "Oh no, she did not say that," she retorted. "I don't know why I'm surprised, but that was a low blow even for her. After all you've done for them, how could she think that, much less say it? You've given them years of your life to help with their daughter, and it sounds as if she doesn't appreciate any of it. Swear to God, I'd have packed my shit right then and ruined her fancy little vacation. She'd have been wearing her tiny bikini to the public pool instead of a five-star resort. Please tell me you went in there and slapped her around. A left hook to that Botoxed forehead would have been a great starting point."

She was so hopeful that Sara hated disappointing her. "Chris changed the subject and I got out of there before they saw me. I was so overwhelmed from what happened with Gabe that I couldn't deal with anything else. I did toss her makeup bag in the kitchen trash, though, so that's something."

"Oh, Sara," Chloe said in a voice full of sympathy. "You've been through hell, haven't you? Why didn't you call me last night? I'd have come right over. I've never been in your particular position, but I certainly know what it's like to be all messed up over some guy. And heartbreak is heartbreak, no matter what the cause. Although at least your man didn't screw around on you, so this can still be saved. You said you've texted him, right?"

"Yeah, but he hasn't responded. Although he did read it," she added glumly. "He's not going to reply. He told me he would cut contact and that's what he's done. I can't blame him after everything that's happened. Any sane person would do the same."

Chloe appeared deep in thought as she settled back

against the padded booth seat. Finally she said, "I can see both sides to some degree. He blindsided you by showing up unannounced. That would have freaked me out a bit, regardless of how long you'd been talking. He's still a stranger, so—yeah, definitely enough to rattle you. But . . . if what he said is true, and I have no reason to believe otherwise, then he had good intentions. I'd say he's certainly thought better of it since then. It was beyond thoughtful of him to want to meet your family and set their minds at ease. As well as keep you from stressing over his visit by not telling you ahead of time."

Sara could almost see Chloe making one of the lists she was so fond of creating for everything. "He has far more checks in the positive category of your imaginary paper than I do, doesn't he? Trust me, I've come to the same conclusion myself."

"Then why are you asking me for advice? It seems to me that you should know what to do next. You've put your family first for the last three years that I know of, and probably longer than that. You've now seen this man in person, actually had a conversation with him face-to-face. Was he everything you'd built him up to be in your head?"

Sara smiled, although she knew it was filled with sadness and not happiness. "Even angry, he was better than my dreams, Chloe. And not just because he was impossibly handsome. It was the whole package. So tall and muscular—but not bulky. Lean, like a runner. His eyes are mesmerizing and so expressive. Which wasn't necessarily a good thing yesterday when I could so easily see how angry, hurt, and disappointed he was with me. Oh, and dear Lord, he smelled delicious. I wanted to keep my face buried against him and never let go."

Chloe leaned forward eagerly. "Wait, you were in his arms? You should have led with that. How did it happen?"

Sara sighed. "I started crying, and he held me for a moment. It felt so good—so right somehow. As if we'd embraced like that countless times before. You know how awkward it usually is when someone touches you for the first time? Well, he didn't seem like a stranger. That must sound insane."

Chloe shook her head. "Not at all. I've had that reaction to people. It's rare, but it happens. And when it does, it's amazing, that connection."

"He meant what he said," Sara said dejectedly. "He's ended contact with me. He might have read my text, but that's as far as it'll go. He'll probably change his number or block me. He was very clear. We learned a lot about each other while he was deployed, and when he sets his mind to something, he sees it through. I just never thought that focus would be turned on me—in a negative way. And so quickly. It was as if I was given only one chance and in his eyes, I failed, and therefore he's done."

"But didn't you say he told you that the ball was in your court?" When Sara nodded, she said, "That implies that he hasn't entirely written you off yet. Let me see if I have this right: If you take the flight he booked for you, then he'll give you another chance?"

"I—guess so," Sara mumbled. "I mean, he said he'd

done his part, and if I wanted to give it a go, then I'd be on that plane."

"That's very direct and to the point. So you do have an opportunity to fix what's happened between you two—if that's what you want to do. I could be wrong, but he sounds flipping awesome." She put her finger against her chin as if deep in thought. "Do you think your ticket is transferable? I mean, I could go tell him in person, let him down gently."

Sara frowned, puzzled by her cousin's offer until the meaning hit her. "Wh—what? Hell no, you won't," she barked out.

When Chloe snickered, Sara knew she'd been played. "That's what I thought. So we have, what, a matter of days to make arrangements? When will your brother and his bimbo be back from their usual child-free vacation?"

"Um . . . five days," she said uncertainly. "I can't leave Kaylee at home by herself, you know."

"Correct me if I'm wrong, but doesn't she have grand-parents?"

"Nicole's parents live in California, and they both have jobs."

"Well, your mother is free as a bird, isn't she? And con-veniently, she's living with you right now. Surely she can watch Kaylee for one day. If there's some reason that she cannot, then I'll take vacation time and handle it."

"You'd do that?" Sara asked, thinking it was the nicest thing anyone had done for her in years.

"Absolutely," Chloe agreed without hesitation. "We probably need to get you some new clothes. You realize it's much colder in Alaska. And there's probably snow on the ground. So heavy winter clothing is a must. Maybe a couple of nicer outfits for an evening out."

Sara's head was spinning. Chloe was clearly in her element and getting more animated by the moment. But she seemed to be overlooking one very important thing. Clearing her throat, Sara jumped in when the other woman paused. "I can't tell you how much all of this means to me."

Chloe raised a brow in question. "I sense a 'but.' Whatever it is, we can deal with it."

"Who is supposed to take care of my niece while I'm gone?"

"Her. Parents," Chloe emphasized slowly. "Sure, it may not be ideal, but if you wait around until they're ready for you to leave, she'll be graduating from college. It won't be a total shock to them either, since they know about Gabe. You said yourself that Chris was concerned about you leaving. That's sort of like giving your notice. Granted, it's not exactly the conventional way, but this isn't a typical situation."

Sara couldn't believe how easy Chloe made it sound to uproot her life and go visit a man she didn't know very well. This was the sort of thing that teenagers without any common sense did. Not women who had no desire to end up in the trunk of someone's car. "Shouldn't you be preaching caution instead of encouraging me?" she asked wryly.

Chloe spread her hands out in front of her. "We know he's pretty far up the food chain in the military. Did he ask for or send you dirty pics during all the time you two were talking a million times a day?"

"Um—no. He never said anything out of line. He mentioned some overly friendly females he'd dealt with through the years and how uncomfortable it made him."

"So another positive for him." Chloe grinned approvingly. "I really can't see a wacko making the effort to come here first to meet your family. That speaks volumes, Sara. At that time, he had no reason to believe you weren't coming to visit him as planned. So why would he put himself in what was likely to be an uncomfortable situation when it wasn't necessary?" She reached out and squeezed Sara's hand. "That was all for you. No guy would do that for a lady he didn't care a lot for. It also tells me that he's a responsible, honorable man, who would never disrespect or harm you."

Sara sighed. "I'm not afraid of him. Somehow, I knew even before he showed up at my door that he was trustworthy."

Chloe sat quietly for a moment before saying, "I can't make this decision for you. But I do want to say one last thing. I—I feel that if you don't go to him, you'll end up alone." Sara's mouth dropped open, and her eyes watered at her cousin's blunt statement. "I don't mean to hurt your feelings. This has absolutely nothing to do with your appearance or who you are as a person. You're gorgeous, funny, intelligent, and quirky as hell. I've told you before, you could have your pick of men—that's not the issue. I don't think you were even aware of it, but you'd given up on yourself until Gabe came along. You were living through your family, and they were more than happy to let you. Kaylee filled the void you might have had to be a mother, and you've been all but running a household for your brother for three years. The only thing missing was male companionship, and when did you have time for it? Without Gabe, you'll go back to what you're used to, like most anyone would. And I'm afraid your family members will be thrilled to encourage it. You won't risk taking a chance with your heart again because you'll be too afraid of getting hurt."

Sara wanted to argue with her assessment, to say she had it all wrong, but they both knew better. If anything, she was understating the fallout from this. "I don't know what to do," she whispered. *Coward. Nicole is right.* "I've never had anything of my own."

Chloe gave her an understanding smile. "Believe me when I say I've been where you are before. The circumstances might have been different, but I've stood at the crossroads, not knowing which way to go."

"I swear if you tell me you took the road less traveled, I may hate you," Sara grumbled, as she used the back of her hand to wipe a tear away. *Why can't I stop crying?*

Chloe burst into laughter, causing Sara to wrinkle her nose in annoyance. *She's perfect. She has no clue what it's like to be me.* "Sorry," she said contritely. "Your expression was so flipping priceless I couldn't help myself. No, trust me, I didn't take a chance. I stuck my tail between my legs and went home. I had a guy that loved me. Really and truly loved me, Sara. He offered me the world and I was too afraid to reach out and take it. All he asked was that I have faith in him—in us—and I couldn't do it. Instead, I went back to guys who treated me like shit. Case in point, my last boyfriend, who dropped his zipper for half the female population of the state, no doubt. Somehow, I felt if I got hurt, it would be easier to handle with a piece of crap like that. But you know what? Getting your heart stomped on sucks no matter who does it. And I realize now that Wes would have never done that to me. We'd have had disagreements like normal people, but it wouldn't have been over infidelity or disrespect."

"Then take your own advice and go to him," Sara urged. "Tell him you made a mistake. Maybe it's not too late. When you love someone, it doesn't simply go away because you're not together." *It rips you up inside instead.*

"He's moved on," she said, wiping her own runaway tear aside. "I can't miss it, as I have a front row seat at the office. Oh, he's too thoughtful to rub my face in it, but I see them together. They were holding hands when she stopped by last week, and he looked at her—the way he used to look at me. Unlike me, though, she was returning his affection."

"He's the real reason you fell apart after your last breakup, isn't he? It wasn't so much the jerk that cheated, but the realization that you loved the one you let go."

"Bingo." Chloe nodded dejectedly. "That epiphany was a sucker punch to the gut."

As they finished their drinks, Sara couldn't help realizing that they were more alike than she could have ever imagined. She'd envied Chloe for years, yet they were so similar. While her family was her excuse to avoid taking chances, Chloe used the illusion that she was a social butterfly who only wanted to have fun. They both pretended to be happy, yet in reality were far from content. No, the two people at this table were both nursing broken hearts, and she wondered if either of them would find the courage to change that. Or would they be sitting here in ten years wondering what could have been? "Thank you, Chloe. Thank you for being real with me. For being honest, but not in a way that belittles me."

"No one should ever belittle you, Sara. And I hope you finally realize that."

Now all I have to do is believe that. Believe her. Believe in me.

Chapter Fifteen

🐾 🐾

"You were pretty late getting home last night," her mother said as Sara poured a cup of coffee and leaned back against the kitchen counter to take a drink. She normally waited until after she'd dropped Kaylee at school to have some so that she could savor it.

Ignoring the critical remark, she asked instead, "Did Kaylee give you any problems?"

"Of course not." Her mother shrugged as if the idea was absurd, although she certainly used it as an excuse not to babysit very often. *Am I the only one in this family who sees how amazing my niece is?* "We played outside until it got too dark. I think it wore her out, because she went to bed right after her bath."

"You got lucky." Sara smiled, thinking of how often she was cajoled into reading one more story.

"I raised two kids. I still remember how to stay one step ahead, although it's a little tougher as a grandmother. I'm not quite as quick on my feet as I used to be."

"That makes two of us," she said, knowing full well how long a few hours with an energetic child could feel. There had been times she'd fallen into bed still fully dressed. Thankfully, Kaylee was better at entertaining herself now than she'd once been.

Sara was looking through the cereal options when her mother said, "I talked to Nicole while you were out with Chloe. Poor thing had been looking forward to her vacation so much, but that stunt you pulled has ruined it for them. They both work so hard and rarely ever have any time to themselves. But now, along with worrying about their daughter, they're terrified that this stranger will show up while they're away." Sara was in shock.

"The stunt I pulled? Mom, I have no idea what I did here that would cause Nicole to lose a moment of sleep. Yes, they work hard, and that's why I'm here. All the time. Because they're not." She couldn't believe that her mother knew and would judge her so harshly. *What's next, an ad in the Sunday paper? Sara, the spinster, is desperate for love. Read all about it!*

Even though she knew it was a mistake, she couldn't stop herself from turning to face the disapproving frown her mother was leveling in her direction. In the most pleasant tone she could manage, she said slowly, but firmly, "Really, Mother, it's none of anyone's business what I do in my private life. As Chris has pointed out several times lately,

I'm an employee here. Therefore, as long as I'm doing my job, it shouldn't matter. Oh—and they took a trip two months ago. Trust me, they're not exactly deprived of vacation time."

If she wasn't so pissed off, she would have enjoyed seeing her mother's mouth flap open and shut in rapid succession. She couldn't remember the last time she'd truly been at a loss for words, but she also knew it wouldn't last. *Batten down the hatches, there's a storm coming. She's going to blow, folks.* "That Chloe is a bad influence on you." She scowled. "You were never so disrespectful until you became friends with her."

"She's my cousin, Mom," Sara pointed out dryly. "We reconnected at the reunion you insisted I attend. She's been a great source of much-needed support for me."

"What she is, Sara, is a troublemaker. There's one on every corner. And you've always been so easily led astray." She was warming to the subject now, her eyes alight with animation. *How is it possible to love someone, yet dislike them?* "It's your father's fault. He sheltered you too much. You have no understanding of what the world is really like out there. Chloe has lived in the city and worked for a big corporation. Whether I approve or not, she has survival experience. Whereas you went straight from our home to living with Chris. You've always been taken care of. Which has clearly affected your judgment. Otherwise, that man wouldn't have shown up here like that." She lowered her voice, looking appalled, as she added, "I'm afraid that one of my friends will call me sometime to say they saw you on the Internet in a dirty video." *Holy shit. Is she really accusing me of making a porno? What have I ever done for her to have such a low opinion of me?*

Sara couldn't help it, she started laughing. She was so beyond angry, hurt, and offended at this point. How could everyone in the family trust her to take care of Kaylee, yet have so little respect for her? What did it say about them? And how had Sara been so blind to it all these years? Sure, her feelings had been hurt before, but relatives knew how to push your buttons. This was something totally different. Gabe's sudden appearance in her life had made an impact in more ways than one. What she hadn't expected from it, though, was how much ugliness would be exposed. She'd come to work for Chris and Nicole out of love. Not only to help them but because she adored her niece. Yet it was now obvious that Kaylee was the only one who appreciated the sacrifices she'd made. Instead of gratitude, the rest of them judged her for the very thing they'd asked of her. She was naive and lacked ambition because she was their nanny. Yet she was their nanny because they'd pleaded. *I can't do this anymore. I will not be their doormat or their charity case. This is not who I am. I choose me.* She straightened away from the counter, all traces of laughter now gone. Her mother eyed her warily, as if aware she might have gone too far. *Too late.* "Thanks, Mom," she murmured. "I needed to hear that." Then she walked out of the kitchen and to her bedroom, where she closed the door and locked it behind her. Although her body was shaking in reaction, she was strangely calm and centered inside. For the first time in so long, she knew what path to take. The only thing left to do was put a plan into place. She had no clue what would happen when she arrived, but in three days she was flying to Alaska, where she intended to put the ball back in Gabe's court one last time.

Chapter Sixteen

🐾 🐾

Gabe had been home for a week, and he was about to lose his mind. After the mess with Sara, the last thing he'd needed was a month off work. So when his boss had come down with the flu and had asked him to take over the training exercises they were in the middle of, he'd all but jumped at the chance. Even in the snow, a few days in the field sounded like a Club Med vacation to him. Especially considering Sara's flight was scheduled to land tomorrow afternoon, and he damn well knew she wasn't going to be on it. She hadn't attempted to text or e-mail him for a few days now, which was more telling than anything.

He reached down and scratched his dog between the ears, then patted his side. "Good boy. Let's head back to the house." He'd taken so many damned walks that even his dog, who was normally thrilled with any outdoor time, was beginning to rebel. If Gabe continued to mope around in the forest as a form of distraction, he'd probably be doing it alone. Trouble could be bribed for only so long with treats before he refused to budge from the front porch. Apparently, man's best friend drew the line at getting frostbite. *Maybe it's me, after all. First Sara and now Trouble.* It made him look forward to going to work tomorrow even more. The soldiers might grumble about it, but they had no choice but to go where he led. *Oh shit. Why did I tell them about her?* He'd always been such a private person, yet not only Jason but several of the other guys knew about Sara. There would be questions. Women might have the reputation for it, but men could be just as nosy. And they were much tougher to dissuade. He thought about calling Jason ahead of time and filling him in to avoid the face-to-face explanation, but he wasn't up to it. The wound was still too raw where she was concerned. *I hate that I miss her. How is that even possible? We're strangers.*

"Hey, handsome, if I didn't know better, I'd think you were trying to avoid me." Trouble made a groan of distress that echoed Gabe's sentiments perfectly. Melanie Trotter was a neighbor who lived a couple of miles from him. Unfortunately, she was also yet another lapse in judgment for him. She had made no secret of the fact that she was interested in him shortly after he'd moved here two years ago. But long hours and a lot of traveling had kept her at bay— for the most part. Her parents had moved to Florida four years earlier and left her their place here. She told him early on that she'd divorced her husband because they weren't compatible. Word around town was that he'd actually left her for another woman. Gabe could see how that would be something you wouldn't want to advertise. Everyone had their pride. It hadn't seemed to put her off the idea of another relationship with a soldier, though, because she'd done everything short of proposing to him. Last year in a weak moment, he invited her to the annual military ball, thinking it might be nice not to fly solo, as he normally did. He should have left it at that. But a few too many drinks had led to subpar sex and a woman who seemed to think they were in a serious relationship. He hadn't wanted to hurt her feelings, so he let things continue on longer than he should have. They dated casually up until he got the word of his last deployment. Then he used the excuse of not wanting her to put her life on hold. She hadn't taken it real well. In fact, she'd thrown a glass at his head with impressive accuracy. Luckily, his reflexes were honed from years of training. She apologized the next day, but he brushed it aside and reiterated that it was over. He felt like an asshole, but it had to be done. He wasn't in the market for a wife, and if he were, it damned sure wouldn't be her.

"Hey, Melly, how've you been?" *Shit, she'll take the nickname as encouragement.*

Sure enough, she was beaming at his slipup. She was dressed in formfitting jeans, knee-high boots, and a thick jacket that was so tight, it drew attention to her breasts. *She came to play ball tonight.* A few seconds later, those tits were squashed against his chest as she gave him a hug that was far from neighborly. "Your garage door was open and

I saw your truck there, so I thought you might be out here. Anyway, welcome home, Gabe. I've sure missed you."

He stepped back, putting some distance between them. "Thanks, it's good to be back. Everything been going okay around here?"

She shrugged nonchalantly. "Ah, nothing ever changes. Old Man Jenkins is still nuts, and Mrs. Jenkins loves him anyway. That's about as exciting as it gets." She reached out and laid a hand on his arm. "You're some much-needed excitement, Gabe." When he didn't take the bait she was clearly dangling, she gave what he'd come to recognize as her fake smile. "How about a good, home-cooked meal? I'll fix all your favorites." *Bet I know what you're planning to serve for dessert.* He loved everything about his cabin in the mountains—except her. He didn't want to hurt her, but he felt like it would eventually come time for a less diplomatic chat. But not tonight. He didn't need any additional drama.

"Thanks, but I've got to get up early tomorrow for a training exercise. I'll be away for several days."

"Well, whenever you get back, then. I'll text you and we can set it up." Trouble flopped over on his back as if to say, *Damn, I give up.* A sentiment Gabe shared.

"We'd better get back; the sun is beginning to set." He covered the rest of the distance to his house a little faster than was polite when there was a woman along, but she kept up without complaint. Even managing to talk the entire time without sounding winded. He knew she spent a lot of time in the gym, and her trim figure attested to it. Although he admired her dedication, he'd always preferred a woman with curves. *Like Sara's.* She and Melanie were as different as night and day in almost every way. He knew she was hoping for an invitation when they reached his place, but to extend one would give her the green light, and that's the last thing he wanted to do. So he nodded politely before saying, "Roads are clear, but better take it slow going home. Have a good evening."

His manner bordered on impolite, but there wasn't much he could do about it. It wasn't all Melanie's fault, though. His mood had been in a steady downward spiral all day, as his subconscious insisted on counting the hours until Sara's flight. The one he knew without a doubt she wouldn't be on. To him, it felt like the final death knell of their unorthodox relationship. *How many endings do you need? Wasn't the one in North Carolina enough?* A part of him had hoped that she'd take the next plane and show up in Alaska within hours of his arrival. But that hadn't happened. No, instead, after a flurry of e-mails and texts, she went quiet. *Did she care so little?* Even as he tried to tell himself that she was simply abiding by what he'd said, it still bothered him. *Were you hoping for another Melanie?* He'd never liked the way his neighbor all but stalked him. Then he grew upset because Sara wasn't doing that very thing—it made no sense. *Because she's different.* No doubt every person who'd ever been a fool for love thought that same nonsense.

As he walked through the home he usually considered his refuge, tonight he felt nothing but loneliness. She'd made him want things that he'd never desired before, and even though he blamed his reintegration for the restlessness that was driving him crazy, he knew it had little to do with that. No, the thing he was having the toughest time adjusting to was not the change from Iraq to Alaska. It was the transition back to solitude after feeling as if he were part of a couple. And the perplexing question that if they hadn't been in a relationship, then why was this the hardest break he'd ever made?

Reality didn't truly catch up with Sara until she exited the plane in Anchorage, Alaska, and it dawned on her that she didn't know where to go. The last few days had been a hellish emotional roller coaster of anger, guilt, and finally excitement. She'd done it, she'd actually quit her job—or her family—and was following her heart. Chloe had been thrilled. In fact, none of this would have been possible without her encouragement. Not only had she backed Sara's decision, she'd also managed to get her mother, Ivy, on board. They'd both shown up at Chris's house to lend their moral support when Sara told her own mother what she was doing. As predicted, her mother had been speechless at first, then furious. Oddly enough, it was her aunt Ivy who soothed the troubled waters for her. In the midst of her mother's guilt-inducing tirade, Ivy had walked up to her sister and thrown an arm around her shoulder. Then she'd said, "Joan, at some point in every parent's life, we have to trust we raised our kids right and let them go. Momma and Daddy did the same thing with us." She then turned to Sara and took her hand. "Your daughter is an amazing woman, and I know you're proud of her. She's given three years not only to her brother but to you as well. I know you'll miss her, we all will. But it's time for her to spread her wings and see where they take her."

"But what will we do? Chris depends on her . . . and so do I. You know I've never handled my household stuff alone. I wouldn't know where to start."

"I'll help you get organized," Ivy said firmly. "I've always taken care of things like that, and there's nothing to it. As for Chris, he can either hire someone from an agency or maybe it would be something you'd like to do. Kaylee is in school all day now, so the hours are less. And I think it would be good for you to have a purpose again."

Her mother had been rather subdued after that. She hadn't tried to discourage Sara, nor had she offered any assistance. She had agreed to watch Chloe for a day until Chris returned. They had all jointly decided not to tell him the news while he was on vacation. Ivy had even said she'd watch Kaylee until they made other arrangements. Everything had gone much better than Sara had imagined. Except saying good-bye to her niece. That had been sheer hell, and she'd come close to calling the whole thing off. Weirdly enough, it was her talk with Chris on the day Gabe had shown up that kept her from backing out. His unhappiness over not having a stronger bond with his daughter and his resolve to do better. Yet that would get pushed to the side with Sara there. They'd settle back into their old routine, and before any of them knew it, Kaylee would be grown.

And second chances might be possible in some things, but you couldn't relive a childhood once it was gone.

Even if things didn't work out with Gabe, she had no intention of picking up where she'd left off. It was time for a new chapter—some kind of change was in everyone's best interest. *How simple it was to walk away from my life.*

Sara shook off that depressing thought as she followed the signs to baggage claim. She was determined to surprise Gabe, but she had no clue how to accomplish it. She couldn't show up at his house, because she didn't know his address. She did know the name of the military base he worked at—hopefully she could find out more there. She collected her suitcase and walked outside to hail a taxi. When they reached the base, she asked the driver to wait for her near the gate while she walked over to talk to the soldier stationed there. His expression remained impressively impassive when she said, "Um—I'm here to see Major Gabriel Randall." Before he could respond, she added quickly, "I know he's supposed to be on leave for the next month, but I . . . don't have his address, and I wanted to surprise him."

She saw it then, a glimmer of amusement that was so brief, she wondered if she'd imagined it. "Do you have an appointment with Major Randall?" he asked, seeming to already know the answer.

"No, this is personal." Lowering her voice, she added, "I came all the way from North Carolina. Major Randall bought my plane ticket, all right? I think that implies that he wants to see me."

He glanced around to where a couple of other soldiers were talking a few feet away. "Listen," he said in the same hushed tone she'd used, "even if I wanted to help you, lady, I couldn't. We're under strict orders that no one goes past these gates unless they've been cleared ahead of time. And I gather that Major Randall didn't do that if he wasn't expecting you. So you'll need to contact him and make other arrangements." When she opened her mouth for one last plea, he shook his head. "I'm sorry, but even if I let you pass, you'd be stopped and escorted out at the next checkpoint."

She thanked him, then returned glumly to the car. "Where to, miss?"

"Well, unless you know how to find someone who lives here without an address, then I have no idea," she grumbled.

"He's in the military?" he asked, waving a hand around.

"Yeah. It's a really long story, but I wanted to surprise him. And I don't have his address. He, um, just moved here recently, and this is my first visit." *I sound like a stalker.* "Er he's my boyfriend, and we had a fight a few days ago. So I didn't want to let him know I was coming. Plus, he's not likely to respond anyway—you know, due to the argument. But—"

"If you show up at his door, you figure he'll have to hear you out," he guessed, shaking his head as if to say, *Women.*

"Yep, that pretty much covers it. Only now, I don't see that happening. I hadn't counted on this area being so big and the military being so . . . uncooperative." *God, he must think I'm an idiot.*

"They can't just let anyone in, right? But I do have

a suggestion. My aunt runs a restaurant in town called Maxi's. Lot of the soldiers hang out there. If anyone'll know your guy, it will be her. And if she doesn't, she could ask around for you."

"Really?" Sara said excitedly. "That would be amazing. Could you take me there? Heck, I'll even buy you lunch."

He nodded, giving her a big smile in the rearview mirror. "You got yourself a deal. My name's Hank. How about you?"

"It's Sara. You have no idea how much I appreciate this, Hank. I was about ready to go back to the airport and fly home."

"No promises," he warned. "But my aunt never forgets a face, or a story connected with it. If your man has been in there or is known to anyone around these parts, then she'll remember it. Plus, she's buddies with every local business owner, and I know if I ask, she'll check around for you."

"Thank you, Hank. Truly, I'm very grateful that you're doing this for a stranger."

"Hey, we all need a helping hand sometimes. And you seem like a nice person. I hope everything works out for you."

As it turned out, she owed Hank a huge debt of gratitude. Maxi didn't know Gabe personally, but as Hank had promised, she had a vast network of connections. One of which turned out to be Gabe's neighbor. Hank stuck around, appearing just as anxious as she was to know what would come next.

"So what are you gonna do now, kiddo?" Maxi asked from behind the bar that Sara had been sitting at for the last hour. "Hank can take you to his place if you're sure he's home, or you could call and ask him to swing by and pick you up." She scratched her head thoughtfully before adding, "But that would ruin the surprise." Then she snapped her fingers so loudly that Sara jumped. "I got it, give me his number and I'll tell him he needs to head this way."

"What will you say when he asks why?" she asked, thinking surely Maxi's request would seem a little unusual to Gabe.

"I can talk my way around anyone. Boy won't even realize 'til later that he doesn't know any more than he did to begin with."

Hank nodded in agreement, obviously having firsthand experience with it.

Sara wrote down Gabe's number and handed it to the other woman before turning to the man who had been so much help to her.

"How much do I owe you, Hank?"

She was surprised when he waved her off. "No charge, my friend. This is the most fun I've had in a long time. I should be paying you."

"No way." She frowned as she began peeling off bills. "I don't want you to get into trouble with your employer. I've tied you up for hours now."

He turned sideways in his chair, giving her a kindly smile. "I work for myself, so it's not an issue. Really—I want to do this, all right?"

Sara was so touched by his kindness that mere words didn't seem adequate. As if sensing her struggle, Hank got to his feet, probably wanting to avoid a sappy moment. But she stood as well and gave him a shy hug. "Thank you so much, for everything. You have no idea how much I appreciate it. I couldn't have gotten this far without you."

His face reddened. "You're welcome, Sara. Call me if you need a ride . . . or anything else. I'm happy to help," he added as he handed her his business card. "I hope everything works out. I'm sure my aunt will update me later," he said, and laughed. They chatted for a few more minutes, and then he was gone, and she felt rather forlorn without her new friend.

"All right, I'm going to call your fella. Keep quiet so he doesn't hear your voice," Maxi instructed as she pulled a phone from under the bar and pressed some buttons. "Hey, Gabe, this is Maxi from Maxi's Diner. Listen, I've got something of yours here. So you need to swing by and pick it up. And don't be putting this off 'til tomorrow, it can't wait. We're open until ten tonight."

When Maxi put the phone down, Sara asked the question she feared the most. "What if he doesn't come?"

Maxi shrugged, not appearing concerned in the least. "Then I'll take you to his place on my way home. But I'm betting he'll be here. Just a feeling I have. Now, why don't you go freshen up in the restroom, and when you come back, I'll get you some dinner. It might be a while before he makes it here, so you can take a nap on the sofa in my office after you eat. Poor thing, you must be tired by now."

"That sounds amazing," she said. She felt oddly at peace as she walked to the back of the diner. This whole thing might blow up in her face, but she'd done it. She was taking charge of her life and doing things on her own terms.

Whether things worked out with Gabe or not, she knew she'd be okay. She was no longer a secondary character in someone else's life; she was the star of her own. She'd taken the risk, and she desperately hoped that Gabe was going to be the reward.

Chapter Seventeen

🐾 🐾

Gabe was exhausted when he walked to his truck. He'd been at the base since five that morning, and it was nearly nine at night now. They decided not to spend the night in the field due to the fresh snowfall and some computer problems, so he was headed home. He started his truck, hoping it warmed up quickly, as he was chilled to the bone. He pulled his phone from the glove box, since they weren't allowed to have them during training sessions. The screen showed he had a voicemail from a number he didn't recognize. He considered leaving it until later, but it could be one of his soldiers. So he clicked the button to listen. Then he replayed it twice more. What could he possibly need to pick up at Maxi's Diner? He'd have thought it was a wrong number if she hadn't said his name. "Shit," he mumbled as he turned his truck toward town instead of his place.

He wasn't sure what he was expecting when he walked into the restaurant, but other than a few lingering patrons, it was almost empty. He stepped up to the counter just as a tall woman with short gray hair came out of the back. He thought he remembered her as the owner, but he wasn't positive. She tilted her head to the side before saying, "Gabe, I presume?" Even though it was more of a statement than a question, he nodded. "You cut it kind of close. Were you at work?"

"Yes, ma'am. I got your message and came straight here. Would you mind telling me what this is about? *Why do I feel as if I'm on some kind of job interview?* It wasn't so much what she said but the way she appeared to be assessing him. He'd been in here only a few times with Jason, but he knew it was popular with the soldiers at the base. He wondered if one of them was playing a prank on him. *So not the time for it.*

She hesitated briefly, "How about I show you instead?" *Damn, this is getting weirder by the moment.*

His first inclination was to decline her strange offer, but he wanted to get the hell out of there. "Um—sure."

She pointed to the rear of the building. "What I called you about is at the back table. Be quiet, though, you don't want to disturb—it." He could only stare at her retreating back in amazement. He almost left at that point. He was too damned tired for this bizarre intrigue.

But once again he ignored the voice in his head that urged him to run. Instead, he moved in the direction she'd indicated and was surprised to see someone either sleeping or passed out in the last booth. When one of his boots made a loud squeaking noise on the floor, not only was he startled, but the person a few inches away sat bolt upright. *It can't be.* She was blinking at him as if just as shocked. "Gabe?" she finally croaked out.

"Sara? How—when did you get here?" *She came. She took the flight.* He still couldn't quite believe what he was seeing. He never seriously considered that she'd actually do it.

"Er—around five, I think. I was sleepy, so I must have drifted off after I had dinner. I—I'm not sure how long I've been waiting." The indentations in her face said she'd been out for some time.

"Shit, that was hours ago. Why didn't you call me yourself? I almost didn't come tonight since the message was so . . . odd."

"I . . . was afraid you wouldn't show up if you knew it was me. We didn't exactly part on the best of terms." She let out a huge yawn. "I'm not sure I'm making sense. I've been up forever. Well, other than the nap I took."

It suddenly hit him that it was eerily quiet. When he glanced around, he saw Maxi, along with another couple of employees, standing next to her. And being caught eavesdropping didn't seem to bother them at all. Heck, Maxi had the audacity to give him a jaunty wave. He was momentarily nonplussed. Stuff like this didn't happen to him. What was the protocol? Take her to a hotel or to his place? He didn't feel right about leaving her in a strange town where she knew no one. But he also hadn't thought about how awkward it would be to have her stay with him. Wasn't she his responsibility, though—at least for now? This could wait until they both had some rest and could talk without an audience. "Are these all your things?" he asked, pointing to the bag and suitcase near her.

When she said they were, he bent down to pick them up and then put an arm on her elbow to steady her when she stumbled to her feet. "Thanks, Gabe." The shy smile she gave him was so damned sweet and trusting that he had to look away. *She came. I don't know what to do.* "I'm going to say good-bye before we leave," she said softly. Instead of joining her, he waited at the door. She hugged Maxi and said something before approaching him. "Okay, I'm ready when you are, Gabe." He always liked hearing her say his name, but tonight he found it rather disconcerting. It implied an intimacy between them, making it difficult to remain aloof. *Would you rather she call you Mr. Randall?*

"It'll take about half an hour to get to my house," he said as he led her to his truck. He opened the passenger door and put her things behind the seat. She stepped forward and placed one of her boot-covered feet on the side rail, but still struggled to pull herself up. He sighed and put his hands on her waist, trying not to look at her jean-clad ass only inches away. She squeaked in surprise, but didn't protest when he lifted her up and onto the seat. He returned to his side quickly and noted that she had her seat belt in place and was staring straight ahead.

They'd been traveling a few moments when she broke the silence. "I know I blindsided you by showing up, but after what happened, it seemed like the best idea."

He smiled ruefully, but kept his eyes on the road. He knew from experience that even though it appeared to be clear, there could still be black ice on the surface. "I can see why you'd want to do that. After all, it worked out so well for me."

His hands tightened on the wheel when she laughed. He'd heard her do the same thing dozens of times on Face-Time, but it was different now. He felt like he was dealing with a sensory overload. He'd caught a hint of her perfume when he was picking her up and he'd come close to dropping her. Thankfully, she didn't seem to notice the close call. There was no escaping it now, though. Her scent was all around him. Considering it was twenty degrees outside, he couldn't very well roll his window down. And there was also her voice to contend with. Was it bad manners to ask her to remain completely silent until further notice? "When I didn't have a clue as to how to find you once I got here, I thought it could be a sign that I should go back home."

It wasn't his fault, but he still felt guilty for not meeting her at the airport. "If I'd had any inkling that you were coming, I'd have been there to meet you."

"It was quite an experience," she admitted. "You might get some funny looks when you go back to work. The guard was nice, but there was no way he was letting me in that gate."

And the surprises just keep coming. "You went to the base?"

"Not the brightest decision," she acknowledged. "Naturally they weren't going to take my word for anything."

He shook his head. He was surprised word hadn't gotten back to him yet. He knew what the security forces who guarded the entrance would be thinking. "It was nothing against you, but we've had women show up looking for some of the guys—for various reasons. So even if there weren't strict regulations in place, you still wouldn't have been allowed in unless I made arrangements ahead of time. And they know to never give information out."

"Yeah, my cab driver pointed that out. In case you're wondering, Maxi is his aunt. That's how I ended up there. He said that either she'd know you or one of her friends would. When you didn't answer your phone, though, she thought you might be at work. So she came up with the idea of leaving you the message and having you come there. I'm sorry for that. You probably didn't know what to think. If I hadn't been so tired and overwhelmed, I'd have gone about it differently."

He felt himself relaxing, as if her voice had lulled him into a kind of trance. He was drawn to her, as he'd always been. He knew it wasn't rational, but his reaction to her—or weakness where she was concerned—pissed him off. He couldn't afford to lower his guard. He gave her credit for keeping her word to come, but that didn't change her dishonesty. She hurt him more than he was willing to admit. And with her there in the flesh, the fallout would be much worse should he discover she was playing games. *I won't be a fool again.* She yawned, and he took the opportunity it presented for a quiet ride back to his house. "Why don't you lay your head back and rest. I'll wake you when we get there." He wondered if he sounded as stressed as he was beginning to feel.

Maybe she picked up on it. Because she shifted, as if getting comfortable. "I think I'll do that. Being this tired and seeing all the snow around us has me feeling disoriented. Plus, it's always made me nervous to travel in snowy conditions." After growing up near Boston, and dealing with this type of weather in a few places he'd been stationed, he didn't give it much thought. But he knew that the states with heavy snow in winter had the equipment on hand to deal with it quickly. The South didn't see a significant enough amount to invest in a lot of expensive snow plows.

"That'll happen until you adjust to it," he replied. He wished he'd kept that comment to himself, as it sounded for all the world like he expected her to stay. But when he heard a soft snore, he figured she'd likely missed it. Now that he'd gotten what he wanted, he found that he missed hearing her talk. After all, they'd spent hours on their computers together daily for seven months. To say it had been tough without her would be an understatement. A part of him was downright giddy to have her here, but the rational side was freaking out. How was he going to survive her physical presence when he hadn't been able to resist her via e-mail? When he paused at a yield sign, he chanced a look at her. A nearby streetlight illuminated the interior of the truck, allowing him to make out her features. She was so beautiful. The fact that her mouth was hanging open slightly only made her more so. As he turned back to the road, the only thought that kept running through his head on an endless loop was *I'm so screwed*. Because how could he possibly guard his heart from someone who already owned it?

Sara woke again with a start. *This is beginning to be a bad habit.* Gabe stood a few feet away, obviously having disturbed her slumber when he opened the truck door. *Gabe? I'm dreaming.* She reached out and touched his arm. *Feels so real.* Then she squeezed it. *Weird, it's never been like this before.* She was debating exploring further when he said, "Um . . . your fingernails are kind of sharp."

Then it all came back to her. "Wait—you're here. You're real. And . . . I'm me." Okay, that last part made no sense, but she was disoriented from the nap, and she couldn't seem to stop the flow of words that were tumbling out.

"Technically *you're* here. And I'm Gabe." She thought she detected a hint of amusement in his voice when he added, "We all clear now?"

"Is this where you live?" she asked, noticing they appeared to be in a garage. *Or a basement. He is kind of a stranger.* She discounted that notion immediately. She might not be the best judge of character, but she'd stake her life on him being a good man. *That's exactly what you've done.*

He helped her out, and she shivered as the cold air hit her. "We need to go around front. Trouble is kenneled in the kitchen, and if we walk through that way, he'll lose his shit. He's not used to a lot of company, so he'll be excited. Better to bring him to you."

She buttoned her coat and dug the hat she brought with her out of her handbag. "All ready."

He put his hand in the small of her back and led her slowly down the drive and to a connecting pathway. "Be careful. I have someone who keeps the main areas clear, but they're probably still slick in spots." The floodlight at the corner of his house was on, giving her a view of the exterior. It was a log cabin with large picture windows and a porch running the entire length. She couldn't tell much about the yard since it was blanketed in white stuff, but she didn't see any lights indicating nearby neighbors. They climbed two steps and he moved forward to deal with the lock. The door swung open and he waved a hand for her to go inside. There was a light on in the entryway—and that's as far as she got before she jumped backward in fright. She heard Gabe's shout a split second before something knocked her off balance and she went crashing into what she suspected were the shrubs. "Trouble! Shit, Sara." He sounded alarmed, and she would have put his mind at ease, if not for the tongue licking her face. If she opened her mouth—yeah, that wasn't happening. Suddenly, the dog was gone and he was there. "Are you all right?" Her coat kept the branches from doing anything other than scratching her hands and the back of her neck. No, the only serious injury seemed to be the one to her pride. She could only imagine how she must look right now. If his face was any indication, it was pretty damn bad.

"I—I'm okay," she mumbled as she struggled to sit up without embarrassing herself further.

"Hang on," he instructed as he put his arms under her

body and lifted her against his chest. "I'm so sorry. That must have scared the hell out of you. I should have checked before letting you go in. Sometimes Trouble manages to escape the kitchen. It doesn't happen often, but every once in a while, he gets lucky—and lives up to his name," he chided as he gently moved back toward the doorway with her. The dog in question was sitting a few inches inside looking sheepish. He whined as if to say, *Whoops, my bad.*

"S'okay." She shivered as the moisture began to seep through her clothing. She'd gone from cold to freezing in the blink of an eye.

"We need to get you warmed up." She had no idea where he was taking her, but she was on board if it would stop her teeth from chattering. *What must he be thinking?* He reached out to flip on a light, then lowered her to her feet. He kept a grip on her waist, though, for support. "Why don't you take a hot shower while I fix you something to drink? You should find everything you need in the cabinet over there." When she nodded, he added, "Call out if you need me."

When he was gone, Sara closed the door and leaned back against it. What a disaster this had been so far. Seeing Gabe again was amazing—and being with him felt oddly right. Yet she had sensed him shutting down during the drive home. She'd been enjoying their conversation, and thought he had been as well, until he abruptly suggested she get some rest. There was something in his tone that alerted her to the fact that he needed space. She had been tired and had fallen asleep again easily, but she would have preferred to have continued talking to him. The bond was still there but was in need of repair, and she wasn't sure how to go about it unless he was willing to help her. *What did you expect? Give him time to adjust.* But how long could this go on before he expected her to go home? They'd never really discussed the length of her stay. The return date on the ticket was open ended, but he hadn't asked her to move in with him. She nearly jumped out of her skin when a knock sounded. "Everything all right?"

She placed a hand over her heart, trying to catch her breath. She'd taken years off her life today with all the shocks to her system. "Um—yeah. I'm good. Just . . . using the toilet." She slapped a hand over her mouth. She'd blurted out the first thing that came to mind. And considering the water wasn't running in the shower, that didn't leave many options. *Oh my God, he thinks I'm pooping.*

It may have been her imagination, but she could have sworn there was laughter in his voice when he said, "Oh . . . just checking on you. I'm leaving your suitcase outside the door so you can put on some dry clothes. Well . . . I'm going back to the kitchen now."

She dropped her head back in embarrassment. He'd actually been stumbling over his words at the end. She might as well have told him she had her period. It would probably have the same effect. *I need to keep my mouth shut and go to bed.* She tended to say the wrong things when she was nervous, and the jet lag was making it even worse. She was practically a loaded gun at this point. *Get in the shower before he comes back.* Peeling off the soggy denim turned out to be the biggest challenge. She hadn't realized how cold she was until the warm water hit her body. She put her head back and let the stress of the day wash away. She would no doubt revisit everything that had happened in the last twelve hours later, but for now, she would focus on nothing more than embracing the new beginning she had undertaken.

Chapter Eighteen

🐾 🐾

Gabe was still smiling when he walked back into the kitchen and pulled a saucepan out of one of the cabinets. He was fairly certain she hadn't intended to blurt out that she was on the toilet. He could sense her mortification. He thought it was more likely she'd been using the time and space to collect herself just as he was. He knew she must be overwhelmed after the day she'd had, as who wouldn't be unsettled by it. He'd certainly been rattled in North Carolina from his visit. Although that had possibly been a bigger train wreck. They had both taken a chance by dropping in unannounced, and neither had been a smooth experience.

As wary as he was, he couldn't help being impressed by her courage. It had been daunting for him, and he was used to being in places and situations that were damned uncomfortable and dangerous. But from what he'd learned, she lived a fairly sheltered existence. He also knew that she was shy and appeared to have a tough time with confidence. He'd been surprised when she agreed to the trip in the first place, but for her to come here after all that had happened, especially not knowing what kind of welcome she'd receive—it had taken guts. *Or it was part of some master plan.* One of the worst things to come from this whole mess was how badly his trust had been shaken. Even though they'd never met, he had grown to believe in her and everything she represented to him. She was goodness, light, laughter, and a soft place to land. *Why did she have to ruin that?* Rationally, he understood her individual reasons, but it didn't change the fact it had dealt a serious blow to the connection they'd established during his deployment. He couldn't deny he enjoyed what she brought into his life, but the last few weeks had been the type of drama that he didn't need. Only now that she was here—in his house—he wasn't sure how to evade it. He also had no clue what her plans were. He hadn't put a return date on her ticket when he bought it, because he knew that flexibility made travel easier. That was coming back to bite him in the ass now. The only thing he had to go on was the fact that she hadn't brought a lot with her. So she either packed lightly, or this was to be a short stay. For his peace of mind, he had to hope it was the latter option.

Trouble's head jerked up from where he was sitting at Gabe's feet a split second before she came into view. He wasn't sure what he was expecting, but she managed to surprise him again. The outfit she was wearing was one he'd seen when they talked near her bedtime. Even though the

SpongeBob lounge pants and matching top were far from formfitting, they still managed to be sexy on her. As were the fuzzy blue socks that Trouble was currently inspecting in fascination. She gave Gabe a questioning look, and he nodded to let her know it was safe to pet his dog. She extended a hand, letting him sniff it. As usual, he took it one step further and licked it. She didn't appear to mind, though, because she giggled as she squatted down to his level. "Hey, Trouble, aren't you a beauty." Trouble cocked his head to the side, as if spellbound by their visitor. *You and me both, buddy.* She trailed her fingertips lightly over the bridge of his nose. Even though his dog had never been anything but friendly to everyone he met, Gabe still kept an eye on them as he poured the milk he'd heated into a cup for her. Trouble didn't seem alarmed by her touch in the least, quite the opposite. He rolled onto his back, presenting his belly for scratching. "Well, aren't you a sweetheart," she cooed. *Great, I'm jealous of my dog.* Trouble had largely ignored Melanie, as if sensing that the small amount of attention she gave him was all for Gabe's benefit. But with Sara, he was rolling around on the floor with a blissful expression on his furry face. *At least it's not just me*, Gabe thought wryly. The Randall boys seemingly had a thing for Southern women who smelled good. Okay, there was more to it than that, but damn, having her this close, with that scent filling the air, was doing a number on his head—the big one and the little one. Both were riveted by the beauty who invaded their space. But what was the proper protocol to follow here? Gabe knew how to run military operations with precision. Years of training had given him confidence in his job. He was damn good at it. But matters of the heart? Why did he feel so out of his depth? Without a clue how to navigate this . . . *whatever this is*.

Gabe forced himself not to stare at the outlines of her nipples, which the baggy top didn't quite conceal. *Down, boy*. Sadly, that warning wasn't for his dog. Clearing his throat, he said, "I figured it was too late for coffee, so it's milk with some cinnamon in it. The spice makes it taste a little better than plain. My mom always made it for us when we were sick."

She smiled up at him as if he were her hero. "That sounds amazing." She gave Trouble one last pat before getting to her feet and moving over to the sink. After cleaning her hands, she took the cup from him. He watched her take a drink and wasn't sure if the color that flooded her cheeks was from his attention or the warm liquid. "Mmm, wow, it tastes like a latte. This is really good." Then she sent his blood pressure up several notches by licking her lips. *I'm dying here. Help, someone . . . anyone.* Dammit, he was thirty-seven. Far too old to experience this type of hormonal overload. At this point, if she bent over, he'd likely come in his pants. That alarming thought gave him a much-needed reality check. He wasn't fool enough to continue testing his shaky resolve tonight, though. They needed to go to bed—alone. He'd feel better after some sleep. He'd be back in control tomorrow. And he was on field duty. *Thank God*. He was absurdly grateful at the thought of rolling out of bed in five hours.

He chanced a quick look in her direction and noticed that she looked wiped out as well. Trouble was sitting at her feet, gazing at her in utter adoration, while one of her hands rubbed his ear. "Hey, I don't think I mentioned it, but I have to work this week. I'm supposed to be on leave, but I'm filling in for my boss. We're doing some training, and one of us needs to be there."

Was it his imagination or did she appear relieved? Could it be that she needed some space as well? Made sense. She had to be as overwhelmed as he was. "That's okay, Gabe, I understand. I don't expect you to drop everything to entertain me. I realize that you have obligations and I'm perfectly capable of taking care of myself."

"Oh, I don't think you'll be completely on your own," he smirked as he indicated the sappy expression on his dog's face. "Pretty sure he'll be following you around like a love-sick puppy." *At this rate, both of us will be.*

"He's so sweet. I haven't had a dog since I was a kid, but that may need to change."

Giving Trouble a pretend scowl, he said, "You might not have a choice. He'll likely run after your plane when you leave." Sara rinsed her cup, and he told her to leave it on the counter. "I don't know about you, but I'm ready to crash. I'm sure I'll be gone by the time you wake up. I have to be at the base before five. Just make yourself at home. I can't take my phone into the field, but if you have any problems, leave me a message and I'll check them as soon as I can. If there is any type of emergency, my contact information will be on the table. The switchboard will know how to reach me. Please don't use it unless it's really an—"

"I get it," she interrupted. "I'm not one of those people who calls someone at work just for kicks. Trust me, if I do it, you'll know it's something dire." He didn't think she'd appreciate him sharing the fact that Melanie had done it twice. Once to ask what he wanted for dinner, and another time to tell him she was going out with friends. Neither of which he needed to be pulled out of a meeting to hear. A fact that he made clear after the second instance.

"Good deal. Let me show you to the guest room. The bathroom you used is right across the hall so feel free to make it your own. I have an en suite, so I rarely ever use that one."

"That must be why it's so immaculate." She laughed, then seemed to think better of it. "Um, not to say that the rest of what I've seen of your home is untidy. It's actually really clean. But the bathroom didn't look as if anyone ever used it. Which, hello, it's kind of one of those places you can't avoid—" She stopped so abruptly, he wondered if something was wrong. Then he noticed the color in her cheeks a split second before she murmured sheepishly, "Sorry, you know how I am. I tend to overexplain when I'm nervous—or sleepy. And I'm probably a bit of both, so you're really getting hit with it."

You know how I am. Her casual remark implied that he wasn't the only one feeling the intimacy between them. He wondered if she was struggling with it as much as he was.

He thought maybe she was. *But what do we do if none of this is real?* He needed to get away from her for a while until he had time to process and deal with it. He knew his sudden movement was abrupt when Sara and Trouble both jumped slightly. He almost apologized, but didn't want to make a big deal out of the already stressful situation. Instead, he glanced back and asked, "Ready?" He saw her nod and fall into step behind him, with Trouble bringing up the rear. She'd left her suitcase outside the bathroom door, so he picked it up and moved it to the room she would be using. He flipped on the light and nearly stopped breathing when she brushed against him as she entered her temporary digs. "The remote for the television is on the bedside table. And there are some extra pillows and blankets in the top of the closet." She ran her hand over the quilt on the bed admiringly, and he shrugged. "My family came for a visit right after I moved here, and my mom bought that. Anyway, I'm a couple of doors down, so let me know if you need anything." He stood there for another moment as they stared at each other. If not for what happened in North Carolina, he would have at least hugged her, but now, he wasn't in the same frame of mind. He was probably overthinking things, but he was too unsure of where he stood with her to jump right back in. "Sleep well," he said instead, and walked away. Trouble would have normally been right on his heels, but he stayed behind. Gabe might be hesitant, but his dog had no such qualms. It was survival pure and simple. If one of them had to be brokenhearted when she left, he was determined that it wouldn't be him again. *Sorry, pal.*

Chapter Nineteen

🐾 🐾

The glare of sunlight reflecting off the snow woke Sara from a sound sleep. She stretched under her warm cocoon, then squealed when something licked her face. She'd assume she imagined it if not for the moisture she felt when she wiped her cheek. She turned a few inches to see Trouble's brown eyes staring at her from a few inches away. She wasn't sure how she'd missed him when she opened her eyes the first time. "Well, good morning to you as well," she mumbled.

He'd obviously had enough of her neglect, because he moved closer and rubbed his head against her shoulder in a blatant bid for attention. "Have you been here all night?" She could have sworn he nodded, but he was likely responding to her scratching him behind the ear. "You're such a good doggy. Kaylee would love you. I'll take a picture today and send it to her." As soon as the words left her mouth, she felt a pang of sadness. *That's probably a terrible idea. They're all pissed at me.*

Chris and Nicole should have returned home from vacation by now. She was surprised she hadn't received an angry phone call yet. Or had she? She'd plugged her phone in to charge before passing out the night before, and now she reached out her hand to retrieve it. A quick glance at the screen showed a couple of messages from Chloe, but that was all. *Nothing from Gabe.* How foolish. Had she expected him to leave her a wake-up text as he had every morning in Iraq? Oddly enough, that was probably one of the things she missed the most after his visit. She'd come to expect those, and it had been beyond painful when they stopped. A large part of her hoped that by coming here, things would instantly go back to normal between them. But it was apparent that just because she was here, it didn't mean he was ready to forgive and forget. After all, Chloe had cautioned her about that very thing.

She knew her cousin was at work, so she sent her a quick message letting her know she'd arrived safely and that everything was okay, although a bit tense between them. Then she pushed the cover aside for a trip to the bathroom. After that, she made her way to the kitchen. She wanted to explore his house, but coffee was the first order of business. True to his word, there was a piece of paper on the table with a number written on it. That was it. He hadn't wished her a good day. Again, those omissions were very telling about how he felt about her now. He was still the same man, but they were basically back to the beginning. He was reserved and standoffish, and she was nervous and wary. Not the best combination, given the fact she was staying with him. *Should I leave?* Instinctively she knew that was the absolute worst thing she could do. Regardless of how uncomfortable it might be, if she bolted, it was over. She at least had a chance here. And if she wasn't willing to endure some awkwardness, then what did that say about her feelings for him?

Gabe had left the coffeepot on, and she opened a couple of cabinets before finding the cups. A search yielded some half-and-half in the refrigerator and the sugar in a canister inside a cabinet. She moved to the window as she took the first sip. It looked like a winter wonderland outside. She could still see the driveway so she didn't think any new snow had fallen. If they had this much of it at home, the state would have to shut down. But from what she could see yesterday, it didn't really slow people here down. They couldn't very well close all the schools and businesses for six months of the year, so it made sense that they would be diligent about keeping the roads clear.

Trouble was leaning against her side, patiently awaiting her next move. "How about we go explore, boy? I promise not to look through your master's dresser drawers if you don't rat me out." She had to laugh at the expression on his furry face. It was uncanny how much his reactions went along with the things she said to him. Finding him at that rest area had been a stroke of luck for Gabe.

They started the tour in the living room. The windows

made up one wall, with a rock fireplace in the middle and a staircase going up to what appeared to be a loft area. The walls looked to be made of pine that had been stained a light color. The house wasn't huge, but the tall ceilings gave it an open and airy feel. Next, she retraced her earlier steps, only this time she walked past the guest room and glanced in the next room. A desk sat against the wall, with a laptop in the center of it. There were some pictures on the wall and she moved over to study them. They were all awards and commendations that Gabe had received in the military. *God, he looks hot in that uniform.* If the sheer number of certificates were any indication, he was very successful at what he did. He was a runner, so the treadmill in front of the window wasn't unexpected.

When they reached what was obviously his bedroom, she paused at the threshold, feeling very much like she was trespassing even though he hadn't closed the door. But since Trouble walked in ahead of her, she took that as a sign that she could follow. *Hey, Gabe, your dog made me do it.* She couldn't help laughing to herself as she imagined using that excuse should she be discovered snooping. Somehow, she didn't think Gabe would buy it.

He was a tall guy, but she was still surprised to see what appeared to be a king-size bed dominating the space. As with the rest of the house, his personal domain was neat and clean. No dirty clothing lying around anywhere. His bathroom contained a shower and a Jacuzzi tub. There were also double sinks, with his toiletries arranged near the first one. She inspected the contents as if it would tell her something she didn't know about him. He appeared to like Axe products because the deodorant and the shaving gel were both that brand. He kept his hair buzzed so short, she doubted he really needed the comb sitting to the side. She picked up a bottle of cologne and held it up to her nose so she could savor the intoxicating scent she recognized from the card he'd sent her. She hadn't given much thought to men's fragrances before Gabe, but now she'd always be a fan of Fahrenheit by Christian Dior. As far as she was concerned, it fit him perfectly. Subtle, sexy, and oh so manly. If she thought it had been arousing from afar, it was nothing compared to getting a whiff of it on the man himself. She might love the scent, but it was the combination of it on his skin that she found heady. She felt certain it wouldn't be the same with anyone else.

Trouble, having obviously lost his patience, licked her hand. That seemed to be his unspoken way of saying, *Can we move along, please?* She put everything back exactly as it had been and retraced her steps. She unpacked her suitcase and kept out an outfit for the day before putting away the rest. She hated for it to appear as if she were moving in, but she also didn't want what little she'd brought along with her to wind up a wrinkled mess. At some point, she would need to make use of the laundry room she'd seen off the kitchen.

One thing that was very different and somewhat unexpected was the silence. Apart from the sound of Trouble's feet tapping along behind her in every room, the house was utterly quiet. Chris and Nicole's house was large, but not as secluded as Gabe's cabin. And not hearing Kaylee's incessant chatter was . . . *heartbreaking*. She already missed her beautiful niece, but it was the silence that was almost deafening.

After a shower, Sara dressed in jeans and a sweater, then found her boots sitting neatly in the mudroom. She also spotted a leash, and her new canine friend barked in approval when she reached for it. "I take it you're up for a walk, huh?" He took the lead line in his mouth, apparently indicating his agreement, and she fell head over heels in love with him in that moment. He'd stolen her heart in a more direct way than his owner, but the end result was the same. She was smitten with another Randall, and this one wasn't shy about his feelings. Although they took the form of slobber more often than not. She hoped Gabe was a little less exuberant with his affection. *Please, you'd take him any way you could get him.* She couldn't argue with that. She'd gladly pat his head as well if he wanted to hump her leg. She couldn't help it; she giggled at that silly thought. She had to hope this was one time the intelligent dog at her feet couldn't read her thoughts. Because if he could, he was going to have some interesting things to tell his master tonight. But until then, they were going to go outside so she could get her first real look at the landscape—hopefully a glimpse that didn't end with her lying on a shrub, flailing around like a fish out of water.

As she stepped carefully off the porch with Trouble at her

side, Sara couldn't help stopping and staring. *Wow.* Somehow, she'd never imagined how beautiful Alaska was. It was like being transported to a white fairytale world. The snow looked like diamonds trickling through the air as the wind shook it from a nearby tree. *Magical.* If asked for a one-word description, that's what she'd say.

She was no stranger to snow, although nothing like the level of what they had here. Yet she had mostly viewed it as a nuisance. Something that made travel hazardous, thereby making her life harder. But the hustle and bustle of Charlotte was nowhere to be found in this serene setting. The dazzling landscape could almost make you lose sight of the cold temperature.

Trouble began digging in the snow and soon came up with a stick, which he promptly dropped at her feet. Gabe had mentioned that she could let the dog off the leash as long as they were in the backyard, so she did just that before bending to pick up the stick. "Not exactly subtle, are you?" She laughed as she tossed it a few feet away and watched him bound after it. They played until her teeth were chattering and she knew it was time to go back inside. "We'll do it again tomorrow," she promised her new furry friend as she scratched his ears and put him back on the leash. Neither of them wanted to leave the beauty of the outdoors, probably for different reasons. To Sara, it was the first time she'd felt at peace since Gabe's surprise visit to North Carolina. Maybe it was simply wishful thinking, but something about this place felt right to her. Almost as if she'd come home after a long journey. *I've been reading too many ro-*

mance novels. That warm feeling lasted for another two minutes until she had a reality check she had not been expecting.

Gabe wasn't sure what he was expecting to see when he walked in the door that evening, but Sara and Melanie sitting in the living room had never entered his mind. He'd texted her before he left work and offered to bring home something for dinner. But she declined, saying she'd eaten a late lunch and wasn't hungry. He'd managed to block her out of his mind for the most part while he worked. Jason had given him a few odd looks, but hadn't questioned him. They'd known each other long enough to understand when they could push the issue and when they should back off. His sister was another situation altogether. Jennifer had had thirty years of experience on how to read Gabe. He'd called her after he left North Carolina, needing to keep his head out of all things Sara. Jennifer had, of course, pried more information out of Gabe than he'd hoped. She knew how disappointed he was, but she also suggested that there were always two sides to every story, and that Gabe was quick to draw conclusions—something that made him an excellent soldier but which sometimes caused him to be unyielding and implacable. *That had saved lives. Even my own once.*

His apprehension had begun to return on the drive home, and seeing Melanie here was about the last thing he wanted. Hell, on a good day, it was at the bottom of his list. Trouble, he noticed, had once again aligned himself with Sara and had his head in her lap, while she stroked his fur absently. The only indication he gave that he was glad to see Gabe was the thumping of his tail. Sara, though, dazzled him with a warm, welcoming smile. One that had his insides firing in all directions. Until his eyes landed on Melanie. Then it was more of a crash-and-burn feeling.

"Gabe, I met your . . . friend today when I was out taking a walk. Imagine my surprise. I've never known you to have a visitor, other than family."

He refused to explain himself to her. He had no idea what Sara had told her, but obviously she'd gone the safe route if Melanie was fishing for information. Once again, he knew he was being rude, but he didn't feel like dealing with her. *Take a fucking hint.* "Did you need something, Melanie?" He knew she caught his deliberate omission of her nickname. He didn't miss the tightening of her lips, before they curved into one of her fake grins.

"Oh, I just popped inside to wash my hands after petting the—Trouble. And you know how us girls lose track of time when we're chatting."

"I didn't notice your car out front. Did you walk all this way?" *Shit, I'm not taking her home.* He was grateful when she waved a hand before saying, "Oh, I left it at Mr. Jenkins's place. I got some of his mail by accident, so I had to drop it off. Figured I'd get in some extra steps while I was out."

He was still screwed because it was dark outside, and regardless of how he felt about her, he would never let a woman roam around alone at night. Especially when she was at his house. "I need to take Trouble out, so if you'll get your things, we'll make sure you get there safely." He saw it, the gleam of satisfaction she didn't conceal quite fast enough.

She stood and turned to Sara. "It was lovely to meet you. It's great having another woman around my age up here. Let's get together for lunch one day. If the weather cooperates, we could even drive into town. I don't know about you, but I could use a dose of civilization."

Sara shrugged her shoulders. "I really enjoy being away from the hustle and bustle of the city. It's so peaceful and relaxing here."

Melanie smirked. "Let's see if you say the same thing after a long winter. Oh wait, you won't be here that long, will you?" It was all said in a friendly tone, but she didn't fool him. Unless he missed his guess, Melanie was anything but thrilled to have Sara here. She was the type who liked men—period. Women, not so much, as she inevitably viewed them as competition. She didn't discriminate by age either, as far as he could tell. He had discovered from spending time with her that she was basically an insecure person who needed her ego fed on a regular basis. He figured it was a by-product of her husband's infidelity, although she'd never admitted that.

Sara didn't comment, but he thought he saw her jaw clench. There was no way she could have missed the underlying meaning in the other woman's comments. Heck, even Trouble had probably picked up on it. If he'd paid attention to his dog's disdain for Melanie when they'd first met, he'd have saved himself a lot of aggravation.

Trouble jumped up when he opened the front door. Gabe usually didn't bother putting him on a leash when they were staying close to home. He'd never had an issue with him running off. Melanie said good-bye to Sara before sauntering ahead of him. The whole sexy stride was wasted on him, since he wasn't vaguely tempted to check out her ass. *Now Sara's was a different story.* If she caught him even half the times he'd been staring at her body, she'd have gone home by now. He couldn't help it. Despite his reservations, the attraction he felt toward her was stronger than ever. "I'll be right back," he told her, and she nodded in acknowledgment. His last thought as he turned away was how natural she looked there among his things. As if both he and the house had been waiting for her. *Am I losing my mind? First my dog loves her and now my house? Maybe I—*

For once, he was actually grateful to Melanie for distracting him from the disturbing place his mind was intent on going. "Well, she certainly showed up out of thin air, Gabe. Imagine my surprise when I ran into her near your driveway. I thought maybe she'd gotten lost or her car had broken down on the main road. But—I recognized your dog." She paused, waiting for an explanation that he wasn't inclined to give. After a long moment passed, she made a sound that was full of exasperation. "Are you sure she isn't related to you? Because both of you are so evasive."

He smothered a grin at the frustration in her voice. Apparently Sara had closed her down, and she wasn't happy about it. He'd always been a private person, and he liked that Sara was as well. "Possibly because it's none of your business, Melanie," he said pleasantly. She'd fallen a few steps behind him, but he didn't miss her gasp.

"We—we're all friends, Gabe. We watch out for each other. Don't you think you should tell the rest of us when you have a visitor staying with you? What if I'd called the police, thinking she was a burglar?"

He'd had it. He was sick and damned tired of these games with her. The gloves were coming off, and she wasn't going to like it. When he reached the next streetlight, he stopped, pivoting to face her. She was momentarily startled, then wary. "Let's cut the shit, shall we? You couldn't care less about any of that. What you're outraged over is that a woman is living with me and you know nothing about her or our relationship. And guess what? You're not going to, because I don't owe you or anyone else here an explanation for what I do, or who I do it with."

She held out a placating hand, knowing she'd overplayed her hand. "Gabe—I didn't mean—"

But it was far too late for that. This talk was long overdue. He tried to avoid conflict, but in his line of work, he knew how to push emotion and sentiment to the side and focus on the task at hand. "What we had is over. You've mistaken politeness for permission to meddle. And that is my fault for leaving any room for doubt. So let me be very clear, Melanie. I do not have feelings for you. Nothing is going to happen between us again. We are neighbors—and that's it. I'm not playing these games with you, nor will you attempt to do it with Sara. Truthfully, I've never trusted you, and I certainly don't now. Do you understand me?"

She averted her eyes, but he still saw the anger there. "I apologize for overstepping," she said stiffly. He half expected a show of fake tears, but she was either too startled or too pissed over what he'd said to fake it.

They resumed walking in silence. Even Trouble was subdued, as if sensing the tension in the air. *She'll probably run us over with her car.* When they reached Old Man Jenkins's place, she went directly to her vehicle. "Drive safely," he said in way of good-bye. She tossed a hand up that was more in line with giving him the finger than a wave. He didn't care, though. He'd been the bad guy more times than he could count in his career, and he'd long ago learned not to lose sleep over it. He was never an asshole without it being warranted. If someone did right by him, he'd do everything in his power for them in return. But he absolutely loathed people who said one thing but did another. The pretenders of the world were toxic and would contaminate everything around them if left unchecked.

As he made his way back home, he couldn't help wondering if he'd escaped one deceitful person only to end up falling for another. But unlike Melanie, Sara had a power over him that no one else ever had. If he gave her a chance, would his heart survive the blow or would this one be a mortal wound?

Chapter Twenty

🐾 🐾

Tense. If asked, it was how Sara would have described the evening after Gabe returned. She had no idea what had occurred, but it couldn't have been good. She had been startled to literally run into the other woman when she was out exploring the neighborhood with Trouble. At first, she had seemed so friendly, but it hadn't been long before Sara sensed something amiss. Melanie hadn't come right out and said it, but she alluded to the fact that she'd been intimate with Gabe. "Extremely close," was the way she'd described their relationship. Yet when he'd found her there, he hadn't looked thrilled. Quite the opposite. He had mentioned dating a neighbor, but said it ended before he deployed. She knew it had to be her. It was clear that Melanie wanted him back, which put Sara in an awkward position. Should she come right out and ask him about her? Their relationship was undefined at best and downright shaky, but didn't she have a right to know? Was that one of the reasons he'd been so standoffish last night? What if he'd slept with Melanie after he returned home? It wasn't out of the realm of possibility, considering how angry he was when he left North Carolina. And she knew he didn't expect her to come to Alaska. Heck, she never seriously thought it would happen either. *Yet here I am. Now what?*

She offered to make him something for dinner while she tried to work up the courage to talk to him about Melanie, but he declined. Instead of spending time with her, he used the excuse of showering and didn't return for nearly two hours. Realistically she knew he was tired from a long day at work. Plus, he was used to living alone and not having to entertain anyone. But . . . they'd spent all their free time together happily for the last seven months. Was it wrong of her to expect at least a little of that to continue? Otherwise, why extend the invitation? Would it have been any different if not for his surprise visit to her? Chloe had mentioned more than once that they had only gotten the best parts of each other's personality. Was she seeing the other side now?

When Trouble's tail began wagging, she looked up to see him standing a few feet away. He'd changed into jeans and a flannel shirt. *Wow.* Gabe in uniform was hot, but this casual version was seriously sexy. *Mmm, and that cologne. He smells delicious. Roll your tongue back in, girl.* Poor Trouble, she was practically petting the dog's fur off as she attempted to keep herself from drooling over the object of her affection. It was hard, though, because he had the dark, brooding thing down. And it was so effortless. "I'll light the fireplace. I prefer wood, but with all the snow here, gas is more practical," he said quietly as he pulled the safety screen over it. The room felt instantly cozier with the flames dancing brightly.

"That's great," she murmured. "Oh, I saved you some of the tomato basil soup I had for dinner. I know you like grilled cheese sandwiches, so I made you one of those as well. I mean—if you're hungry. Why don't you have a seat and relax while I go heat up everything." He appeared almost shocked by her statement.

"I—thank you. That sounds really good. I can get it, though, Sara. You're a guest, not my maid." He winced as soon as the words were out, obviously remembering the comments she'd made about Nicole and Chris taking advantage of her kindness. "I didn't mean that the way it came out. I'm just . . . not used to people doing things for me."

"Melanie mentioned cooking for you. I think that was why she was here. Something about confirming your plans." She wanted to kick herself for mentioning the other woman without having figured out exactly what to say. His expression told her he wasn't happy with her comments, and the last thing she wanted to do tonight was cause more tension. *Way to go, big mouth.* It had been jealousy pure and simple. She longed for an explanation, but was too afraid to question him. *I would have asked him anything a month ago.* She hated the distance between them now. She felt as if she'd lost her best friend, and in his place, there was a reserved stranger who only looked like Gabe.

He took a seat in the recliner across from her and picked up the television remote from the table. *He's ignoring me?* She stood, figuring she'd give him a little space while she fixed his plate. She was almost to the kitchen when he said so quietly, she almost missed it, "I won't be seeing Melanie socially. I can't tell you what to do, Sara, but I will say that she's not a trustworthy person. And she's jealous of you, so I would exercise caution if you cross paths again."

When she glanced back, he was staring at the television, but she knew he was aware of her scrutiny. She also understood that, for now, she needed to let this go. Gabe was ruled by logic, not emotion. Having this type of discussion was something most men would avoid, but for Gabe, it was pointless. He saw things in a certain light, and to continue asking intrusive questions would only irritate him. If Melanie showed up again and Sara thought it was a problem, then she would revisit the issue with him. "I appreciate the warning," she replied.

Their stilted conversation that evening set the tone for the rest of the week. He was gone when she woke up every morning, and she spent the day exploring his property, inside and out. She had dinner ready when he came home in the evening, and they usually ate in front of the fire. He seemed to want to avoid the intimacy of the kitchen, which she understood. He always complimented her on whatever she'd prepared and thanked her for doing it. Then he cleaned the kitchen and brought her a cup of coffee in the living room. She'd been surprised to discover the first time that he'd been so observant of the way she added extra cream and sugar to hers. That small thing had gotten her through those first days. But by Friday, she'd begun to think it was time to consider returning home. Christmas was only a few weeks away. In all the excitement, she'd actually lost sight of one of her favorite times of the year. And she seemed no closer to bridging the gap with Gabe. Instead of the rapport they'd once shared, they had settled into a polite friendship. One where you said "please" and "thank you" but didn't joke around, nor share any secrets. Instead, their dialogue was limited to "good morning," "good evening," "how did you sleep," "how are you," and "how was your day." After that, they talked about Trouble and, of course, the weather. It was like a wash, rinse, and repeat. It wasn't that it was necessarily bad, and if not for what she'd had with him, she might have been content. But she couldn't help remembering how they'd once covered so many varied topics and laughed so much. After the initial awkwardness, it had been so natural. But now, she had no clue how to break past the barriers he'd erected, and truthfully, she didn't have enough confidence to do any of the radical things Chloe suggested. Most all of them consisted of her dropping all her clothing and letting him take it from there. *But what if he didn't?* Chloe had assured her that he wouldn't turn her down, but Gabe wasn't like other men. He was different—which was one of the main reasons she was attracted to him.

"I think it was a mistake to come here," she admitted to Chloe that afternoon. "Neither Chris, nor my mom, are taking my calls, and I haven't talked to Kaylee since I've been here. I turned my world upside down because I have feelings for Gabe and I thought he felt the same. Yet nothing is changing, Chloe. And if I try to talk about anything personal, he changes the subject. It's like he throws up a roadblock at the very hint that our conversation might become anything other than generic chitchat. Honestly, I can't see that getting any better. Don't bother encouraging me to seduce him either. Trust me, I'm so far out of my element in that area that it would be a joke. I'd likely either trip and knock myself unconscious, or elbow him in the crotch. Sadly, those are the better outcomes."

"My mom has visited Joan a couple of times, and she says everything is fine. Your mom is watching Kaylee when they need her and seems to be enjoying it. Although I'm sure she would never admit that to you. And you know my mom would not sugarcoat it if things were going badly. So don't worry about them. When Chris pulls his head out of his ass, he'll see that it's the best for all of you."

Sara didn't want to admit it to her cousin, or even to herself, but she was having moments of regret. Her life hadn't been exciting, but it had suited her. There were some daily irritations, but there was also laughter, and people who needed her. Gabe didn't appear to care if she was there or not. In fact, how long would it take him to notice if she left? She felt like it would be a relief to him if he found her gone. "I think Gabe regrets buying me the ticket," she admitted on a sigh. "He's too nice to say it, but I don't believe he's . . . attracted to me. I mean, I realize I hurt him in North Carolina, and he probably has doubts about my sincerity. But . . . he's so blank when he looks at me. And if you could see the neighbor that he was dating before his deployment, you'd know that I'm not his type. She's tiny. Like zero body fat. She probably works out for hours a day. And she dresses so trendy. I felt frumpy next to her."

"Oh, come on, you know men can separate their feelings from the women they bang," Chloe inserted. "He's probably had sex with a lot of different types of women."

"So not helping," Sara muttered. "Let's just look at the facts. I've been in his house for almost a week, day and night. Wouldn't you think he would have at least found some excuse to touch me? Yet he goes out of his way not to. Our fingers bumped when I was handing him a cup last night and he couldn't jerk away fast enough." She reached up to wipe a tear away, feeling emotional as she gave voice to her fears. "He doesn't want me here. I—need to go home. But—I don't really have a home anymore. I gave it all up because I thought we had something. I want to be angry at him for leading me on, but I was right there with him. I could have pulled the plug at any time, but I didn't. It felt so good—belonging to someone. Being cared about. The possibility of a future that didn't involve me being on the outside looking in at other people's happiness."

"Sara," Chloe whispered, sounding as if she were in tears as well.

"You tried to tell me that it was too good to be true, but I didn't want to listen. Yeah, I had reservations. I was afraid to believe in it—but somewhere in my heart, I thought it could happen. I let myself fall in love with a man I'd never met in person. I've read about it working out for other people, and I believed it could for me as well. But he doesn't want me, and I'm just embarrassing myself by remaining here, because really, why would he pick me, when he could have anyone he wanted?"

Sara heard a sigh on the other end. "I'm beginning to regret encouraging you to do this," Chloe admitted. "I still believe that you needed to break free of the rut you were in, but hell, so do I. It just seemed like this was your shot at everything we all dream of finding in life. But if it's doing nothing but making you doubt yourself more, then screw it, North Carolina is waiting. You can stay with me for as long as you like."

She was touched . . . and relieved at her cousin's offer. It gave her some sense of security amid all the turmoil she was feeling. She was also a little embarrassed to have poured out her innermost thoughts and insecurities. It wasn't something she usually admitted in such detail. "Thanks, Chloe, that means a lot to me. You know, he doesn't even have a Christmas tree. Somehow that makes it even more depressing. And I didn't think that was possible." Sara laughed, running a hand through her hair. "That was random, geez. Listen, I need to get off before he gets home. I'll call you later on, okay?"

She ended the call after promising Chloe she'd be in touch soon. She wanted nothing more than to lie on the sofa and have an epic pity party, but she didn't want him to find her like that. So she got up and walked to the bathroom to compose herself and hide the evidence of her tears. She hoped she could also find the strength she needed to talk to him—to tell him good-bye, because in her heart, she knew she was out of options.

Gabe stood frozen in the kitchen. *Bastard.* He felt like a complete and utter bastard. He'd come home a little early, since training ended ahead of schedule. He had also used the kitchen entrance, instead of going around front. With Trouble no longer being confined, it didn't really matter which door he used. He was a few steps from the living room when he heard her talking. At first he'd been afraid that Melanie had dropped by again. But a glance around the corner showed that it was Sara on the phone. Not wanting to intrude, he silently returned to get a drink until she was finished. Yet the close proximity meant that he could hear some of her end of the conversation, and even though he knew it was wrong, he couldn't move when he heard his name. *I turned my world upside down because I have feelings for Gabe and I thought he felt the same.* The anguish in her words tore at his heart. This was a very private moment, and unbeknownst to her, he was eavesdropping on it. *He's too nice to say it, but I don't believe he's attracted to me. I let myself fall in love with a man I'd never met in person.*

He knew she was talking to her cousin, since she called her by name. He could only imagine what the other woman was saying about him. *Nothing you don't deserve.* She ended the call abruptly, and he stepped out of sight and prayed she didn't come in his direction. A moment later, it sounded like the bathroom door had closed, and he sagged back against the wall. She blamed herself for everything, yet he knew differently. He had been angry and hurt over the confusion when he visited, but that wasn't the real reason he'd been so distant. *Coward.* There was no way to sugarcoat it. He panicked when she showed up, and it had nothing to do with her physical appearance. If anything, she was even more beautiful to him now than the first time he'd laid eyes on her. Her personality, her mannerisms, her quirks. He could go on and on. He discovered a different thing each day about her that captivated him. And ironically, the stuff he liked the most was what drove him away. He'd fallen for her in Iraq, and he was even more smitten now, and it terrified him.

It wasn't that he thought she was too weak for the military way of life, although he wondered how she'd deal with the isolation it could bring. He also thought there was a strong possibility that he would have a very hard time leaving her behind. *If you don't get your shit together, you won't have to worry about that. You'll lose her.*

But how? He could handle hundreds of soldiers without breaking a sweat. He'd dodged enemy fire, for God's sake, and had returned to do it again and again. Yet matters of the heart were a mystery to him. He broke out in a cold sweat just considering all the things that could go wrong. *He doesn't even have a Christmas tree.* It didn't seem like much, but it was a starting point. He always felt better with a plan of action. She'd been trapped here alone, without a vehicle, for a week. With only his pitiful company in the evenings. And what entertainment had he provided? She claimed to like *The Walking Dead*, but watching an entire season wasn't exactly romantic. Plus, he always took the chair, while she sat on the sofa with his dog. Well, actually, Trouble adored her so much, he couldn't claim total ownership of the dog these days.

He moved into the living room to wait for her, hoping she didn't return with her suitcase. About fifteen minutes later, she came into view, with her faithful companion trotting happily at her side. *Trouble is smarter than I am. Maybe if I licked her hand?* He couldn't help smiling at that thought. Of course, that was the exact moment that she spotted him and halted in her tracks. "Oh—hello, I didn't realize you were home."

Her face was flushed and he knew she was wondering how long he'd been here. "I just walked in." He shrugged. "Hey, how about we go out tonight? Feel like dinner at Maxi's before we go shopping? I didn't bother to get a Christmas tree last year since I was busy getting ready for my deployment, but I think we should rectify that, don't you? Trouble will probably chew all the lights off it, but it'll be nice while it lasts."

She appeared stunned. She probably had no clue how to deal with him not only interacting normally with her but also suggesting an outing. The look on her face would have been comical, had it not been further proof of how shitty he'd been the entire time she'd been staying with him. *I can do better, Sara, give me a chance.*

"I—er . . . sure. If that's what you want. Just let me change clothes. I'm covered in dog fur."

He motioned toward what he was wearing. "Yeah, I need to do the same. What say we leave in about thirty minutes? Will that give you enough time?"

When he recalled how long it had taken Melanie to get ready, he wondered if he was rushing her. But she merely shrugged. "Sure, that'll work." She gave him a last perplexed stare before disappearing once again.

Only this time Trouble stayed behind. He ambled over to Gabe and nudged his leg, as if congratulating him on pulling his head out of his ass. "I know, buddy. You've been trying to tell me, but I'm a little slow sometimes." He could have sworn the dog nodded. "You're entirely too smart, boy," he murmured as he scratched him between the ears. "Actually, you're the brightest male in this house."

Gabe spent a few more minutes with Trouble, then headed to his room. For the first time since Sara had arrived, he was strangely excited. It was what he'd expected to feel when they met in person. But instead they had been plagued by misunderstandings and mixed signals. And most of those lately had come from him. He'd put the ball in her court in North Carolina, and she'd passed it back to him by taking the flight to Alaska. She made the leap of faith, only he hadn't been there to catch her. He wasn't naive enough to think it would be smooth sailing. They were still essentially strangers. But neither of them could deny they cared about each other. She'd told her cousin that she'd fallen for him, and he'd been fighting the fact that he felt the same way about her. He didn't know if what they had was a forever thing, but he did know with certainty that if he didn't give them a real shot, he would always regret it. He only hoped he hadn't already lost her.

Chapter Twenty-One

🐾 🐾

Sara felt as if she'd landed in the Twilight Zone. As she sat across from Gabe in Maxi's, she couldn't help thinking that he wasn't the same man she'd been staying with. No, in fact, he was the Gabe she'd come to know in Iraq. The warm, funny, thoughtful, and caring version that she was beginning to think she'd imagined. "So what'd you decide on?" he asked as he looked up from his menu. If he thought it strange that she was staring at him, he didn't mention it. In fact, he smiled, offering her a genuine expression. Not the fake kind he'd been using. *What is going on? Pity date?* And they were going to pick out a Christmas tree next. That was maybe the weirdest thing of all. She wondered if he was doing it for her benefit. She'd mentioned how she loved Christmas and how much fun it was to decorate the tree with Kaylee. The fact that he wanted to get one was oddly touching.

The past week had been a roller coaster of emotions for her, and she was more than a little overwhelmed by it all. Today was the first time she allowed herself to fully consider all that she'd walked away from to go to him in Alaska. Her relatives might not be perfect, but she'd always known she had a family to rely on if needed. Yet now, she wasn't sure that was the case. They had every right to turn their backs on her, as she'd basically done to them. "Sara, are you ready to order?" When Gabe touched her hand, she realized she'd been lost in her thoughts and hadn't noticed the waitress standing there.

"Oh, sorry," she murmured and quickly selected the lasagna. "I don't see Maxi," she noted as she glanced around. She felt awkward and uncertain, which made it difficult for her to relax.

A fact that Gabe seemed to notice. Because when the server returned with a glass of wine, he motioned for her to put it in front of Sara, and he took the tea she'd ordered. "Listen, I know it's been tense since you've been here, and I apologize. We could sit here and rehash everything, but I don't think either of us is up for that." He rubbed the bridge of his nose before continuing. "What I'd like to do, if you're agreeable, is to start over. Try to get back to where we were during my deployment. There's a reason we wanted to meet. We enjoy each other, and there are feelings there. Granted, we have to make the adjustment to being together in a more conventional way. It might not have been easy on us, but we've at least broken the ice this week."

She wondered for a moment if he was joking. This was

the exact opposite of what she'd been expecting. She had been ready to throw in the towel and return home because he'd been so cool and distant toward her. Maybe he had sensed it somehow. Because he was opening up to her— and did this mean he was giving them a real chance? *Is that what I still want?* "I'm scared," she admitted. If they were going to attempt to restore their former bond, she needed to be completely honest with him. And if he couldn't handle that, it was better to know now.

He leaned forward and put his hand over hers, giving it a squeeze. The gesture was unexpected and she assumed he'd release her, yet he didn't. Instead, his fingers curled around hers as if it were completely natural. "So am I. Terrified, in fact. I've never done this, Sara. My parents and my sister are the only constants in my life, and I haven't seen them in over a year. They might not be thrilled, but they're used to me being a mostly absent son and brother. I've dated and had some short-term relationships, but they were never serious, nor was I unhappy to see them end. The Army has been my life, and pretty much my wife, for the last sixteen years, and I haven't wanted to subject anyone to it. You already know I deploy and relocate on a fairly regular basis. It's hard on anyone left behind. I haven't been in that position personally, but plenty of my soldiers have, and it's tough on everyone involved. Even knowing all that, I couldn't stop myself from becoming attached to you. You gave me something I've never had before: a sense of belonging. I can't give you a guarantee that this will work out. It hasn't been smooth sailing thus far. But we're still here.

If you're willing, let's take it one day at a time, and see where it goes. Try to push the fears and bullshit aside, and be the Gabe and Sara who've spent the last seven months talking together."

"Well, well, look at you two sitting here all happy and glowing. I've been wondering how things were going. Seems like they worked out fine." Maxi stood next to their table with her hands on her hips, beaming down at them like a proud parent.

"Things are definitely looking up." Sara smiled as Gabe gave her a wink. Her words were not only a response to Maxi but also her acknowledgment of everything Gabe had just said. His answering grin told her that he understood. She found herself relaxing and enjoying his company. They both made an effort to keep the conversation lighthearted, which meant a lot of joking around. And when they left Maxi's, he took her hand and led her to the truck. She had to fight the urge to pinch herself to see if she was dreaming. This was exactly what she'd envisioned all those nights she'd lain awake and dreamed about being with him.

Shopping for a Christmas tree and decorations was the most fun she'd had in longer than she could remember. He urged her to pick out whatever she liked. When she attempted to be conservative, not wanting to choose items that were so costly, he'd gone behind her and put everything in the cart that she'd admired.

She was studying the lights when he excused himself. She thought he was going to the restroom, so she was surprised when he returned with three red stockings. "I think you forgot something. I don't know about you, but I'm not going to piss Santa off by not being prepared. One for you, me, and Trouble. You know he'd be hurt if we left him out."

In that moment, he reminded her of Kaylee. His expression was a mixture of sheepish and expectant. As if hoping for her approval, but a tad embarrassed at the same time. She didn't have to pretend to be pleased at his thoughtfulness, because she was thrilled. Not only was it sweet, but it showed her more than words that he wanted them to be a couple. A tree was great, but what he'd done on his own was so touching. She swallowed past the lump that was wedged in her throat, knowing he might take it the wrong way if she burst into tears. "I couldn't agree more." She nodded. "I'm glad you thought of that. Christmas wouldn't be the same without them hanging above the fireplace." He laid them in the cart, then put his hand in the center of her back and rested it there while they finished.

He surprised her again on the way home by turning on the radio and finding a station that played holiday music. It was a perfect evening, and much different from the other ones she'd spent there. Trouble was ecstatic when he saw all the bags they brought in. They'd decided on an artificial tree, knowing it would be easier. So when Gabe sat the big box down without opening it, both her and Trouble were disappointed. He took his coat and gloves off, then turned to see her expression. He chuckled, shaking his head. "I guess you wanted to do all this now, huh?"

She knew he was tired after working all day, but it was hard to think of going to bed and waiting until tomorrow.

"If you're not up to it, I could do it myself. If you'll help me open the box, I'll take it from there." Trouble barked once, as if volunteering his assistance as well.

"I can see now that I'm going to be outnumbered." He scowled at his dog, adding, "Who's fed you and picked up your poop for years now? I thought you had my back." Trouble flopped down on the floor in a move that clearly said he was remorseful but still wanted to see the damn tree. "All right, let's do this," Gabe said, and got started.

Sara unpacked the decorations and tried to hide her smile as he cursed his way through the directions. "Need some help over there?"

"Hell no," he mumbled, then flashed her a boyish grin. "Sorry. I keep putting these damn things in the wrong spot. Whoever heard of color coding something, then having all of them look alike? Is this yellow or orange?" As she moved to offer her assistance, he held up a hand. "Oh no, baby, this right here is personal. You stay over there because shit just got real. I'm going to war against this plastic monstrosity."

Sara pumped her fist in the air, letting loose a roar that made Trouble jump. "Go, tiger, you totally got this. I believe in you. Winners never quit and quitters never win." He smirked when her motivational chant finally ended. "Too much?"

Holding up two branches that didn't appear to belong anywhere, he said, "You better keep going. Maybe sacrifice something to the PVC gods who made this crap. For this to actually look like it's supposed to, we might have to promise them our firstborn." He kept working as if he had no clue what he'd said. *Our firstborn?* She knew he was joking around, but still—images of her pregnant with his child flooded her mind. They'd never really discussed any desire for children, and now certainly wasn't the time. *But what if?* She didn't know how long she stood there daydreaming, but she was abruptly pulled back to the present when he shouted, "The enemy has been defeated." He motioned her over and put his arm around her shoulders to pull her closer. "Behold the beauty of this masterpiece."

So sexy. Kiss me. As they admired his handiwork, she longed for him to do more than hug her. Considering how timid she'd been during her few sexual experiences, it was hard to believe that she wasn't nervous with him. Anticipation and desire far overshadowed any anxiety she might have. And unlike the reserved stranger he'd been since she arrived, this was her Gabe—the man she'd been in love with for months. "It's perfect," she whispered, and it had little to do with the tree before them and everything to do with him.

Even though she would have been content at that point to snuggle on the couch for the rest of the evening, Gabe's renewed enthusiasm was infectious. She put the hooks on the ornaments, and he hung them. A few times she had to chase Trouble through the house when he pulled something off and ran with it in his mouth. Luckily, they'd anticipated that very thing and had purchased all nonbreakable items. When she returned to the living room with the snowman she'd wrestled away from him, Gabe was standing on a stepladder waiting for her. "Think we're finished." He rearranged a few lights near the top as he said over his shoulder, "Angel, if you'll hand me the star, I'll put it up."

"*Angel?*" She hadn't realized she'd said it aloud until Gabe flipped around slowly to face her. He appeared almost embarrassed, which she found fascinating. *Oh my God, what if he accidentally called me the wrong name?*

That horrifying thought had barely flitted through her head when he said, "I guess I should admit that I—gave you that nickname after you sent me the picture of you and your niece playing in the snow while I was in Iraq. That's how I came to see you, Sara. You appeared in my life seemingly out of nowhere and made it so much better. It was the toughest deployment I've ever been through for a variety of reasons. And you . . . you became the beautiful angel who saved my sanity on the long days and nights. Every time I needed an escape, I looked at that photo. To me, it wasn't rabbit ears above your head, but a halo. When I was so physically and mentally spent that I didn't know how I'd deal with the seemingly endless months ahead of me, you soothed me. Made me smile and see each day as a new opportunity to hear your laughter and see that gorgeous face."

She tried to blink the tears away, knowing they would make him uncomfortable, but it proved impossible. "Gabe," she sighed, putting a wealth of emotion into his name. Trouble approached her and dropped a toy Santa at her feet, as if apologizing for upsetting her.

"I really suck at this," Gabe joked weakly. He stepped down from the ladder and took her into his arms. She slid hers around his waist and they stood there, finding comfort in each other. His hands rubbed her back, and she thought she felt him drop a kiss onto the top of her head a couple of times. She didn't do an all-out ugly cry, but if that would keep him close, she was willing to try. "All better?" he asked as he pulled back to survey her face.

She nodded shyly, thinking, *Kiss me, dammit.* And he did—on the forehead. *So close. The lips, Randall. A little lower.* It didn't happen, and she couldn't really complain. He held her as they watched *It's a Wonderful Life.* When it was over, he surprised her by getting their boots and coats, then returning with a comforter to bundle around them. "What?" she asked sleepily, thinking maybe she was dreaming the entire thing. But the cold air hitting her face a few moments later let her know she was definitely awake.

She shivered and buried closer into his side, as Trouble voiced his displeasure at being left inside. "I know it's freezing, but it's clear tonight and I wanted you to see the Northern Lights."

Intrigued, she looked up at the sky, expecting to be awed, but instead there was nothing more than some milky-looking clouds present. She thought she detected other colors, but they were too faint to detect for sure. Obviously, Gabe was wrong about it being clear. "We can try it again tomorrow," she murmured, not wanting him to hear the disappointment in her voice. She'd seen so many magnificent pictures of the bright dancing lights, and what she was seeing wasn't even remotely close.

"Here, try this." Gabe laughed softly as he handed her a camera.

She shrugged as she brought her hands up to grasp it, thankful he'd had her put on her gloves as well. It took a moment, but suddenly everything changed. The camera lens brought to life a scene that took her breath away. Shades of green, purple, yellow, orange, red, and blue shimmered in the night sky. "Oh my," she hissed in wonder. "Gabe, I see . . ." Her voice trailed off as she stared, mesmerized by the sight before her.

Gabe leaned closer as he said, "They say human eyes often can't see the faint colors of the aurora at night. But this type of camera doesn't have those limitations. I bought it right after I moved here on the advice of the locals, and it's been worth every penny." Sara would have likely remained spellbound on the porch until she froze to death had Gabe not ushered her back inside. They discarded their outerwear and rushed to the fire to warm their hands in front of the flames. Then he pulled her down onto the sofa next to him, and she cuddled into the warm curve of his body. "Thank you," she mumbled sleepily. Lying with her head on his chest, hearing the beat of his heart, Sara knew that every moment in her life had led her here, to this man. Against all odds, their paths had intersected. Whether he was her final destination, or a stop along the way, she didn't know, but she'd never been more excited to take the next step than she was now.

Chapter Twenty-Two

🐾 🐾

Gabe stood in the kitchen waiting for Sara. They'd both fallen asleep on the sofa the previous evening, and he woke her after two for bed. He'd wanted nothing more than to take her to his room and make love to her, but he didn't want to rush things. He figured she was dealing with enough shock from the sudden turnaround he'd made in his attitude toward her. And he didn't want her to know that it stemmed from the phone call he'd eavesdropped on. That had been an extremely private moment for her, and he felt like an ass for intruding on it. Yet had it not happened, she might well be on her way home.

Trouble's ears perked up, a clear indication that she was awake. He'd taken the dog out to do his business earlier and fed him when they returned. The lure of food was the only thing that kept him from being in the bedroom with her. He couldn't fault him, though, since Gabe felt the same.

A few moments later she came in rubbing her eyes and yawning. When she noticed him, she abruptly stopped. "What're you doing here?" When he raised an amused brow at her blunt question, her face turned an adorable shade of pink. "I mean—um, good morning. Shouldn't you be at work?"

"Well, hello to you, Angel. I thought I mentioned that I'm now officially on leave until after the holidays. We finished up in the field yesterday. So . . . I'm afraid you're both stuck with me." Her nickname once again slipped out, but she didn't appear to mind. In fact, he thought she looked pleased. He'd felt awkward when he accidentally called her that last night. He could have attempted to brush it off. But he hadn't wanted her to possibly think he'd mixed her up with another woman. *As if that were even possible.* Once he started talking, it all came pouring out. Even though he was uncomfortable revealing so much of himself, in the end he thought it brought them closer. And if this was going to work, they both needed to learn to open up more, no matter how hard it was.

She winced, shaking her head. "I completely lost track of the days if you can believe that. Do you go in on weekends normally?"

"Just depends." He shrugged. "It's not unusual, but I try to have Sunday free when I can. Anyway, you're quite possibly going to hit me—or at the very least, say no. But I realized earlier that tonight is the annual holiday ball." When she looked faintly alarmed, he rushed ahead. "I know what you're thinking. I hate these damn things too. I've never been good at shit like this. It's expected of me, though. Lead by example and all that." He paused before adding, "It's formal, Sara. I realize you likely didn't bring anything like that with you. So if you agree to be my date, we'll go shopping, and I'll buy you a dress. I'm sorry to spring this on you so suddenly. Between the fieldwork and . . . other stuff, I've been kind of distracted." *Why isn't she saying anything?* Gabe put his hands in the pockets of his jeans and rocked back on his heels. He felt as if he were inviting Abby Johnson to the junior prom all over again. Only she'd been a little more enthusiastic than Sara was so far. "Hey, it's no big deal. I'll make an appearance, and we can do something when I get home."

He'd turned away to pour her a coffee when he heard her say, "I'd love to go with you. Just give me a few minutes to get dressed and we can go shopping."

She made it a few steps when he put a hand out to stop her. "Thank you, Angel, I—this makes me happy." There was no way he could resist the urge for a good morning kiss. His mouth was inches from its goal when he suffered a sudden hurdle. "What . . . ?"

"No way," she mumbled as she backed up. "I haven't brushed my teeth yet. I refuse to go down in history as the chick with morning breath." He smiled, wanting to assure her that he was willing to risk it, but not if it would make her uncomfortable. She surprised him, though, when she winked and said, "But please try again later. I mean—don't forget." *Damn, she's cute.*

After she was gone, he replied to a few e-mails in his office, then went outside and started the truck so that it would be warm. When he came back in, she was dressed and pulling on her coat. *No time like the present.* She glanced up at him and her eyes widened, as if sensing what was to come. *She's not running, good sign.* She inhaled sharply when he raised his hand and ran a thumb over the curve of her lower lip. "Gabe," she whispered, just as he lowered his head and took her mouth in a gentle kiss. He could feel her heart thudding against his chest as he pulled her closer to his body. The feel of her arms wrapping around his waist told him better than words that she wanted this as much as he did.

The connection they shared long distance was even more potent in person. He wanted to explore every inch of her body. She was like fire in his veins. He'd never reacted this strongly to a woman before. He was almost afraid to test his control by deepening the kiss, but the slide of her tongue against his took that decision from him. His hand had just made contact with the curve of her ass when something wedged between them. One of them protested—heck, possibly both. They strained forward, not wanting to let go . . . but Trouble was out of patience. Unfazed by Gabe's command to stop, the canine continued until he was leaning against Sara. *I've been dog-blocked,* he thought incredulously.

Sara dropped her head, and for a moment, he was afraid

she was upset over the embrace. But then a giggle erupted . . . and another, until her entire body was shaking. He found himself laughing as well, unable to ignore that Trouble was jealous. "Buddy, I thought we were friends," he grumbled. As much as the interruption sucked, it was undoubtedly for the best. As it was, his zipper was digging painfully into his dick. Another few minutes and he'd have taken her against the mudroom wall. *Damn, don't think about that now.* He reached over and cupped her cheek. "We'd better get out of here before I get carried away again and he mauls me."

Her face was flushed, but there was a sparkle of satisfaction in her expression that made him feel good. Any question of how their relationship would handle the transition to the real world was answered fully. *We almost threw this away.* She pulled her coat back around her and buttoned it before telling Trouble good-bye. As they walked to his truck, Gabe found himself wondering how someone who had been there only a week could make such an impact on not only him but his dog as well. He also wondered how they would ever go back to the life they'd lived before her should she leave. He pushed that sobering thought aside as he took her hand. He didn't want to miss out on the joy of being with her by worrying over the future. Instead, he vowed to savor each day with her as if there were no tomorrow.

Sara stood before the mirror in the bathroom and studied her reflection carefully. Penny, her helpful sales associate, had assured her that the red mermaid dress she'd picked out was perfect for her. And it had seemed to be. In fact, Sara had never worn anything so sexy and glamorous before. The formfitting, off-the-shoulder lace gown was gorgeous.

She'd also stopped by a salon that Maxi recommended and had her hair styled in a loose French twist, which made her neck seem impossibly long and slender. The nude-colored pumps had a higher heel than she would normally wear, but they were surprisingly comfortable. She rounded out the ensemble with a matching bag that was just big enough for lipstick, her phone, and some tissues.

She couldn't believe how inexpensive the dress was. Apparently the store was having a clearance sale on last year's styles, and everything she tried on was less than half what the tag showed. It was a stroke of luck, considering she refused to let Gabe pay for any of it. She was already staying with him free of charge. She didn't expect him to clothe her as well.

"Angel, are you almost ready? I'm sorry to rush you, but we need to leave in about fifteen minutes."

"I'll be right there." She inspected her makeup one last time. Squaring her shoulders, she walked out of the bathroom and nearly crashed into him in the hallway. "Whoops!" She teetered for a moment before he reached out to steady her. *Why is he staring at me like that?* "Gabe?" She glanced down, thinking there was a wardrobe malfunction. Yet nothing seemed amiss. *Both nipples are covered—check.*

"You're absolutely beautiful," he breathed out shakily. He took her hand and swiveled her around slowly. "Wow. I know I should say something more refined, but that one word keeps going through my head."

When she got her first real look at him in his dress blues, she knew exactly how he felt. *Damn. Did I say that out loud?* The look of confusion on his handsome face said that she had. She cleared her throat before trying again. "You're like seriously hot, Major. I mean you're always sexy, but this is smoking." *He's blushing. Ah God, I'm so in love with him.* Luckily, it didn't appear that she had shared the last thought.

"Um—thanks," he murmured as he tucked her hand into the crook of his arm. "Might as well get some practice in on this. You have no idea how badly I want to kiss you right now. But even if you'd let me mess up your lipstick, I still wouldn't trust myself." They chatted easily on the drive to the hotel where the ball was being held. Traffic was heavier near town, and Gabe mentioned the night skating at Westchester Lagoon. "I'll take you there one day. They have big fire pits for warmth and there's hot chocolate and music. No way I'm getting on a pair of ice skates, though," he added on a laugh.

"I'd love that," she said softly. "And I think we can both agree to remain safely on our feet as spectators."

When they arrived at their destination, Gabe helped her from the truck, then handed his keys to the valet. After dropping their coats off, he put a possessive hand on her hip, guiding her into the room. She knew it was likely her imagination, but it felt as if every eye was on them. Gabe kept her close as they slowly made their way through a long receiving line, where she met Gabe's boss and his wife, along with a bunch of others she would never remember. Truthfully, she was so giddy over him introducing her as his girlfriend that she hadn't heard much after that. She hoped she hadn't missed a question from anyone. When they made it to the end and had a moment alone, she motioned him closer and whispered, "See, I told you. It's the uniform miracle. Everyone looks amazing."

He laughed, shaking his head. "Naturally, it's my date that notices."

She batted her eyes at him. "None of them hold a candle to you, muffin. You're like the prize in a box full of Cracker Jacks."

"Bro, did she just call you 'muffin'?" Sara whirled around, surprised to have been overheard. The man looking back at her in amusement was handsome—there was no disputing that. But he didn't compare to the one who owned her heart. Speaking of Gabe, she was afraid she'd embarrassed him with her silly comments, but he appeared unfazed.

"You're just jealous, Keller," he said dryly. He winked at her before adding, "Sara, this is Captain Jason Keller."

She understood their camaraderie immediately. She knew they were not only colleagues but friends as well. Jason took her hand between both of his. "Sara, it's a pleasure. I've heard a lot about you."

"Likewise." She smiled shyly. "Gabe mentioned you many times during his deployment."

At Gabe's pointed look, Jason released her. "Oh, I'm

sure he did. He's always been jealous of me. I'm good-looking, intelligent, popular with the ladies, and—"

"Full of it," Gabe tossed in. "Angel, he's a prime example of why your uniform theory is incorrect."

She giggled at their private joke while Jason rolled his eyes. "I'm not going to dignify that with a response." He eyed her curiously, but she could detect nothing negative there. "Sara, on behalf of myself and everyone we were stationed with in Iraq, I'd like to give you our heartfelt thanks for making our time there more pleasant." He nodded his head in Gabe's direction. "You turned this irritable grouch into a ray of sunshine. Granted, it scared the hell out of us when he began flashing those dimples, but eventually we figured out he was actually smiling. Well—either that or he had a severe case of gas, possibly both."

"What is she doing here?" Both Sara and Jason turned to follow the direction of Gabe's stare. *Melanie? Why?*

"Hey, isn't that your old . . ." Jason's voice trailed off as he winced at his friend. "Yeah, a lot of us wouldn't think anything of it, but that's a little awkward for you, isn't it, buddy? That's why I always fly solo to these events. I've witnessed too many *Jerry Springer* moments over the years."

"It's not a big deal," Gabe muttered, but Sara could tell he wasn't happy with the other woman's appearance. It didn't thrill her either. She saw enough to know that Melanie was wearing a sexy black dress that made her appear even tinier. *Great, she looks like a size 0, while I probably resemble Clifford the Big Red Dog.* As if sensing the direction her thoughts were taking, Gabe pulled her into the crook of his arm and whispered against her ear, "She's not even in your league, Angel—never was."

"I need a drink before you two get any mushier," Jason joked. "I swear, I don't know how to deal with this kinder, gentler version of you, Randall. Can we at least go glare at some of the newbies? Make their balls draw up around their throat? You know how much you enjoy that."

Sara cocked her head up at her date, who gave her an innocent smile. "Have no clue what he's referring to. I'd never do anything so juvenile."

The banter continued as other soldiers joined them. Soon, she had forgotten all about Melanie's presence and was enjoying herself. "Hey, we better find our places, the Color Guard is getting into position." Sara glanced in the direction he pointed to see a group of soldiers holding several different flags. Everyone seemed to be of the same mind, because they were forced to walk single-file through the crowd until they reached their table. She was startled when the soldiers suddenly stood at attention. After the national anthem, it was a blur of toasts, speakers, and even a cake cutting. She was moved to tears at the ceremony around the missing man table. Gabe explained it was in honor of fallen, missing, or imprisoned military service members. She was also fascinated by the history of his unit. The only downside to the evening was Melanie seated at the table beside them, and the fact that she caught the other woman staring at Gabe more than once. It was obvious she still had feelings for him, even if he didn't return them.

When Gabe's boss called him over after dinner, Jason

leaned closer and said, "He was never into her, so don't let it bother you. I've known Gabe for a long time. We met years ago when we were stationed in Florida. We've been split up a few times, but we ended up here together. He's always been very careful about getting seriously involved with a woman because of the military lifestyle. It's tough to keep a relationship intact with the separations." He took a drink from his beer before adding, "You've been good for him. He was the most human in Iraq that I've ever seen him. Normally he's kind of like a machine. Focused on the mission to the exclusion of all else. That shit will take a heavy toll on you unless you learn how to decompress. If it means goofing off with the other soldiers, you do it. It's survival—it's sanity. And I think he's finally seen that. Knows there's more than the job. Doesn't matter what you do, or who you are, there must be balance in all things."

She smiled, touched by his insight as well as the trust he was placing in her. He might seemingly be the less serious of the two men, but she sensed that he could be just as intense as Gabe. She also knew instinctively that by telling her what he had, he was giving her his approval. "It's something I'm learning too, Jason," she admitted. "Coming here was the biggest leap of faith I've ever taken. And I still have a near panic attack several times a day over it." Just then she spied Gabe holding center court in the midst of a dozen other soldiers, and she was filled with a sense of pride. *That's my man.*

Sara had no idea how long she'd zoned out, but the amusement in Jason's voice said he'd noticed it. "You two crazy kids will figure it out. The best advice I can give you is not to do anything stupid. My father imparted those wise words to me when I was a kid, and they cover damn near everything."

"That was deep, Captain. You should have that put on a patch for your uniform." He chuckled in response. She hated to leave the amusing conversation, but she was in serious danger of peeing herself. "Do you know where the restrooms are?" she asked him as she got to her feet.

"They're out in the hallway, right outside the doors," he replied as he made a show of stretching his neck. "I think I'll go dazzle your boyfriend and his cronies with some of my wit."

She waved, then walked in the direction he indicated as fast as her heels would allow. By the time she opened the door to the ladies' room, she almost had her knees crossed. She was a timid tinkler from way back, so she took the last stall and heaved a sigh. It was nice to have a quiet moment. It had been a great evening, but she wasn't used to being around so many people. Thankfully, Gabe and Jason's banter kept it from being too overwhelming.

Unfortunately, her peace was short lived because she heard voices a few minutes later. It sounded as if several of them had had too much to drink. Not wanting to walk out while they were there, she decided to stay where she was. She had texted Chris earlier, so she removed her phone from her bag to see if he had responded. She had all but tuned out the ruckus a few feet away when one of them slurred, "Mel, who's the girl all over Gabe?" *Oh my God.*

"Is that the one who's living with him?" another voice asked.

There was laughter, and she instinctively knew it was from Melanie. "Yes, that's her. I can't believe she's still hanging around. Poor, deluded thing, I almost feel sorry for her. She probably thinks she's special to him." Her words might indicate sympathy, but her tone was full of sarcasm.

"She was flirting with Gabe *and* Jason. Maybe she's doing them both."

"That would explain the slutty red dress."

"If I were her, I'd have picked something a little more figure friendly. She looks as if she has a good twenty pounds on Gabe."

Sara didn't know who the other hurtful comments were from, but once again, she recognized Melanie's voice. "What'd I tell you? I've been around him long enough to realize it's Army first and everything else last. But how can you have such high work standards . . . and rock-bottom personal ones? I mean, aside from her appearance, she's also very unkempt. The day I met her, she was covered in dog fur. She even let that mutt of his lick her in the mouth."

"Ugh, that's nasty. Don't worry about it, though, honey, we've all given a few mercy dates. Aren't you glad you dumped his ass?"

"Looks like he's found the perfect woman for him now." One of them cackled so loudly, it hurt Sara's ears.

"Exactly. I've moved on. He was never anything more

than a stepping-stone for me. Now Jared, he's on the fast track—and I'll be along for the ride. I'll be a colonel's wife by this time next year."

She heard the sound of the door opening, then their voices faded away. The quiet was almost oppressive now. Her chest was so tight, she felt as if she couldn't breathe. When dark spots began to dance before her, she knew she was going to pass out unless she got control. Picturing Melanie and her friends standing over her should that happen was the only thing that centered her. She stood up on shaky legs and forced herself to inhale slowly. She didn't know how long she'd been gone, but it had obviously been a while.

GABE: Angel—where are you?

She knew he wasn't to blame for what happened in the women's restroom, but facing him now was the last thing she wanted. There was no way she could go back out there and sit for hours while pretending to be okay. Because she was far from that. The happy glow of the last few days was ruined, and she needed space to process.

SARA: I'm in the bathroom. Not feeling well.

GABE: I'll collect our coats and be right there, sweetheart.

Much like the man himself, his response was perfect. Which somehow made it even worse, with her own self-confidence in tatters.

There's no way he could love me. They were right.

She had barely processed that depressing thought when he sent her another message.

GABE: I'm outside the door. Do you need me to come in and help you?

SARA: No, I'll be right out.

She quickly washed up and attempted to steady herself. She hoped that he would attribute her pallor to illness rather than what it really was. *I don't want to face him. Should have never come.*

His eyes were full of concern when she stepped out. She had to blink back tears when he extended a hand to feel her forehead for fever. "What happened, Angel? Should we stop at the emergency room?"

She looked away, hoping he couldn't see the truth. "It's—probably something I ate. Could we go now?"

He put his coat on, then helped her do the same. His arm went around her shoulders, cradling her gently against him. "Absolutely. The valet should have the truck waiting out front."

They were almost to the front door when Jason stopped them. "Hey, you all right, Sara?"

Please let me get out of here. She knew she didn't have to pretend to be sick because she sounded so shaky when she said, "Just—want to lie down. I'll be fine."

"Call me if you need anything, brother," he said in a voice devoid of humor for the first time that night.

She glanced up briefly when he said good-bye, and wished she hadn't. *He knows.* Which seemed impossible. Yet it was there, as he studied her thoughtfully. She turned away, not wanting her face to reveal more. The trip home seemed endless. Luckily, Gabe suggested she put her head back and close her eyes, which she did. Even so, she could feel his gaze on her at times during the drive. She knew he was worried, but short of telling him exactly what happened, there was nothing she could do about it. And that was something she wasn't ready for yet—if ever. She knew it was simply the opinions of a handful of mean women. Yet their arrows had struck every weak spot that existed in her armor.

"We're home, Angel," Gabe said softly as he rubbed her arm. He came around to her side and helped her out. When they walked into the kitchen, Trouble barked in excitement from his kennel. As if sensing something amiss, he quieted after a few whines. "Let's get you changed, then you can lie down, sweetheart."

"I'm going to wash my face and go to bed," she murmured. "Really, I'll be just fine." She forced herself to lift her eyes from his chest, to his face. He was worried, that was clear. And he didn't like leaving her alone. *Please go. Just—go.*

He dropped a kiss onto her forehead. "Call out if you need me." She nodded, and once she'd walked a few steps away, he added, "Thank you for tonight . . . you made this the best event I've ever attended."

She murmured something she hoped he'd take as a passable response and shut her door behind her. She crossed to the bed and sank down on it, expecting the floodgates to open wide. Yet—strangely enough—they didn't. After barely holding herself together for the last hour, it was almost anticlimactic. She was curiously blank. She had no desire to get up, nor did she fall asleep. Instead, she stared at the wall for over two hours. At one point, she heard Gabe pause in the hallway before continuing on to his room.

She needed her cousin. She still had no desire to talk to Gabe, yet she did want to unburden herself to someone. So she pulled off her dress and tossed it in the corner. She couldn't imagine wanting to wear it again. They had ruined what she'd once considered so beautiful. Removing it somehow helped to cleanse away some of the pain.

Her purse, which contained her phone, was nowhere to be found. Then she vaguely remembered Gabe carrying it from the truck. She stood, undecided, not wanting to risk waking him. Finally, she eased the door open and crept down the hall. She checked the kitchen first, but ultimately found it on the couch in the living room. Unfortunately, Trouble appeared, startling a small squeak from her before she clamped a hand over her mouth. She lowered herself into Gabe's recliner and flipped the nearby lamp on. She sat quietly, listening for any sounds from the other end of the house, but there was only silence. She patted Trouble's head while feeling around for the bag she had dropped next to the chair. Her fingers touched something, and she lifted it. Only instead of her purse, it was a manila envelope. Shrugging, she put it on the table in front of her, then froze.

She picked it back up, inspecting the front of the envelope, where her name was carefully written. But other than that, there was no other writing on it. She knew it was an invasion of Gabe's privacy, but she couldn't stop herself from sliding a finger under the edge to carefully break the seal, before upending it onto the table. She wasn't sure what she was expecting, but the stack of envelopes that fell out took her by surprise. Then the smell of her perfume reached her and she knew. *My letters.* Her gaze fell on one after another, surprised to find them so worn. They appeared to be years old, instead of months.

The sudden thump of Trouble's tail was the first indication that she wasn't alone. She tensed, hoping he wasn't standing there—but her luck had completely deserted her tonight. Gabe's eyes went to the stack of mail, then back to her. "I meant to put that away." She swallowed hard when she saw he was wearing only a pair of boxer briefs. Even in the midst of emotional turmoil, she couldn't help admiring his lean, chiseled body.

"You kept them," she murmured as she laid aside the letter she was holding.

"Of course." He moved closer, taking a seat on the couch. He picked up the same paper and brought it to his nose. "I loved that my locker in Iraq smelled like you. Hell, my whole room did. And it was oddly . . . soothing. It made it feel as if you were there. Like any moment you would come through the door. I had a routine I followed almost every day. I'd read your e-mails, then go through all of these. They made me smile. Gave me hope for something outside my military service." She felt a tear trickle down her cheek, but she didn't bother brushing it away, since another was already falling. He paused so long, she thought he wasn't going to say anything more. He appeared to be lost in his thoughts as he stared at the floor.

"Gabe," she prompted, sensing there was more.

"Falling in love with you before we even met was the most fanciful thing I've ever done. There is absolutely no reason it should have made it past me coming home. Yet— even when I was angry, I still craved your presence. Being back in the States only made me want to be with you so badly, it was damn near a physical pain." He moved closer and reached out to cup her cheek. "If you hadn't come here, I wouldn't have been able to stay away for long. Regardless of what I said about ending anything between us, I was losing my mind. I've never been in love before. I was determined not to put the stress of my life onto the shoulders of another. But—I never counted on you, Angel. I knew for certain I was in love with you when I became incapable of rational thought. I've had an explanation or a plan of action for everything in my life—until you. I finally came to the realization that things are different with you because I lead with my heart. It doesn't have to fit into some neat, logical box. There's simply the way I feel."

Sara felt as if she'd been given everything she could ever want—and more. The crippling doubts and insecurities she'd suffered earlier were clearing—and, in their place, was an affirmation that this amazing man was not only her present but her future as well. She wanted to belong to him in every way. It was past time to cement their bond. And she needed to be the one to take the leap, not only for him but for herself. She would not let a bunch of jealous, catty women ruin what they had. Gabe had made himself vulnerable to her several times now, and he deserved no less from her. So she took a breath and she jumped, never doubting he would catch her.

Chapter Twenty-Three

🐾 🐾

Gabe felt sweat beginning to bead on his forehead. Even with Sara's sudden illness at the end of the evening, this was the best night of his life. Having her with him at the ball had been so natural—so right. He'd proudly introduced her as his girlfriend to his colleagues and their spouses. But secretly, he longed to call her his wife instead. Was that crazy to have such a sudden bond with someone? Yes—and no. They had known each other for seven months. It may not have been a conventional courtship, but he knew instinctively that they were meant to be together. Hell, he'd sensed it from the very first e-mail. No matter how much he tried to second-guess it, his gut said it was right.

When a sound had woken him, he figured it was either Trouble destroying the Christmas tree or Sara being sick. He saw the light in the living room and stopped in his tracks when he found her with the letters. He was almost as surprised as she likely was when he poured out his heart. He thought her tears were the happy kind, yet she still hadn't said anything. *Should have stayed quiet. Too soon.* She stood, and he thought she was leaving. Only instead of walking past him, she came to a halt inches away. Then she shocked the hell out of him by lowering herself onto his lap until she was facing him. "Angel, what—" He didn't finish his sentence, though. How could he when she was lowering her mouth to his? She moved slowly, as if unsure of herself, and he was too riveted to be of much help. He was as alpha as the next guy—probably more so—but he wanted her to be the one to initiate anything between them. He'd been so damned unsure of where they stood lately, so this was an important, and much needed, step forward. She kept her eyes open as she made contact. The fact that they were staring at each other while kissing would be comical if it wasn't so hot.

He was tempted to take control, but he held off, waiting for her next move. When her tongue darted out to lick the seam of his lips, he could take it no more—and apparently, neither could Trouble. The dog let out a howl that was clearly meant to ruin the moment, but there was no way Gabe was going to let that happen. They needed to relocate, but he couldn't bear to let her go. As he shifted, attempting to get to his feet, she muttered crossly, "Can you work with me here, Randall?"

"I am, Angel." He grinned, nodding in Trouble's direction. "Unless you want a threesome, we need to move." She giggled when the dog whimpered again. "Wrap your legs around my waist," he instructed as he put his hands on her ass. Then he stepped around his dog and walked down the hallway. By the time he made it to his bedroom, he'd bounced them off the wall twice. In hindsight, sucking on her tongue while walking in the dark wasn't the best idea. *But it was fucking hot.* He set her on her feet before flipping on the bedside lamp.

She stepped back when he attempted to undress her. He almost panicked, thinking he'd surely die on the spot of blue balls if she was having a change of heart. *She's still here, that's a good sign.* "I—want to do it . . . for you. Is that okay?" It was too dim to see if her face was flushed, but he would bet anything it was flaming. Seriously, though, it was the sexiest thing she could have said to him in that moment.

"Angel, I'd love it." He took a seat on the edge of the bed, leaving his boxers on, even though his cock was damn near bursting out. *Let her set the pace.* She grasped the waistband of her bottoms, then seemed to think better of it, and started with the top instead. Hell, he didn't care either way as long as the end result was naked. The strip show wasn't exactly what he imagined, though. Her movements were so fast, he could hardly track them. He thought he caught a glimpse of a nipple before she bent to deal with the last of her clothing.

He was pretty sure pants were normally dropped that fast only in the event of an emergency. *Now that's what I call enthusiasm—or terror.* He hoped it was the former. He wondered fleetingly if she had been commando. That question was answered in the next moment when Trouble appeared from seemingly nowhere with something in his mouth. Gabe figured it was another ornament from the tree. Thank God they'd bought plastic ones.

It must have been one of her favorites, because Sara shrieked and began trying to wrestle it from his mouth. "You bad boy! Give those back. I swear, where did you come from?" She glared over at Gabe as she continued to struggle with her furry nemesis. "If you weren't going to shut the door, why did we come in here? We could be getting it on out there. That's on my bucket list, you know."

He was so distracted by her bouncing tits, and her ass, that he could hardly focus. The only things he picked up from the exchange were the words "getting it on" and "bucket list." "Um—Angel, just let him have the damned thing. I don't care if he eats it, as long as he goes away. They're all a dime a dozen anyway. His slobber might be an improvement."

He got to his feet, intent on getting rid of the little cock blocker. But she blocked his path, scowling at him with her hands on her hips. *Sweet Jesus, I want to suck those.* "Baby?" She called him an endearment, and he loved it, yet—the tone was all wrong. *Go ahead and apologize. You screwed up somehow. I swear that mutt is getting the cheap dog food for this.*

He struggled to make eye contact with the naked woman of his dreams. *I'm a mere guy, not a saint.*

"You do realize he has my panties, right? Granted, they might not be the most expensive ones a woman can buy, but

I assure you they cost more than the figure you named. And—having your dog eat them is *not* one of my kinks." *Oh shit.* Her serious expression slid away, and a giggle escaped. He found himself grinning as well. There was no possible way that either of them would ever forget their first time. Between her frantic disrobing, and Trouble turning into some canine panty pervert, it was one for the record books. If he got lucky after this, it would be a miracle. *Speaking of.* She was so close to him now that her nipples were nearly touching his chest. *One step forward and we have contact, folks.*

"I'll buy you more," he offered. "I say we call them collateral damage for now and think big picture. I'll shove him out into the hall and then we pick up where we left off."

He half expected her to change her mind, but she nodded in resignation. "Oh, all right. Hurry up, I'm getting cold." *Again, with the enthusiasm.* He wasn't offended by her sarcasm, though. In fact, he thought it was an indication of how comfortable they were together. They'd teased each other all the time when he was in Iraq. But there was an adjustment period in a situation such as theirs, and they had both struggled with it.

Gabe took Trouble to the kitchen and bribed Sara's panties away from him with some dog treats. He resisted the urge to gawk at them as he tossed the scrap of silk into the trash. He'd replace them with a new, slobber-free pair. He shook his head as he retraced his steps. *You can't make this shit up.*

His body was in overdrive when he returned to find Sara on her side, fast asleep. He couldn't believe it at first. *Re-*

ally? Clearly, he'd pissed off the man upstairs at some point. A snore filled the room—wait, was she choking? He inched closer, peering down at her. And she almost gave him a heart attack by rolling over onto her back and laughing. "Angel—are you stoned?"

"I couldn't resist." She chuckled. "This whole seduction I attempted to pull off has been a train wreck. I figured the only thing left was one of us passing out."

He shifted until his cock was an inch away from her face. "I can assure you that it won't be me, sweetheart. I've managed to stay hard through my dog eating your undies, and you being bored-to-sleep in my bed." He bent down until he was hanging over her. "But now I'm going to take the edge off by devouring you. Sound good?"

She inhaled audibly. "Yes—please." Now that he knew it was going to happen, he attempted to slow the momentum, wanting nothing more than to fully pleasure her. He took her lips, letting his tongue explore her mouth, while he nudged her legs apart and lowered his body onto hers. The thin material of his boxers was all that separated them as he ground against her. The friction was exquisite torture, but her moans told him that she was enjoying it. Between the endless kiss and the damp heat he could feel through his briefs, he was getting closer to the edge. *Time to shift the focus.* He stepped off the bed and put his hands on her hips, turning her until her legs were dangling over the side. "What are you doing?" she asked in a voice heavy with desire. *You haven't seen anything yet, Angel.* He didn't respond until he was on his knees between her spread legs. "Ohhh." He detected a hint of embarrassment, but she wouldn't be able to focus on that for long, he'd make sure of it.

The glow from the lamp highlighted every peak and valley of her gorgeous body. And for a moment, all he could do was stare. *Mine.* "Do you have any idea how beautiful and sexy you are, Angel?" She shook her head shyly, but he could tell that she was pleased. Wanting to keep her off-balance so she wouldn't have time to overthink, he slid one finger inside her, and she moaned as she tightened around it. He let her adjust to the invasion as, aided by her slick arousal, he glided in and out. He used his thumb to rub her clit, then added another finger. *So tight.* He lifted her hips and breathed in her heady scent. *Heaven. Peaches and cream.*

She knew what was coming; he could tell by the tensing of her thighs. He understood this was a very intimate thing for a woman, but if they had any idea how freaking much men loved their taste, they would learn to embrace the power. He lightly circled her sensitive nub, smiling when he heard her ragged groan. He savored her sweet nectar as he dipped his tongue into her before sucking her clit into his mouth. "Oh my God," she hissed as her body shook. She was so amazingly responsive, which only fueled his own desire. Soon, the combination of his fingers, along with his mouth, had her flying over the edge. He was surprised, and thrilled, to discover that his Angel was a screamer. He fucking loved knowing that she was possibly waking the neighbors. Not to mention the fact that poor Trouble was probably plotting a rescue attempt. "Jesus, Mary, and Joseph," she choked out. "That was better than the best vibrator I've ever owned."

Whoa. Vibrator? They would definitely revisit that topic at a later date. But right now, he'd rather come inside her than on her leg. And thanks to the naughty image she'd given him, there was little time to waste. So he lowered her and opened the nightstand drawer to find a condom. He removed his own briefs as fast as she'd dropped her pants earlier. Her eyes widened at his size as she returned to her previous place on the bed. He planned to try every single position he could think of with her, but tonight, he wanted to be face-to-face. He moved his body over hers once again, only this time there was nothing between them. He supported his weight on his elbows while he kissed her thoroughly. Then he licked and sucked her tight, rosy nipples until she was shuddering in reaction. He returned to her mouth as he slid his cock up and down her slick entrance before sinking an inch inside. "Angel, you feel so damned good," he groaned as he trailed kisses down the curve of her neck. Each time he pulled out, he eased back in a bit farther. As much as he longed to bury himself to the hilt, he waited, taking his cues from her.

When she locked her legs around his hips, he knew she was there. He growled, afraid of hurting her, yet so damned hard he was light headed from it. "Gabe, please!" The raw need in her voice was his undoing. With a muttered oath, he buried himself inside her.

They both froze, equally overcome by the wonder of being joined together. Her eyes were closed, and her face was contorted. "Sara, are you okay?" No matter how painful it was for him, he refused to move until she answered.

He ground his teeth together, striving for control. "Sara?" *Please.*

He jolted when her legs suddenly tightened, sending him impossibly deep. "I'm good, Gabe. I'm—just, it's the best thing I've ever felt, and I want to make sure I remember every moment."

So perfect. "Baby, this is only the beginning for us," he assured her. "Now let me love you the way you deserve." He had just enough restraint to make sure she was with him every step of the way. He plunged into her wet heat again and again, feeling a type of pleasure he had never known before. This woman—the one he had met against all the odds—was his perfect match in every way.

She hit her peak, crying out seconds before he reached his own climax. He managed to toss the condom in a nearby trashcan before he pulled her onto his chest and they lay spent. In her, he'd found not only Nirvana—but home. If he were an overly religious man, he'd even call it heaven. Tomorrow they would face a new set of challenges, as every couple does, but at that moment, there was only the here and now. And oddly enough, he had no desire to look beyond it. She made him want to savor every second, instead of constantly scanning ahead to avert a crisis.

When he heard a soft snore, he knew it was the real thing, unlike earlier. He yawned as well, allowing sleep to take him. There would be no need to dream of her tonight, because she was where she belonged at last—in his arms.

Chapter Twenty-Four

🐾 🐾

Sara cringed as she took a seat at the kitchen table. After making love with Gabe last night, and this morning, she was a bit sore. It had been so long since she'd had sex that it was kind of like being a virgin again. She'd read that women actually paid money to get back to that state, which she thought was insane.

She'd been grateful when Gabe left to help his neighbor, Mr. Jenkins, start his car. It gave her a chance to pop some Advil without him noticing. She could easily picture him bundling her up and taking her to the hospital when he caught her holding her crotch.

What seems to be the problem, Ms. Ryan?

Well, my boyfriend has a huge pecker, and he wrecked my va-jay-jay.

Ah, I see. Happens all the time.

Truthfully, she wouldn't care if he had broken it. Because the orgasms alone were worth the small discomfort she was feeling. The man was seriously talented between the sheets. He seemed to be more in tune with her body than she was. Last night had been raw and explosive. But when she'd woken this morning to find his cock pushing against her ass while he kissed her neck, she'd been breathless with anticipation. Heck, she hadn't given a thought to morning breath as he made her come three times before finally joining her. Then they'd taken a shower together, which was a little unsettling for her at first, but with Gabe gently washing every inch of her body, including her hair, she'd quickly lost her inhibitions and simply enjoyed the intimacy between them.

She couldn't quite believe how much everything had changed in the last few days. He'd gone from being stiffly cordial to sweet and loving. It was as if he'd known she was on the verge of giving up and going home. Chloe had even texted the next day to see when her flight would be arriving. Thank God he came to his senses in the nick of time. *Wait—what if he heard our phone conversation?* It was an unsettling thought. She didn't recall exactly what was said, but she had been upset and depressed over their situation.

As she sat there running through it in her head, a part of her wanted to ask him, but then again, why? What did it matter if it had resulted in them being together now in every sense? After all, she certainly hadn't shared with him what happened at the ball. Eventually she might. But there were a couple of reasons she wanted to keep it to herself. The main one being that he might take it as a sign she couldn't handle the demands of being a military wife. She knew he worried about that very thing. And second, he'd be pissed, and no doubt he would confront Melanie. And that, she didn't want. She was still angry and hurt over the entire incident, but she was also less emotional and more objective now. It was unfortunate, but it opened her eyes to a brutal truth. There were mean girls everywhere, and their ugliness was usually fueled by jealousy and bitterness. The other woman was clearly distressed over Gabe breaking things off. She'd undoubtedly planned to win him back when he returned home, but now, with her in the picture, it wasn't happening.

Sara, better than anyone, knew what it felt like to lose a man like that. She'd been devastated after he cut contact with her. Except that still didn't excuse the other woman's behavior. And even though she had always shied away from confrontation, she knew in this instance that if she didn't stand up for herself, Melanie would continue to escalate her ugliness. The fact that Gabe was off work for a few more weeks made confronting her tricky.

She was still pondering the dilemma when the front door opened and she heard Trouble's excited bark. He nearly slid sideways on the slick kitchen floor in his haste to reach her. "How's my favorite guy?" she cooed as she scratched him behind the ears.

"I never thought I'd envy my dog until I met you." Sara's head jerked up to see Gabe leaning against the wall as he smiled ruefully at her.

Holy crap, he's so sexy. I can't believe he's mine. "I love you," she blurted out. *No way, I didn't just say that.* So much for making it a special moment.

She put a hand over her face, inwardly wincing, before glancing at him once again. There was laughter there—but it was the softness in his eyes that had her riveted. He crossed to her, nudging his protesting dog to the side, and sat down. "I don't know, Angel, I found that to be incredibly special."

She blinked, wondering how he knew—"Crap, I said all of that out loud, didn't I?"

"Yep." He grinned before putting a hand on her thigh. "And do you seriously imagine I give a damn when or how you speak the words? Baby, you could have screamed them out in the middle of a wet T-shirt contest, while showcasing your stripper moves, and it would still be the second-best moment of my life."

Sara put her arms loosely around his broad shoulders, absolutely enchanted by this handsome man. The fact that she wasn't in the least concerned by his ranking of her declaration was further proof of how much she not only trusted him but understood his humor. *What's the punch line, baby? I know there is one.* "Wow, you're a hard sell." She faked disinterest, even adding a yawn.

He shrugged, pulling her off the chair and into his lap. He dropped a kiss onto her upturned nose, then her forehead. "It would be rather impossible to have reached this point without first finding each other. Your envelope didn't contain just a card, Angel, it was also an introduction to the love of my life—and my future." *How? What did I ever do to deserve this—this kind of love from such an amazing man?* She wasn't aware that she was crying until he used his thumbs to wipe the moisture away. "I love you, Sara Ryan." He moved one of her hands until it was resting over the steady beat of his heart. "There will be times that I'll say the wrong thing, drive you nuts, and generally be a pain in the ass. I'm stubborn, overly serious, and according to Jason, completely anal." When her lips twitched, he rolled his eyes. "Yeah, I wish he'd use a different word, even if it is basically true. My point is, on the days you're ready to throw in the towel, remember this: No one has ever, or will ever, love, appreciate, and cherish you the way that I . . ." His voice trailed off when Trouble wedged his head between them. "Um, the way *we* do. In case you've missed his . . . subtle hints, Trouble and I are very much a package deal."

Normally she would have fallen back on sarcasm to deal with this emotional moment, but it simply wasn't there. Her heart was too full to pretend she was anything other than a pile of mush. "I wouldn't have it any other way, Gabe. I'm so blessed to belong to the Randall boys." She kissed his lips while patting the dog's head. "And we all have our difficult days. So when we're at our worst, we'll simply love each other through it."

"I like that, baby." He smiled down at her. "You're getting the bad end of this bargain. There are two of us to misbehave. And from what I've seen, you mostly live up to your nickname."

Her humor picked that moment to make a reappearance.

She shifted until her lips were at his ear before whispering, "Think PMS, honey."

"Oh shit, please have mercy." When she lifted a brow, he added, "Do it for your country. I'm a soldier, you know."

As they continued to tease each other, she couldn't help thinking that even without the words of love, this would be one of those moments that she would remember for the rest of her life. But then again—she was finding that most days with this man were too memorable to ever forget.

Sara couldn't believe it when the opportunity to confront not only Melanie but possibly some of her minions as well came about that very night. Gabe was surprised at her enthusiasm when Jason called to invite them to meet some of the soldiers at Maxi's. She knew Gabe mostly avoided those types of informal events, and he likely wasn't that keen on this one either. Outside the fact that she hoped Melanie would be there, she also felt it was important that he continue building upon the bond he'd formed with the other soldiers while deployed.

They were both dressed casually in jeans and boots. Instead of trying to hide her body for fear of drawing attention to herself, she had chosen a green sweater that hugged her curves in all the right places. Gabe certainly appreciated it. So much so, in fact, that they were fifteen minutes late arriving at Maxi's. They hadn't made love, but her man was well satisfied ahead of dinner. Being secure in Gabe's feelings for her gave Sara a type of freedom she'd never thought possible. She was surprised to find that she was a far more sexual person than she'd imagined. Of course, when your boyfriend looked like Gabe, dropping to your knees to pleasure him with your mouth wasn't exactly a hardship. She'd never been so glad that Trouble was already in his kennel. Otherwise, her first attempt would have likely been a disaster, rather than a fervent success.

Gabe took her hand as they walked through the parking lot to the restaurant. "Still got time to back out," he teased as he helped her over a slick spot on the pavement.

"Aw, we'll have fun, I promise."

He stopped and kissed her soundly. By the time he pulled back, she was beginning to reconsider. "What a shock," said a resigned voice behind them. They both swiveled to see Jason a few feet away. She was surprised to see him take a draw off a cigarette before putting it out beneath the bottom of his shoe. "Should have figured if you actually showed up, you'd spend most of the evening sucking face." He rubbed his hands over his shoulders before adding, "I believe I'd do it in the stockroom, though, since it's damn well freezing out here."

Sara giggled as Gabe flipped him off. Then they did the universal bro hug, which was actually rather touching. Gabe might be reserved around the other guys, but there was a relaxed closeness between these two. "She made me come," he admitted to the other man. "I'd rather be home with my woman and my dog."

"That's the saddest thing I've ever heard," Jason mocked jokingly. "Let's go inside. I'm terrified I won't die of hypothermia, and I'll be forced to watch you two braid each other's hair and talk about your feelings."

Sara laughed at the absurd notion that a macho guy such as Gabe would ever be anything but ultra-manly. She linked one arm through Gabe's and the other through Jason's. "Don't be sad, cupcake—we'll find you a woman. I have a cousin who might be perfect for you."

"She better be homely, or I'm not interested. I'm talking plain times about fifty, Ellie."

Ellie? "You realize her name is Sara, right?" Gabe asked dryly.

"Um—yeah," Jason muttered as he reached out to open the door. "She's one of us now, though, so she gets a nickname."

Sara was beyond touched at his acceptance. Even though he was matter-of-fact about it, she sensed it was a high honor from him. "So, why Ellie?" she asked curiously. It seemed so random to her.

"Ellie Mae Clampett," they both said at once. "I'm surprised you didn't come up with it first, dude," Jason said. "With that accent, it's perfect."

"Hey, what's wrong with my voice?" she asked in mock anger.

"Absolutely nothing," Jason assured her. "There isn't a man alive who doesn't get weak in the knees over a girl with a twang."

"I knew we should have stayed home," Gabe grumbled. "I'd sleep better at night if you'd stop hitting on my girl-friend."

"Better take her off the market, then," Jason goaded before turning to greet the rest of their battalion at the back table. "Hey, does everyone remember Major Randall?" It was obviously a shared joke, as they all laughed and called out greetings. Apparently Gabe hadn't been kidding about not attending these things. Then all eyes were on her as Jason pulled her forward. "And this is the lovely Sara, Gabe's much better half. I'll go ahead and warn you, they're big fans of PDA." Gabe punched him in the shoulder while she simply shrugged and grinned. *It's true, we are.*

Most of the tables had been pushed together to accommodate the large group, so it wasn't until they were seated that she noticed Melanie at the opposite end. When the other woman met her gaze, Sara forced out a friendly smile; after all, she had no clue that Sara had overheard them that night. She could tell by the tightening of Gabe's jaw that he saw her as well. It wasn't difficult to understand why Melanie was bitter. If the man with his arm around her chair was Jared, then she'd taken a big step down. *No—more like a free fall.* He was balding and out of shape, with an obnoxious laugh that grated on Sara's nerves. Something about her brittle grin told Sara that Melanie was having a tough time in her quest to be an officer's wife. She couldn't help pitying her. *Is it really worth it?*

After dinner, everyone moved over to the pool tables. Sara had never played before, but she loved how Gabe put his arms around her to help line up the shot. When she made it, he hugged her to him, before dropping a kiss onto her forehead. *That cologne. Dear God, it's like sex in a bottle.* "Having fun?" he asked as he smiled down at her.

Even though he joked around with the other soldiers, he always made a point to keep her near. As if not wanting to be apart, which she kinda loved.

She rubbed his back as she rested her head against him. "Yeah, I am. How about you?"

He nodded, then leaned forward briefly to answer a question from Martinez. "Yeah, Angel, it's been good. But mainly because you're here. One of the reasons I love Alaska so much is the peace and quiet I have at the cabin. And even though I realize it's necessary to socialize at times, I'd always rather it be me, you, and Trouble."

"Me too," she murmured. "I love you, Gabe." *Wow, that one even surprised me.*

His eyes went liquid soft. "I love you too, Angel. Let's get out of here."

She had completely lost sight of her mission. Gabe had stepped away to collect their coats when she saw Melanie going toward the restroom. *Game time.* She almost chickened out. Thinking about what she'd do when she saw her was one thing, but actually confronting the other woman was quite another. Yet she knew that if she didn't have the courage to say something tonight, she never would. She was not a mean person, but she also couldn't be the woman that Gabe deserved if she let others disrespect not only him but her. *I can do this.* She was so focused on her goal that she didn't notice Jason until he touched her arm. "Oh hey, I didn't see you. We're getting ready to leave. Gabe is getting our things." *Shit, I'm rambling.*

He looked from her to the nearby restroom, then back again. "I see," he finally said. He rubbed a hand over his neck as if debating his next words. "I know something happened with her at the ball. I was talking to a few people and saw her, and the others, go the bathroom not long after you. And they came back out first."

"Did you tell Gabe?" she asked, hoping he hadn't. She needed to handle this on her own.

He shook his head. "No, I didn't. Probably should have, but it wasn't my place. I think you've already figured out that you have to be able to handle yourself among this crowd. This isn't a place for the weak or faint of heart. Not to say you need to be a bitch like some of those ladies are, but don't take any shit either. It's no different than anything else—if you stand up for yourself, they'll move on to an easier mark." The serious tone was gone as he smirked down at her. "Along with the ever-popular 'Don't do anything stupid,' I'll also add, 'Never be a victim.'" She saw Gabe looking around for her at the same time Jason did. "I'll tell him you're in the bathroom. Better be quick or he'll probably break the damn door down." He gave her a wink and added, "Go get 'em, Ellie Mae."

The fist bump she gave him was a little shaky, but he didn't comment on it. She quickly crossed the remaining space and opened the door. She stopped short as she saw Melanie and the blonde she had been sitting near standing in front of the mirror. She recognized the blonde's high-pitched voice as she laughed over something Melanie said.

They both looked over at her in surprise when she stepped up next to them. She pretended to smooth her hair as she said pleasantly, "We need to stop meeting like this."

The blonde rolled her eyes and smirked at Melanie, who said, "Sara, how lovely to see you again. Mindy, have you met Gabe's little . . . friend?"

Instead of being offended, she wanted to thank Melanie for her condescending words and tone. Because they gave her the courage to do what needed to be done. She turned, putting her back against the counter and crossing her arms over her chest. "Actually, *Mindy*, I'm Gabe's girlfriend. Although he just calls me his Angel." They both appeared wary now, which proved they had some self-preservation instincts, if not intelligence. "I hate that the rest of the gang isn't here, but since you two are, I think we should get a few things straight."

"Really, *Sara*, what is this little scene all about?" Melanie asked snidely, but it was hard to miss the look of unease in her eyes.

"Well, *Melanie*, I just happened to hear everything you said about me and Gabe in the restroom at the ball."

"Oh shit." Mindy grimaced. Melanie stood her ground, but she had visibly paled.

I've got this. "Let me assure you that I don't give a damn what anyone here thinks of my weight, or my clothing. Because guess what? I'm fit, healthy—and I have a man who loves me *and* my curves. Oh, and that 'mutt' is a Randall boy—and I belong to them, just as they belong to me." Mindy's eyes were bugging out of her head by that point, but it was Melanie who held Sara's focus. She stepped closer until they stood toe to toe. *She's afraid.* "He dumped you, Mel, get over it. A word of advice, though—find someone who makes you happy . . . because obviously Jared doesn't. Otherwise, you wouldn't feel the need to tear others down, just to raise yourself up." It was probably her imagination, but Melanie appeared almost ashamed. She hoped that some of what she'd said had gotten through to her.

She had just opened the door when someone cleared her throat. "Er—Sara. I—wanted to apologize for . . . everything. Major Randall is Matt's boss, and I should have never . . ."

Sara stared at Mindy, not really knowing whether she was sincere in her apology. Truthfully, she didn't care. "You're right, you shouldn't have." With those final words, she walked away, and she never looked back. Only Gabe and Trouble mattered. *I am theirs, and they are mine.*

They made love when they got home, and unlike the other times they'd slept together, this time they took things achingly slowly. Gabe gave the impression he was intent on kissing every inch of her body before sliding inside her. She had fallen asleep in his arms once again, and wondered how she'd ever slept without him holding her

She woke with a start. She had dreamed of Kaylee. The little girl had asked her over and over why she didn't love her anymore. When Sara tried to assure her that she did, Kaylee said, "If you loved me, you wouldn't have left." She was so shaken, there was no way she would be able to relax again anytime soon. So she eased slowly out from beneath

Gabe's arm and tiptoed down the hallway to the kitchen. Even though his kennel was rarely locked at night, Trouble still chose to sleep in it most of the time. But when he saw her, he jumped up and followed her to the living room. She curled up on the couch, and he settled next to her, with his head in her lap. She knew he sensed her sadness and was offering her comfort the only way he knew how.

Kaylee. She missed her niece so much. For days she had been texting Chris, and her mother, but neither of them responded. She loved Gabe deeply, yet wondered what kind of person she was if her happiness was at the expense of others. *Am I any better than Melanie?* Even though before she left she'd tried to explain to Kaylee why she needed to go away for a while, she knew the little girl was too young to understand her absence. Heck, she had been confused herself. And she could only imagine the things Nicole had possibly been filling her head with. She loved her family, and she didn't want to lose any of them. But Kaylee—she was the child of her heart. It might not be every day, but she couldn't fathom a world where they weren't in each other's lives on a regular basis.

"Angel—what's wrong?" She hadn't heard him come into the room, and neither had Trouble. Gabe was very much like a ghost when he wanted to be. No doubt from years of training in the military.

She wiped her hands across her eyes as she looked up at him. "I had a bad dream."

He eased down beside her before picking her up and settling her in his arms. "Tell me about it."

And more tears fell as she did. "I don't know what to do. Chloe is the only one I have any contact with. I know they're physically okay, but that's it. I . . . miss Kaylee so badly. We spent almost every moment together for years. Being here with you is the best thing that's ever happened to me. But—I feel like a piece of me is missing."

"Oh, baby," he murmured as he held her close, rocking her gently. "I know you've been trying to reach them. I can see the hurt in your eyes every time you check your phone and there's no message. And I know how you feel about that little girl. You always glow every time you speak of her. Even when things were strained between us, I wondered when this would happen."

"But, Gabe, I love—"

"Angel, I know you love me," he interrupted her gently. "And just because you do doesn't mean you care for her any less. But we've got to figure out how to bridge the two parts of your life. I'd never ask you to completely give up the rest of your life for me. Just—let me think about it. I'm still on leave for another few weeks, so maybe we should fly to North Carolina and work this out in person."

She sat up quickly, hardly able to believe what he was suggesting. "Really? You'd go with me?"

When Trouble whined, Gabe shook his head. "Package deal, remember? We'll go."

"I love you." She kissed him, then yawned, suddenly feeling drained. *Kaylee.* With Gabe's arm around her, they walked back to his bedroom, and she easily drifted off to sleep while the Randall boys watched over her.

Chapter Twenty-Five

🐾 🐾

The situation with Sara and her family weighed heavily on Gabe's mind as he checked some work e-mails. He was past due for his post-deployment physical, so he'd reluctantly headed to the base earlier to take care of it. Normally he would have stayed the rest of the day, because really, other than Trouble, there had been no reason to rush home. But everything was different now. He had a life outside the military, one that he loved more with every passing day.

Yet even if Sara stayed with him in Alaska, she would eventually come to resent him for taking her away from her family in North Carolina. He knew he loved her before she came to Alaska, but truthfully, in his wildest dreams, he hadn't thought they'd mesh together so perfectly. He not only loved her—he needed her. And that was a first.

He had suggested taking her home for a visit soon, but

he'd never believed in putting off until tomorrow what could be done today. The first logical step in doing that was calling her brother. He might be avoiding his sister, but Gabe wouldn't be so easily ignored. He was betting on the other man being curious enough to answer an unknown number. Especially when it rang his phone in five-minute intervals. *Just try me.*

It took exactly eight attempts before Chris Ryan gave in. "Ryan."

Despite being generally pissed off at what the other man was putting his sister through, Gabe found himself grinning at the irritated tone in his voice. He'd likely sound the same if he were on the receiving end. "This is Gabe Randall, your sister's—"

"I know who you are," he snapped. "What I don't know is why you're calling me."

Gabe leaned back in his chair, getting comfortable. This was clearly going to be an unpleasant conversation. "You left me no choice when you refused to extend Sara the courtesy of a response."

Chris laughed, but there wasn't an ounce of humor there. "I'm not sure why this is any of your business, but I'm simply following the example she set by taking off on us. Much of which I blame you for."

Gabe shrugged, fully in agreement with the last part. "Fair enough. Giving her that ultimatum in North Carolina wasn't my finest hour. I should have handled it differently. But why punish her for my transgressions?"

He heard a long sigh on the other end of the line. When

Chris spoke again, his tone was more resigned than angry. "Because she's too old to act so damned recklessly. And you—I've checked around. You're very well known and respected in the military. Likely to make lieutenant colonel in another year. Not the type of soldier to fill a woman's head with a bunch of lies and lure her away from everyone she knows. I—I just don't get it, man. What's your endgame here?"

"I love your sister," Gabe said bluntly. He didn't like what Chris's behavior was doing to Sara, but he understood his frustration . . . and mistrust. It was the very reason he'd gone to her first, in hopes of setting their minds at ease. "In your position, I would question my intentions as well. Which is why I showed up at your place originally. Unfortunately, that didn't go as planned. I thought I'd been played. I was shocked when Sara came here. I didn't think I'd see or speak to her again."

"You expect me to believe you'd have let her go that easily after claiming to love her?"

"Knowing what I do now, absolutely not. But it wasn't a situation I ever dreamed I'd find myself in, hence the uncertainty and mishandling."

Chris was quiet for a long moment before asking, "What do you want from me?"

It wasn't in his nature to overexplain his feelings, but he sensed his usual approach would only antagonize the other man. Sara needed her family, and Gabe wanted to give them back to her. "I found her on the couch last night crying. She had a dream about Kaylee. Your daughter thought she left because Sara didn't love her." He paused at Chris's harsh intake of breath. "I've watched her check that damned phone of hers a dozen times a day, and I've seen the sadness when there's nothing from you or her mother. When we first began talking, it didn't take me long to see how family oriented she is. Her face would light up each and every time she spoke of her niece."

"Then why did she take off like that?" Chris snapped in frustration. "Do you have any idea what kind of upheaval it's caused? I have a daughter who is so upset, she's not sure who her mother is anymore. And a wife that tells me constantly what a horrible person my sister is. Oh, and then there's my mother, who complains constantly about picking Kaylee up from school yet gets angry when I mention hiring someone to do it. Since things seem so much better in Alaska, I'm about ready to pack my fucking bags and move in with you as well."

The pieces were all falling into place for Gabe now. Even though some of what Chris said didn't make sense, he'd picked up on enough to figure out the main issue. "So . . . you're not taking Sara's calls because of your wife. It's a damned if you do, damned if you don't thing."

"Exactly. I'm not blind. I know my wife lets her guilt at being a working mother cloud her judgment where Sara is concerned. Nicole loves Kaylee, but she lacks the maternal instincts that my sister has. She thinks Kaylee should be a little adult, like her friend's unusual child."

Gabe really wanted to tell him to grow a pair, but being caught in such emotional chaos had to be tough. He wondered why Sara had stayed with them for so long, with her sister-in-law clearly acting like a bitch to her. *For Kaylee.* Sara was so selfless. The environment she had lived in for the last three years had been toxic for *her* soul. Yet she'd stayed so that that little girl knew she was loved unconditionally. If Sara's own brother and mother hadn't stuck up for her, hadn't appreciated her, how on earth was she still so wonderful? How had she remained so incredible through that? It's time her brother took on the role of a *brother.* Time he showed his sister how much he valued her. "I realize you're in a difficult position, but it's not fair that Sara gets shut out of Kaylee's life because your wife can't accept all that she has done for all of you."

Chris ignored his criticism of his wife. Instead he said, "I knew the day you showed up from out of nowhere that she would leave. She'd been different for a while, but I couldn't put my finger on it. Then I found out she was talking to some guy, but she wasn't dating, so it didn't seem like a big deal. Everything clicked, though, when I saw her reaction to you. I told Nicole that night I was worried about it, and she brushed it aside. But I—just knew. Hell, I was the only one who wasn't surprised when it happened. I'm sure this sounds absurd, but what are your intentions where she's concerned?"

"I'm going to marry her," Gabe replied without hesitation.

"Isn't that a little fast?" Chris asked skeptically. "She's been there for less than two weeks."

"We've talked every day for nearly eight months. We

know each other better than a lot of people who've been married for years." *Better than you and your wife, I bet.* The animosity was gone as they continued to converse. He was surprised to see he'd been on the phone for over an hour. Other than Sara, this was a record. He was on the verge of ending the call when a sudden thought occurred to him. It was a long shot, and unlikely to work, but it was worth the effort. Either way, he felt certain that something could be resolved soon. Now that he understood the real problem, he wouldn't stop until he found a solution. He didn't know if it was the military way, but it most certainly was the Randall way.

Chapter Twenty-Six

☙ ❧

"Merry Christmas, Angel," Gabe murmured as he slid inside her. With what little rational thought she could manage, she marveled at how romantic her life had become. Their Christmas Eve had been spent on the couch making out. After a while, though, she had begun to think he was either teasing or torturing her. When he jumped to his feet a few moments before midnight and carried her to the bedroom, she was baffled by his sudden urgency.

"Were you waiting until—?" She groaned, feeling dangerously close to orgasm after being on the edge for so long.

"Yeah," he hissed, sounding just as strained. "Should have kept our clothes on longer," he added as he put a hand under her ass to pull her hips closer. "I love you, Angel."

"Me too," she whimpered, so lost in the pleasure wracking her body that she could focus on little else.

Or at least that's what she thought . . . until Gabe brought her abruptly back to the present. "Dasher, Dancer, Prancer, Vixen, Comet, Cupid, Donner—shit, what's the other one's name?"

What the . . . ? Could extreme horniness cause delusions? He froze as his body shuddered. Then for the first time, he came before her. Had she not been distracted by his ramblings, they would have likely peaked together. He dropped his face into the curve of her neck before muttering wryly, "Blitzen—you little bastard."

She couldn't help smiling, even though she had no clue why he felt the need to list all of Santa's reindeers in the middle of doing her. She ran a soothing hand over his back as she asked, "Something you want to tell me, baby?"

He laughed as he got up to dispose of the condom, and then returned to pull her onto his chest. Pressing a kiss to her forehead, he said, "I knew I was going to go quickly after the long buildup. So I went with something festive rather than baseball statistics. But I couldn't remember the name of the last one in time."

"Gabe," she said, giggling, "you're so flipping adorable."

"So it begins," he grumbled. "I'm no longer your 'sex God.' I fail to bring it home once and I'm demoted to 'adorable.' Which, I believe, is how you refer to Trouble."

She bit her tongue, trying to keep a straight face yet finding it nearly impossible. "You're totally smoking hot, baby. I spend most of my time objectifying you."

"Go on," he said, sounding slightly mollified. *I can't help it, he is adorable.*

She wiggled against his masculine frame, enjoying the hiss he emitted. "And . . . you have the biggest candy cane I've ever seen. I've watched porn for years, and have never seen one that compares."

"You watch skin flicks?" *Wow, someone likes that—a lot. He's baccckkk!*

"Well, sure," she replied nonchalantly. "Doesn't everyone? How else are you going to fill your shopping basket?"

"Um—come again? You've got to stay focused during dirty talk, Angel."

"I am. Chloe and I refer to *that* as going to Walmart. It's more kid friendly than saying 'masturbate.' We've gotten pretty creative with it. A quickie is the express aisle, and a long session is browsing. When you're interrupted, the item is out of stock. Oh . . . and when you don't come, it's the dreaded rain check."

"That's a fate worse than adorable. I refuse to go down as a postponed checkout." She squealed in surprise as he surged up, taking her with him. "You've been upgraded to home delivery, Angel. Get ready to sign for the package."

And because she was such a good customer, he included the installation at no charge.

Sara was relentless in her quest for him to open his Christmas present from her. He'd spent the entire morning making one excuse after another, but she would not be dissuaded. He wasn't sure what could possibly be in the small box she was holding, but she was literally bouncing on her feet in excitement. *Maybe she's proposing?* If she dropped down to one knee at that point, he wouldn't be surprised. And, of course, Trouble was even worse than her. He seemed to suspect that some of the packages were for him, because every time he was left unsupervised, he pulled one out and tried to tear off the wrapping paper.

He'd sent his family gift cards for Christmas since he wouldn't be seeing them until the spring. His father hated crowds and wouldn't consider traveling anywhere around the holidays. And after being deployed for so long, Gabe had no desire to leave Alaska for a while. Luckily, his family knew him well enough not to take offense. They'd long ago learned to live with his absences.

He might have taken care of his own shopping, but Sara had wanted to go to the mall. She insisted that they part ways and meet back up a few hours later. Which was fine with him, since he wanted to get a few surprises of his own. She had mentioned several times that their trip to North Carolina was the best gift he could possibly give her, and she insisted that he not get anything else. He might be new to this relationship stuff, but he knew it was always better to do too much than to risk doing too little. After all, they would never have another first Christmas again. He wanted it to be something she'd always remember, and he was well on his way to achieving that goal. *Come on, Jason.*

Shit. His pocket was vibrating. He needed to get rid of her for a few minutes . . . but how? He didn't have to feign panic, since it was genuine. He leaned down to squint at the pile under the tree, then back at Trouble. "Damn, Angel, we're missing one. I thought I found them all earlier, but we're definitely short." The fact that he sounded panicky was clearly unnerving to her, since he was normally so calm.

She put a hand on his arm, squeezing it gently. "It'll be fine, babe. Where did you find the others?"

In the woods? That would be pushing it. "Oh—um, several different places. One was under our bed, and another in the storage closet . . . and the last one was in my dresser drawer."

She blinked once, then again, as if processing his words. "How did the dog manage to get into those last two places? He doesn't have hands."

"I don't know," he said shrilly, "he's not a normal dog." *Sorry, buddy, you've gotta take one for Team Randall.*

"Okay, okay, I'll handle everything." She led him to the couch and pushed him down onto it. "Just relax, I promise I'll find it." She darted one last puzzled look in his direction before walking down the hall with their falsely accused dog at her heels.

When she was out of sight, he jerked his phone out and read the text:

Eta 5

And that was almost four minutes ago. It barely registered before he heard a vehicle. Sara had been watching the Christmas parade on television earlier, so he quickly grabbed the remote and turned the volume up, hoping to block out any other sounds. He reached the door just as Jason stepped onto the porch. Gabe put a finger to his lips as he motioned him inside. They were tiptoeing to the kitchen when Sara appeared out of nowhere. "Baby, Trouble just opened the hand soap and licked some of it. At least his poop will smell like apples for a few—"

She was looking down at the dog, and hadn't yet noticed anything amiss, until . . .

"Sarie!"

Her head shot up as a startled gasp escaped her lips. Kaylee flew out from behind her father and launched herself at Sara. Gabe knew she was in shock. Her face had gone deathly pale and her entire body was shaking. "Kaylee," she whispered as she dropped heavily to her knees to pull the little girl into her arms.

Gabe couldn't make out much of what she was saying, but Kaylee was talking nonstop while tears ran unchecked down Sara's face. Hell, he wasn't far from bursting into sobs himself. He felt a hand on his shoulder as Jason stepped forward. "Shit, that's hard to see," he mused in a voice devoid of the usual sarcasm.

He turned away to give them some privacy, and got his first real look at her family. He recognized Chris from their brief, awkward meeting in North Carolina. Next to him was a very thin woman with long, sandy hair, and what he would bet was designer wear marketed for the ski-resort crowd. Then there was Sara's mother. He'd seen a few pictures of her, but he was still surprised at how young she appeared. *And ill at ease.* Gabe extended a hand to Chris, who seemed relieved at the tension-breaking gesture. "Good to see you again. Trip go all right?"

"It was great, we really appreciate it. This area is beautiful. Kaylee was about to lose her mind when she saw all the snow."

"We can take her out later if she wants. Trouble will be thrilled to have someone else to chase." Gabe smiled as the dog in question stood off to the side, clearly wary of the new arrivals. *Makes two of us.*

He knew it was petty, but instead of greeting Nicole next, he moved on to Sara's mother. He would attempt to be passably polite for Sara's sake, but no one would disrespect his woman in their house—or anywhere else for that matter. "Mrs. Ryan, I'm Gabe Randall. It's nice to meet you."

She glanced from him to her daughter and niece, then back again. That's when he noticed the moisture in her eyes and the telltale trembling of her mouth. He knew that Sara had essentially taken care of her mother after her father died, in much the same way she had Kaylee. If he didn't miss his guess, she was devastated without her. "She's . . . happy here," Mrs. Ryan mused quietly. He thought a part of her was relieved to find her doing well, while another part was hurting. *Abandoned.* It wasn't logical, but emotions rarely were.

When he could put it off no longer, he moved to make the final greeting. The younger woman studied him curiously, as if searching for some explanation of his appearance in their lives. He was taken off guard when she hugged him briefly. Polite or not, he didn't return the embrace. Luckily, it was the equivalent of an air kiss, and over before it started. "Thank you for having us. It's all Kaylee has talked about since you made the arrangements."

He inclined his head in acknowledgment of her statement. "I appreciate everyone altering their holiday plans to make the long trip here."

Chris cleared his throat before speaking. "We're family. We don't spend Christmas apart. If that means driving down the street or catching a plane, that's what we'll do."

Gabe was glad to hear him offering support for Sara. He wondered when, and if, the other two would get on board as well. Since hiding was no longer necessary, he motioned everyone toward the living room. Jason pulled him aside to say good-bye, no doubt ready to leave the tense environment. He walked him to the door, then returned to find only Nicole and Chris on the couch. He looked around, thinking Mrs. Ryan might have gone to the restroom. But instead, she was standing inches away from Sara and Kaylee, much like a child herself, wanting desperately to join in but not knowing how.

"She's had a rough time with Sara gone," Nicole murmured. "We all have."

Have you? Really? Or is this bullshit? He wasn't a man who trusted easily, and this woman had given him no reason to believe her about-face. Yet there was something about the way Chris was interacting silently with his wife that made him pause and reconsider. *Maybe he's finally grown a pair after all.*

The rest of the day was an awkward blur, although things were slowly beginning to thaw between the Ryans. Chris, Sara, and Kaylee found their stride fairly quickly, but it was a work in progress with the others. Mrs. Ryan seemed to hover on the perimeter of a room most of the time. Clearly wanting to be with her daughter, yet not knowing how to deal with a reunion that would inevitably end in another good-bye. The biggest surprise was Nicole. Kaylee blurted out enough for him to gather that Chris had indeed stepped up to the plate, and "a lot of yelling" had occurred as a result.

Gabe, Sara, and her family took Kaylee outside to play in the snow for as long as they could withstand the cold temperature. Trouble was like an exuberant puppy as they chased each other through the beautiful Alaskan snow. When they came back inside, everyone changed before meeting up in the kitchen. Gabe had picked up a turkey from Maxi's that morning, with enough side dishes to easily feed everyone. Maxi always sent too much food, so Sara hadn't questioned it.

Sara leaned over and kissed him softly when he took the seat next to her. Then she smiled shyly at her family. *She's finally at peace.* Even if things weren't perfect, she was centered again. And if he thought her beautiful before, it was nothing compared to now. She was aglow with happiness, and he was humbled to know that a part of that was because of him. *God, I don't deserve her, but I'll never stop trying to be worthy of the gift you've given me.*

It had gone so quiet, it was almost eerie. That's when it hit him. He'd given voice to his thoughts, as she often did. And—she was crying again, but instinctively he knew these tears were the good kind. Strangely enough, it was Mrs. Ryan who broke the silence. She got to her feet and clasped her hands together in front of her. "I don't think any of us have deserved Sara for a long time, Gabe, but she's loved us anyway. I . . . spent the last few weeks being mad at my daughter and . . . blaming you for taking her away from us. But—today I looked at her, and I realized something." She swallowed heavily as she fully faced Sara. "She never belonged to us. She stayed for so long because we needed her. And selfishly, we took advantage of that. She's been a substitute husband, father, and mother." There wasn't a dry eye at the table by this point, including his own. "Now it's time for us to offer you the same support, my beautiful girl." And one by one, they each chimed in:

"As a mother."

"As a brother."

"As a sister."

"As a Sarie," Kaylee added last, bringing some much-needed comic relief. Gabe was working up the nerve to ask Sara a very important question when Kaylee moved to stand next to him. He turned to give her his attention, never expecting to be brought almost to tears by her words.

"I didn't like you, Mr. Gabe, because my mommy kept telling me that Sarie was a shellfish woman. My Sarie isn't a shellfish, but I didn't tell Mommy that. My Sarie is an angel." He heard Nicole's surprised gasp, but didn't bother looking up to see her reaction. *This girl. Now I completely get why Sara couldn't leave.* "But I like you now, Mr. Gabe, because you have a doggie. I want to get a doggie one day. You should share my Sarie, though. She teached me that when I was a little girl." She looked so serious. So utterly adorable. He could see how much love Sara had brought into this little girl's heart.

"I tell you what, Kaylee. Let's make a deal."

Her eyes lit up, and the excitement bubbling out of her was infectious. It made Gabe completely understand why Sara's face had been radiant and carefree when she was playing with Kaylee in that first photo she sent.

"If it's okay with your daddy, how about we set up Skype or FaceTime on an iPad so you and your Sarie can still talk each day? She has tried to read books to Trouble, and he isn't as good a listener as Sara has told me you are. I think she misses reading books to you. What do you think?" Kaylee tossed her arms around his neck and hugged him before running away to get her father's approval on the plan.

As much as he enjoyed the exchange with Kaylee, he hadn't yet taken his turn, and everyone but Sara seemed to understand that. This wasn't the way he expected to do it, but there had never been a more perfect time. So, he slipped from his chair and onto one knee next to his Angel—phrasing his as a question, rather than a statement, "As a wife?"

Thankfully, she didn't keep him in suspense for long. Less than two seconds later, she was in his lap as she cried, "Yes, yes, yes!"

But it was the furry Randall, who was completely smitten with the woman in their lives, that added, "Woof, woof, woof."

As he hugged his new little family close, Gabe thought, *I couldn't have said it better myself, buddy.*

Epilogue

🐾 🐾

Sara and Gabe married on Easter of the next year. Her immediate family along with her aunt and Chloe flew to Alaska for the small ceremony in the chapel on the base. Neither of them wanted a big formal wedding. They'd been married in their hearts for so long that making it official was merely a formality.

She still found it hard to believe that she'd gotten everything she'd ever wanted—and more. Not only did she have a husband who never went a day without telling her how much he loved her, but she had a family who was trying to be there for her in every way possible. Their dynamic had been so one sided for such a long time—and it wasn't a change that happened completely overnight, but it was better than she could have imagined. And last but certainly not least, she had an adorable dog who showered her with slobbery affection so often, she was in need of a bib. But those canine cuddles melted her heart. *God, I love my Randall boys.*

They'd been married about six months when they had "the talk." Gabe knew she loved children, so having a baby was a conversation they'd touched on several times. That time, though, Gabe surprised her with his detailed vision for their future. "Angel, I've thought about what scenario makes the most sense for us at this point in our lives. I know you want to start a family, and even though we're not exactly ancient, I realize waiting for years would put you at a higher risk for complications. Which is not something I'd consider doing if there were other options." He took her hand, lacing their fingers together before saying, "It's taken a while, but I've come up with a workable plan. I—I'm sorry for springing it on you like this, but I didn't want to get your hopes up and then have it not be possible after all."

If not for the hint of excitement she could detect beneath his serious demeanor, she would be nervous. "What is it, baby? You know I hate being kept in suspense."

"I do know that." He smirked affectionately. "I'll be due to change stations in another year. I'm allowed to list my preferences in order and hope for the best. Sometimes that works out, and other times it doesn't. But in my particular field of expertise, I've made some important connections. And that has paid off now." *Geez, spit it out already.* She was on pins and needles, while he appeared to be on some verbal Sunday stroll. Finally, he took pity on her and said, "I've been given early approval for a move to Fort Bragg— in North Carolina."

She gawked at him, hardly able to believe what she was hearing. She was thrilled at the prospect of going closer to home, yet she had also grown to love Alaska. "So . . . we just pack up for good when the time comes?"

He released a breath, which had her tensing once again. "Not exactly, Angel. There's more. You see, Jason and I have been talking for some time about moving into the civilian contractor sector for the Army when we retire. We would still work for Uncle Sam, but not as enlisted men."

"But how would that differ from what you do now?" she asked, not fully comprehending what he was telling her.

"The main two differences for us would be I'll no longer deploy, nor will we be forced to relocate. The only thing you might not like is that the job would likely be here, at my current base. In fact, an offer is already in place for when I retire."

"Would we stay in North Carolina right up until that time, or will there be another stop before we return to Alaska?"

"I'm fairly certain I can remain there for the duration." He reached out to cup her face as he added, "A big reason behind this is so you'll have your family close should I deploy one last time. God forbid, it could even happen when you are pregnant."

"I've always understood that, Gabe," she murmured. "And I know it would be hell for both of us, but you're doing everything you can to make sure I'm well covered."

"I know it'll be hard for you to leave them again, but remember, you can visit as often as you'd like." She could hear the regret in his voice, and she knew he had been tormenting himself over the upheaval the next few years would cause.

"Baby, I love it here. Yes, it will be an adjustment. But now that Nicole has agreed to Kaylee visiting us for a few weeks in the summer, I think we can build on it even more. I was born in North Carolina, but Alaska is where I found myself—and I found my future as well. It doesn't really matter, though, because my home isn't a house with four walls." She placed a hand over his heart as she added softly, "This is where I belong. Everything else is just a dot on a map."

Acknowledgments

As always, a special note of thanks to my agent, Jane Dystel, and my editor at Penguin, Kerry Donovan. None of this would ever be possible without you both, and I appreciate all that you do.

To Marion Archer, you are magic, my friend. Thanks for all that you do.

Ready to find
your next great read?

Let us help.

Visit prh.com/nextread